Apparitions
Ghosts of Old Edo

Miyuki Miyabe

Apparitions
Ghosts of Old Edo

Miyuki Miyabe

Translated by Daniel Huddleston

HAIKA SORU

SAN FRANCISCO

Apparitions: Ghosts of Old Edo (AYASHI)
by MIYABE Miyuki
Copyright © 2000 MIYABE Miyuki
All rights reserved.
Originally published in Japan by Kadokawa Shoten Co., Ltd., Tokyo.
English translation rights arranged with OSAWA OFFICE, Japan, through
THE SAKAI AGENCY.

English translation © 2013 VIZ Media, LLC
Design by Izumi Evers

HAIKASORU
Published by VIZ Media, LLC
PO Box 77010
San Francisco, CA 94107

www.haikasoru.com

Library of Congress Cataloging-in-Publication Data

Miyabe, Miyuki, 1960– author.
    [Short stories. Selections. English]
    Apparitions : Ghosts of Old Edo / Miyuki Miyabe ; translated by Daniel Huddleston.
        pages cm. — (Apparitions)
    ISBN 978-1-4215-6742-6 (pbk.)
    1. Ghost stories, Japanese—Translations into English. I. Huddleston, Daniel, translator.
II. Title.
    PL856.I856A2 2013
    895.6'35—dc23

                            2013036039

Printed in the U.S.A.
First printing, November 2013
Second printing, October 2023

Table of Contents

Introduction...7

I
A Drowsing Dream of Shinjū.....*15*

II
Cage of Shadows.....*45*

III
The Futon Storeroom.....*67*

IV
The Plum Rains Fall.....*95*

V
The "Oni" of the Adachi House.....*121*

VI
A Woman's Head.....*161*

VII
The Oni in the Autumn Rain.....*191*

VIII
Ash Kagura.....*219*

IX
The Mussel Mound.....*241*

Introduction

by *Masao Higashi*

Whenever I read Miyuki Miyabe's historical fiction, I get the urge to go out and walk around my neighborhood, even if I have no errands I need to do.

I rent an apartment in Tatekawa of Sumida ward as my workplace. It isn't far from the Fukagawa area—the home turf of Miyabe's works. Nowadays, "Tatekawa" is written 立川, and if that doesn't ring any bells, I'm sure many will recognize it in its original form, 竪川. Even her short story "Ash Kagura" (included in this volume) contains a scene in which Boss Masagorō, the thief-taker, hurries along the Tatekawa River toward the scene of a crime:

> *The Tatekawa River reflected the sky: leaden, gloomy, and stagnant. There was no sign yet of any cormorants out this morning. A cold wind that stung at the tips of their noses came blowing in from across the water.*

怪

This waterway, once bustling with boats carrying people to pray at Mount Narita and the two shrines in Katori and Kashima, is practically invisible nowadays, blocked off from above by the elevated Komatsugawa line of the Tokyo Metropolitan Expressway. Still, if you go down a little ways south from where the Shumoku Bridge crosses the Ōyokogawa River, it's just barely possible to recall some traces of the past in the flocks of waterfowl skimming the water's surface as they fly and in the swaying willows and rustling reeds along the banks.

At such times, the first thing I remember is Miyuki Miyabe's historical fiction, starting with *Honjo Fukagawa Fushigi Soushi* (The Honjo Fukagawa Book of Wonders) and *Genshoku Edo Goyomi* (An Edo Calendar, Printed in Its Original Phantom Colors).

There is certainly no shortage of authors who have written about the atmosphere and ways of life that live on in the Lower Tokyo area. Kidō Okamoto, Shūgorō Yamamoto, Shūhei Fujisawa, and Ryō Hanmura are four great authors who come to mind right away, whom Miyabe herself praises as having blazed the trail for her own historical fiction, and among them are not a few authors and stories to which I myself feel a great sense of attachment. So in spite of that, why Miyuki Miyabe? I can think of two main reasons.

First of all, Miyabe's stories engender a powerful feeling of immediacy—if we really try to put ourselves in the place where the story unfolds, the sense of distance when the characters move about and the feel of the air that envelops the world of the story both come alive in such vivid intensity and intimacy that the reader is enticed into a vicarious experience transcending the ages.

Should we say that it's her karma, after all, to write such tales, being a local author whose family has lived in Fukagawa for four generations? Of course that's a part of it, but it isn't everything. As is mentioned in the opening of her unique essay on walking, *Heisei Okachi Nikki* (A Heisei Walking Diary), Miyabe has herself walked from Nihonbashi to Monzen-Nakachō and all the way from Yūrakuchō to Kinshichō (!) in order to achieve that "sense of time and distance" when she sat down to write. Indeed, is it not this kind of sincere, refined creative consciousness whose steady devotion to the idea, shared by the artisans of Lower Tokyo, of in all things "learning with your body" that is creating this captivating sense of immediacy?

The second reason is more straightforward and trivial:

Miyuki Miyabe's period stories are often first-rate tales of horror and fantasy. For a ghost-loving child such as myself who grew up to make his living as a "horror critic," this above all else is the point on which she really hits the bull's-eye.

And so among Miyabe's historical ghost stories, which begin with *Honjo Fukagawa Fushigi Zōshi*, a collection of linked stories with the motif of the Seven Wonders of Honjo, and her Edo-period mystery *Furueru Iwa* (The Trembling Stones), whose tale of a psychic girl has its origins in *Mimibukuro*—one of the greatest collections of essays on the supernatural to come out of the Edo period—all the way up to her recent historical novel, the gentle ghost story *Akanbe'e* (Nyaaah!), we find none other than this very volume, *Apparitions* (*Ayashi*), which outdoes them all in the richness of the supernatural.

Actually, even now I can't suppress my excitement when I think back on the shock I felt the first time I read it through. Miyuki Miyabe appeared to be playing in what we should perhaps call a hybrid borderland between mystery, horror-fantasy, and historical fiction, superbly blending logical solutions with the supernatural, but in this book she boldly stepped over into "supernatural fundamentalism," unleashing monsters throughout beautiful old Edo that put to shame the soul-eating devils, the zombielike living corpses, and the ageless, deathless, vampirelike mystery men that populate Western horror novels.

Besides the examples I just mentioned, I think we can also recognize a striking influence in this book from the Western horror stories that the author so deeply appreciates.

怪

"*That thing* is hungry beyond all bearing."

This is a line spoken by the dead elder sister of the heroine in "The Futon Storeroom," and for someone like me, whose future life was pretty much decided in his youth by a secret encounter with the Sōgen Suiri paperback edition of *Kaiki Shōsetsu Kessakushū* (A Collection of Horror Masterpieces), it was a phrase that evinced an irresistible sensation of déjà vu.

I could swear I've seen that somewhere before . . .

Carrying in my mind a dim fog somewhat like the demons that haunt this book, I read on for a while, and then...*Aha!* I slapped my knee in recognition.

"It's Podolo! Look!"

"Before it comes back," she said. And then she said, "It's starving, too, and it won't wait. . . ."

This unsettling, mysterious line appears near the end of L.P. Hartley's short story "Podolo" (translated by Toshiyasu Uno and collected in volume 2 of the aforementioned *Kaiki Shōsetsu Kessakushū*), which Tei'ichi Hirai, the master translator of British and American horror, declared "a veritable model of the modern horror tale."

This is hardly worth going out of my way to mention, but it is fair to say that as works of fiction, "The Futon Storeroom" and "Podolo" have nothing in common whatsoever. I really must doff my hat to the ability and sense of playfulness of an author who can take the famous line above—hinting at the fear of some unknown thing writhing in the darkness—swap it into a completely different situation, and produce the kind of creepiness and lingering echo that lives up to, and even surpasses, that of the original text.

But wait just a minute, you say. How can you confidently draw such conclusions when only those two lines resemble one another? I can practically hear the objections closing in, but fear not, I have a reason.

A few years ago when I was sitting at a roundtable discussion arranged by a magazine publisher (it ran under the title of "The Pleasure of Immersion in <Fantasy and Horror>" in the January 2002 issue of *Shōsetsu Suiri* and was collected in the Futabasha edition of

Horaa Japanesuku wo Kataru [Talking About Horror Japanesque]), and when the subject of "Podolo" came up by chance, I unexpectedly heard the following words casually roll right off the tongue of Miyuki Miyabe herself:

> *That's right. To children, that line toward the end, "It's starving, too, and it won't wait," is frightening, but they don't understand the meaning.*

Well, needless to say I was inwardly shouting "Bingo!"

Incidentally, at that same discussion, I was very much impressed at how Miyabe quoted one after another, which made her superior attachment to and fondness for English and American horror novels plain to see. I also want to add that a fragment of her deep understanding is splendidly realized in *Okuru Monogatari Terror* (publisher: Koubunsha), which was published at the end of the same year.

In addition to "The Futon Storeroom," which I've already mentioned, *Apparitions* as a whole is chock-full of "good stuff" the author has drawn from European and American horror stories and skillfully made a part of her own author's toolbox. I get a deep impression of these things playing off each other in the book.

In the white towel that covers the face of the tragic heroine of the "The Plum Rains Fall," we have a distant reflection of Nathaniel Hawthorne's "The Minister's Black Veil," and in the misshapen, disgusting form that the women of "The Oni in the Autumn Rain" see standing out in the rain, we catch a glimpse of J.D. Beresford's "The Misanthrope." You may well be surprised as you take note of these things.

Or perhaps you might also find pleasure in the colorful monologue styles of the ghastly and lurid "Cage of Shadows" and "The 'Oni' of the Adachi House," with their deep portrayals of the inner workings of life, and be reminded of the works of Sheridan Le Fanu, beginning with "Madam Crowl's Ghost," with their solemn and mysteriously beautiful manner of speech.

Now that I think about it, Kidō Okamoto, who was both the father of the Edo-period thief-taker tale as well as a fine writer of horror stories, was so well versed in Western horror stories that he edited the first volume of *Sekai Kaidan Meisakushū* and even left behind stage adaptations of two masterpieces of British horror: W.W. Jacobs' "The Monkey's Paw" and Frederick Marryat's "The White Wolf of the Hartz Mountains." (It's no coincidence that both of these works are collected together in *Okuru Monogatari Terror.*)

Kidō Okamoto and Miyuki Miyabe—for these two authors who stand at the origin and the leading edge of the historical novel, there is one other point of commonality besides a shared affection for European and American horror novels. That is their native Tokyoite nature, which practically spills out of them. On the point of the culture and the human kindness of Edo's neighborhoods, which engenders a homey feeling, I'd like to bring up one more name, that of the previously mentioned Tei'ichi Hirai. Tei'ichi writes that when he was very young, his grandmother—who was born and raised in Edo Fukagawa—used to tell him bedtime stories, and it seems as if many of the foxes, tanuki, and *yōkai* from the stories he heard have made their way as-is into the world of Miyuki Miyabe's fiction.

In any case, it seems that the atmosphere of old Edo and the horror stories of the West make exceedingly good partners.

The period horror of Miyuki Miyabe, which embraces both of these excellent traditions, will, I am convinced, continue to flower into ever larger, more bewitchingly beautiful blossoms.

—*Masao Higashi*
March 2003
On the day it was reported that early blooming
cherry trees had blossomed along the Sumida River.

I

A Drowsing Dream of Shinjū

The string of double suicides popularly known as the "tea towel *shinjū*" occurred in the city of Edo at the very start of the Kyōhō Period in 1716. They continued for about a year and a half, reaching a total of four cases.

In all four of these incidents, the couples tied themselves together at the wrist using long tea towels so as not to become separated when they threw themselves into the water. In three of these four incidents, things went "well" from start to finish, resulting in the deaths of both partners. In the last case, however, the cloth came loose at the moment they hit the water, and the man—who in spite of himself had begun to beat against the waves with his arms—started swimming and survived. They say that the man who lived was overcome with regret, crying out in a voice that summoned tears to the eyes of his rescuers that if only they had followed the example of the other double suicides before them—tying their hands with a good strong cord instead of one of those fashionable tea towels—he would not have had to endure the living shame of having survived.

But those "fashionable tea towels" had been used in the previous three cases as well. They were produced at a certain wholesaler of dyed cotton tea towels that at the time was located in the Abura-chō area of Nihonbashi-tōri and could only be purchased there. As this was a wholesale business, its activity had originally been limited to selling, with no involvement in dyeing, tailoring, and the like. The change began when its master—a creative man who had always been full of interesting ideas—produced a small lot of tea towels with colorful patterns to pass out as gifts to regular customers on the occasions of Obon and New Year's. He had made them as a hobby, so to speak. These towels generated unexpectedly good word of mouth, and the owner, judging that there was money to be made, offered them for sale to the general public, with whom they were an unexpected hit. No one was more surprised, they say, than the master of the wholesale business himself.

Whenever a product becomes a big hit, there's always a reason for it, and in this case, it was because the designs on these tea towels were very well done. The idea of these so-called *monogatari moyō* or "story patterns" was to draw on the cloth a single scene from some famous story such as *The Tale of Genji, Tales of Ise,* or *Otogi Zōshi,* and then leave parts of the cloth undyed to form a picture. Scenes from love stories seemed to work particularly well, and especially popular were scenes from *The Tale of Genji.* In all four of those double suicide cases, the men and women had bound their hands together using tea towels that bore images from that book.

In the three successful cases, the images on the tea towels had been taken from the chapters "Lavender," "Boat upon the Waters," and "Akashi." In the fourth case, which had ended in failure, the design had come from "Evening Faces." The cloth was said to have had *katawaguruma*—wheel-like patterns common in Japanese textiles—accenting pictorial designs from the story and a floral pattern of the "evening faces" for which the chapter was named. A sad and lonely design, calling to mind Genji's bereavement over a dead lover of his own.

All that aside, *shinjū*—or *aitaijini,* the less romantic term authorities preferred to call double suicides—were strictly forbidden by law. Despite the fact that one had ended in partial failure, the number of incidents had risen as high as four, and the governing

powers at last moved to take action. Although the steady belt-tight-
ening of the Kyōhō Reforms had not yet begun at that time, these tea
towels—which from the start should have been such practical and
useful things—were criticized as being foisted on the public with
unnecessary, luxurious design work that tickled the fancy of the men
and women who were thinking of forming suicide pacts. And so it
was that the master of the cotton wholesaler that had produced them
met with great misfortune: he was banished to a faraway island and
his property was confiscated, ending his business in its first generation. In the end, his hobby had come with a considerable price tag.

In no time at all, however, the general public forgot about these
events. Still, among those who worked in the same industry as that
master wholesaler, the tale of the *monogatari moyō* tea towels continued to be discussed within very limited circles. It became a parable
about what was most important for running a store, and there were
also anecdotes about how interesting the tea towels had been as
handcrafted art. It was hardly surprising that masters and their wives
alike enjoyed talking about them.

At last, the Kyōhō era came to an end. Then, in the fourth year
of Bunka . . .

怪

"The Daikoku'ya employs very harsh discipline with its apprentices. You're gonna have a lot of rough times there, most likely,
but in the end, the hard way is also the easiest. First of all, if you can
make it working there, there'll be no place you *can't* work. And when
people say, 'In youth, seek hard labor,' they're telling you the truth.
In the end, the hard way *is* the easy way. Get it? Got it? Good. Don't
you forget it."

The day Ginji was sent off to work at a cotton wholesaler called
the Daikoku'ya, in Tōri Setomono-chō, the old man at the Mannen'ya
had tilted his bald, rounded head a little to the right and told him

these things in a voice oddly suffused with emotion. Ginji had taken his words to be in reference to his elder brother—the second eldest in his family—who despite having been helped by this office time and again, had never continued for long in any of his apprenticeships. Eventually, the brother had fallen into a reprobate lifestyle of gambling and carousing, and his current whereabouts were unknown. Ginji felt a terrible sense of pathos as he listened to the old man.

The Mannen'ya was an agency for those seeking employment. It was located in Ōdenma-chō Block 1, and although it was operated by a solitary old man, his was a highly trusted business that had long been placing apprentices in the many cotton wholesalers that dotted the way from Ōdenma-chō and the surrounding area on through Muromachi, Takara-chō, Suruga-chō, and Nihonbashitōri-chō. You could search up and down the banks of the Ōkawa River, and not even among its thick stands of reeds could you find a voice that spoke ill of the old man.

This old man had helped Ginji's mother find work when she was very young. She had met Ginji's father at the place of her apprenticeship and had thereafter made a home and born children one after another until there were six of them. Now, in order to find apprenticeships for those children, she was relying on the old man's good offices once more. Ginji had heard of his mother's surprise upon seeing the old man again. It was the first time in fifteen years, but he hadn't changed one bit, almost like some sort of supernatural creature.

Five years ago, the Mannen'ya had placed the family's firstborn son in a wholesaler called Kashiwa'ya in Ōdenma-chō Block 1. He had at last made journeyman and was apparently highly thought of. However, the second son of the family was in the miserable condition already described. This had had the effect of canceling out all of his eldest brother's accomplishments, leaving Ginji incapable of finding an apprenticeship without relying on the old man at the Mannen'ya.

Ginji was fourteen years old and the third born into his family. He had two younger sisters and one younger brother—the latter of whom was the youngest in the family. Despite the fact that they were still only small children, both of his sisters were nearing the age when they could leave home to apprentice as nursemaids or housemaids. Ginji knew he would need to make a great effort in his work so as not to adversely affect their chances for future employment. As for himself, he embraced the firm determination of his childlike heart and found it depressing to have people telling him to "be diligent" as if they didn't trust him.

Maybe that was why, from the time Ginji began his apprenticeship, he was always of a calm, relaxed disposition. He never worried over this and that, he never turned into a pessimist, nor was he ever particularly full of enthusiasm—his coworkers found this interesting. The Daikoku'ya was indeed a rough and noisy place to work, where a newly arrived apprentice could hardly expect to have his name remembered or even be treated like a human being. His daily routine consisted of being ordered around with shouts of "Hey!" and "What's the matter with you!" However, this kind of treatment was something all apprentices had to go through and was simply to be expected. Though his days were spent working so hard that the exhaustion seeped into his marrow, his heart was at peace.

In the past, whenever his eldest brother would come home for his New Year's and Obon visits, he would complain until he was blue in the face about how the seasoned workers at his workplace would arrogantly throw their weight around and about the terrible abuses he was forced to endure at the hands of the senior journeymen: "They make me skip meals." "They shove me into the toilet." "They bury me in futons and laugh at me." "They hit me." "They kick me." It was all he ever talked about, to the point one would think he had been sent to prison rather than to a cotton wholesaler in Ōdenma-chō. However, none of those things ever happened to Ginji at the Daikoku'ya. The old man at the Mannen'ya had indeed been telling him the truth. Maybe this was what he had meant by saying, "In the end, the hard way *is* the easy way."

The master and mistress of the Daikoku'ya were both still in their mid-forties and worked at a brisk pace, taking the lead in the management of the business. The way their eyes penetrated every corner of the place was one reason their business was so clean, tidy, and organized. Ginji remembered that the old man at the Mannen'ya had once told him that such scrutiny was fine because the master was the boatman and the Daikoku'ya his ship. Ginji had accepted this as a child would.

The previous master had retired ten years earlier and now lived a life of ease at a second house in the Mukōjima area, where he busied himself with fishing and long aimless strolls. Under normal circumstances Ginji would never have had the chance to meet him in person. However, when the weather became unstable at the start of spring, the old master suffered complications from influenza and became bedridden. Because of this, the number of messenger errands increased sharply. Some days, messengers had to go back and forth between Tōri Setomono-chō and Mukōjima as many as three times in a single day. Because most of these errands simply involved delivering items and letters and bringing other items and letters back, it was only natural that this work fell to the newest apprentices who had not yet even halfway proven themselves—boys who when told to run something over there would in their simple honesty literally *run*. This being the case, it came to be that Ginji often made trips to the house in Mukōjima. There he had seen the old master's face. He was a thin, small-bodied man, and his illness was perhaps to blame for his ashen complexion and the strange puffiness of his eyelids. When Ginji thought about it later, he got the feeling that his illness might not be influenza but something worse.

The Daikoku'ya did have an heir. The master and mistress of the house had one son, aged twenty, whose name was Tōichirō. Born when the wisteria he was named for was at its peak, he was said to have been a beautiful baby with a doll's features. Even now that he was an adult, the good looks of this young man brought no shame upon his name, and all the young women around Nihonbashitōri-chō squealed with excitement whenever they spoke of him. Young master Tōichirō had been spoiled rotten as a child by the old master in Mukōjima. Even now he was still the old man's pride and joy, and so it happened that from the time his grandfather became bedridden, Tōichirō would often go to the island to visit the ailing old man. Because of this, about half of the time when Ginji ran to Mukōjima on some errand, he ended up accompanying Tōichirō.

Tōichirō treated him with great kindness on such occasions. Perhaps this was usual for well-brought-up youths, or perhaps his kindness and warmth was due simply to his feeling sorry for Ginji, who was as yet an inexperienced child. It may be that the way Ginji ran for all he was worth whenever he carried messages had impressed Tōichirō as well. Gradually, the young master began to summon Ginji whenever he felt like going over to Mukōjima, even when there were no messages to carry. It became his custom to have Ginji hold his umbrella on rainy days and carry the lantern along the dark roads at night. Once this pattern took hold, there were some among the older journeymen who became jealous and started to bully Ginji. For his part, Ginji didn't think he was really of any great use to the young master, and there were times when he considered the attention more an annoyance than a blessing. Still, deflecting the attentions of someone who has taken a liking to you can often be more difficult than escaping the abuse of a hateful enemy. Whenever the young master called for him, there was nothing Ginji could do except follow him wherever he wanted to go.

And so it was that when he was attending Tōichirō, he often witnessed the young master being spoken to by young women. In most cases, the speakers were maidservants or girls from town following behind an older housemaid; in any case, the girl would likely be someone from some shop or other. They would be on the way to or from some training session, shopping trip, or shrine visit, and would suddenly spy Tōichirō and call out to him, "Oh, my! How are you today?" At least that was what Ginji believed was going on at first. As the number of these encounters increased, however, as more frequently he found himself thinking, *Wait, isn't she the same one we saw the other day? And actually, haven't we run into her here before?* he came to suspect these encounters were all deliberately contrived— that these women knew about the young master's visits to Mukōjima and were lying in wait for him along the way.

Ginji, though still a child in many ways, was a young lad as well and as such not without some measure of jealousy when he saw the young master being pursued by all these women. Though he was well aware that no one could choose their own birth, whenever he compared himself—heading out early in the morning for a long day of hard, sweaty work—to the young master—rich, good-looking, and seemingly without a care in the world—Ginji would get the feeling that he somehow understood why his elder brother had stumbled into a life of dissipation.

In early May, right after the end of the Boys' Festival, Ginji encountered the unexpected sight of the young and the old masters engaged in a fierce argument at the house in Mukōjima, where the young master was always going to look in on his ailing grandfather. The argument seemed to have something to do with business, the old man straining his hoarse voice as he spoke with considerable harshness: "That's enough of your cheek! You're a decade shy of 'ready'!" Ginji was in a state of utter shock as he eavesdropped on the proceedings.

Accompanying the young master to the other house by no means allowed him to duck responsibility. Housemaids and man-servants were present to care for the old master, and they would be waiting with bated breath for him whenever he came over from Tōri Setomono-chō, ready with chore after chore for him to do. They were probably getting advance notice of his coming from the shop somehow, and they worked him to the bone, same as at the store. That day, he had already drawn water from the well and chopped firewood when he was handed a hatchet and driven into the shrubbery of the back garden. "That *shinodake* bamboo's overgrown. It's an eyesore, so cut it back. And come right back as soon as you finish." And so it happened that as Ginji was clumsily swinging the hatchet and trying to fend off biting lice, he unavoidably heard the sound of the raised, angry voices coming from inside the house.

Tōichirō was saying something or other about tea towels. "The Daikoku'ya has never sold tea towels before. It doesn't make any sense."

He went on, saying something or other about dyeing, until at last there was the sound of a slap, and the old master said, "Shut up! Who in the world put such a story into your head? And did you not listen to it long enough to hear the ending?"

"I know what happened. They went out of business. But our situation is completely different. The reason everything was confiscated was because they got caught up in the Reforms."

"No, no, that isn't true," the old master cut in. "Listen to me, please! The real problem was that they made something that appealed to men and women who were already talking about forming suicide pacts. That was their original mistake. A business should never, ever do something like that."

"But that doesn't even make sense!" said the young master stubbornly. "Was it the makers' fault those people used their tea towels to kill themselves? No, it wasn't. Using those monogatari moyō cloths was something they decided to do on their own. A true businessman wants to make things that sell."

"A wholesaler's job isn't to manufacture new products. You're going to be in a world of hurt someday if you can't understand that much."

Ginji was listening intently to these exchanges when he became aware of the footsteps of a maidservant making her rounds through the back garden growing closer. She had likely noticed that the stalks of shinodake bamboo were neither swaying nor falling and, thinking he was probably sitting idle, was now headed over to give him a piece of her mind. Ginji hurriedly raised the hatchet. All around him, the bamboo leaves began to rustle, and the noise drowned out the conversation from inside the house.

Walking back to the shop that day, the young master was in a terrible mood. Bathed in the slanting sunlight of an early spring afternoon, Ginji followed along behind the young master, shoulders hunched, in silence. In the shadow of a distant forest, Ginji noticed a pair of carp streamers that had been left out past the end of the Boys' Festival celebrations. Something about them struck him as oddly forlorn.

He wanted to cheer the young master, but he didn't know what he should say and felt that anything he did say would end up missing the mark.

From that day forward, Tōichirō avoided going to Mukōjima and withdrew from Ginji's life to a degree the apprentice found rather refreshing. Judging by the snippets of rumor he picked up from the housemaids, the old master was calling for his grandson, but the young master had no intention of going to him. That quarrel had apparently resulted in quite a grudge.

As he was no longer accompanying the young master, Ginji went back to the busy life of a new apprentice. The rainy season came and the rainy season passed, the summer sun began to burn with blinding whiteness, and even if there was still no one who called Ginji by his own name, the scoldings aimed his way had grown less frequent, and when he was hard at work and drenched in sweat he sometimes wondered if he didn't glimpse a faint smile even on the face of his hard-to-please supervisor. On days like that, his rice was delicious, and when he collapsed in exhaustion onto his futon, thin and hard as a rice cracker though it was, it felt so soft! In his dreams, he heard the old man from the Mannen'ya saying, *The quickest way is to be diligent in your work.* He sounded pleased.

怪

It happened near the end of July.

An offer of marriage was made to the young master.

Though he had been showered with offers before, all of which had ended only in talk, this time it was apparently the real thing. The mood of the Daikoku'ya became suddenly tinged with a bright and festive feeling.

The bride-to-be was the daughter of a miso wholesaler in Koishikawa Denzuin-mae. She was sixteen years old, and her name was O-Natsu. Her family was related to the wife of the Daikoku'ya's current master, and that lady had known O-Natsu well from the time she was in diapers. "This way, there won't be any feuding between mother-in-law and daughter-in-law," the maidservants were saying. They sounded halfway disappointed.

All this seemed rather sudden, but as more and more information came to light, Ginji realized that the marriage was all in accordance with the old master's wishes. The old man probably didn't have all that much time left. Before he died, he wanted to see his dear grandson marry and become a full-fledged adult in truth as well as name, and if there was time enough, he had another heartfelt wish—to live to see the face of his great-grandson.

The master and his wife also had an ulterior motive in undertaking his request: they were well aware of how the young master set the hearts of the neighborhood girls all aflutter, and they knew they needed to get him settled before it was too late to prevent him from making a mistake. Rather than allowing him to fall in love with one of those tomboyish girls and take her to wife, they thought it wiser to find someone related to the family who was well known to them and reliable, who could stand together with their son like a pair of matching *hina* dolls.

The wheels of their thoughts turned in unison, carrying the negotiations forward smoothly like a pair of wheels—at least at first. Even the young master himself, who was being borne along on these wheels, appeared to have no objection. Since Ginji was entirely divorced from accompanying the young master by this point, he had not been around him in his daily life recently, but when he heard the whisperings that passed between the housemaids and the older workers, he thought to himself with relief, *Ah, I'm happy for him!* He suddenly felt very moved as well to think that the young master must in his own way be feeling guilty for having had that argument in Mukōjima. It was most likely to please the old master that he was accepting this arrangement so meekly.

At any rate, I'm happy for him. Master Tōichirō's been really good to me. By the time he becomes shop master, I'll be a genuinely useful worker and a cornerstone of the business. Until then, I've got to focus on my training. I don't have a lot of experience, but if I work hard and honestly give my all for the store . . .

Thinking such thoughts, Ginji felt like he had grown up just a little and was glad.

It is here, though, that a *however* must intrude.

It was just past mid-August when a most unanticipated occurrence took place. Arrangements had been finalized between the two families, and plans had just been made to hold the ceremony in early January of the following year. And then it came out that the young master had a lover.

Moreover, the woman was a housemaid at the Daikoku'ya. Her name was O-Haru. She was twenty-six years old and had come to work at the Daikoku'ya twelve years prior. She was a fine worker whom everyone—even the chief housemaid who managed things indoors—relied on in many ways. In his daily work, Ginji had had little occasion to seek her assistance, but efficient, hardworking

O-Haru had always seemed a very firm-willed, reliable person, though at the same time rather difficult to approach for a newly arrived apprentice like Ginji. She was no outstanding beauty. With rather swarthy skin and a small, pinched jaw that was always drawn inward, O-Haru had an earnest gaze that was ever looking forward. Her mien was less like that of a housemaid than it was of a male apprentice who had been learning the trade and was at last coming into his own.

It was O-Haru herself who had brought the matter to light. She was in charge of certain indoor chores and as such had frequent opportunities to see the lady of the house face to face. On one such occasion, she burst into tears and, weeping almost like a child, confessed to everything. No one else was present at the time, but on hearing the news, the lady of the house became extremely upset and in the heat of the moment summoned the chief housemaid, who in turn became so utterly discombobulated that she violently took hold of O-Haru by the shoulders. She was about to drag her from the room when O-Haru pushed away her hands and cried out, "Be careful! The young master's child is in my belly!"

The lady of the house fainted. It was a terrible thing to be ambushed with. The one whom she should have been on guard against all this time was not one of the shrill city girls who had made such a fuss over her son, but rather a taciturn housemaid who had been at his side all along—waiting on him hand and foot, sharing day by day in his joys and sorrows, and quietly, gradually trekking her way up that narrow path into the mountains of his heart.

When the master of the house heard, he became furious and called for the young master right away. Tōichirō hung his head and confessed, admitting that all was as O-Haru had said. Their relationship had been ongoing for about two years. There had been times when he had tried to break it off, but seeing her every single day, he would ultimately be dragged back into the affair, which had continued in this manner even up to the present time.

However, the young master had no intention whatsoever of making O-Haru his wife. He had even told her, "I can't do that." At such times, O-Haru had reassured him bravely, saying, "I know my station in life." But at that time, the fact of her pregnancy had not been revealed. Though logic dictated that the child was his, the young master was not pleased to learn of the pregnancy, nor was he of a mind to break off his engagement and see his relationship with O-Haru through to marriage.

It was a pity about poor O-Haru, but, well, it was what it was.

While this upheaval was going on, Ginji often thought about something his mother had told him long ago, of how the old go-between at the Mannen'ya had delivered a very stern sermon at the time when she had first left home to apprentice as a housemaid. *There is just one rule*, he had said, *that you must observe if you don't want to stray in a housemaid apprenticeship: never fall in love with the young master of the house.*

At the time, his mother answered, "I can make up my mind not to fall for him, but what do I do if he falls for me and starts making advances?" The old man of the Mannen'ya said, "The young master in love with a housemaid? That does not happen. Ever. Not even in one case out of ten thousand does such a thing ever happen." He had not been smiling as he answered. "Even if he comes to you saying he's in love, he is mistaken. So get it through your head right now that that kind of thing absolutely does not happen. If it looks like he's about to lay hands on you, remember, there are a lot of other people there in the store besides just you and him. If you have the will and determination to do so, you can protect yourself from anything he may try. The important thing is to stay firm in your convictions and never let the rings of your own barrel loosen." This he had also spoken in a very serious tone of voice.

Ginji wondered, *Had O-Haru not come to her apprenticeship through the Mannen'ya? Had she never been given such a lecture? Had she heard one but forgotten it? Could a speech encompassing the most*

important thing for living your life really just slip your mind at the very
moment it was most important to remember?

Ultimately, it was decided that O-Haru would be put out of the shop. However, O-Haru was completely without family who could take her in. With the young master also to blame, his family couldn't really throw her out —or them, rather—all alone. At last they rented a house in a place called Ōshima-mura, located on the newly opened land beyond Fukagawa, for her to live in until the child was born. Afterward, the child would be taken in for a time by the Daikoku'ya, then fostered out as soon as a suitable family could be located. As long as O-Haru agreed to resign herself thereafter to thinking only of her own future—never approaching the young master again and never going looking for the child—no one from the Daikoku'ya would put a word in against her, no matter where she went to work from henceforward. They would also pay her a sum of money suitable for her twelve years of otherwise unpaid service. Those were the terms that the Daikoku'ya offered O-Haru. They made them as favorable as they could.

O-Haru took their offer. She had no other choice. She was lucky in that the Daikoku'ya's master and mistress were both of a mild disposition when it came to their son and had allowed O-Haru to have her say. As one of the workers, she could not have said a word in protest even if they had showered her with invective and thrown her into the street without a single *mon* to her name.

A strong-minded woman, O-Haru had never whined or complained, but because of the attitude she had taken at the time her secret came out, she had made an enemy of the chief housemaid, causing the housemaids working under her to grow defiant. It was under the hail of their icy gazes that she departed in solitude for the rented house in Ōshima-mura. She left by way of the kitchen entrance—as though fleeing—and afterward Ginji saw the chief housekeeper sprinkling salt over where she had passed.

"That shameless little ———! And at her age too! Seducing the young master . . . making him her plaything. Probably thought she could get the property, but this is one wholesaler that won't deal in what she's selling. We don't even know for sure if that baby is his."

At this point, you really don't have to keep criticizing, Ginji thought. But then again, maybe women were harsher than men when it came to this kind of thing. O-Haru had certainly done something she shouldn't have. With that straightforward gaze of hers, she had been staring into dreams she shouldn't have allowed herself. She had loosened those barrel rings that should always remain fastened tight.

The Daikoku'ya, having shaken itself free of her, moved ahead with plans for the young master's wedding, and as this proceeded it was as though O-Haru had never been there at all—as though everyone had comforted themselves not by forgetting O-Haru, but by *erasing* her.

Ginji harbored his doubts about this state of affairs. Was the young master really comfortable with this? O-Haru, with whom he had made a child, had been driven out, and now he was about to make another woman his wife. Ginji couldn't imagine himself doing such a thing. Surely, Tōichirō would remember O-Haru. Surely, Tōichirō would worry about the baby. When Ginji let slip his thoughts on the matter, though, his coworkers at the shop only sneered. "If you had money, people covering your back, and were free to pick whomever you liked from a bunch of women who were all crazy about you, I guarantee you wouldn't be hung up on O-Haru."

"But even the young master—he loved O-Haru once, didn't he?"

"You don't have to 'love' a woman to knock her up. She can end up with one in the oven even if the guy doesn't feel a thing. You're still a kid if you don't know that much."

It was at that time that Ginji hated his work at the Daikoku'ya for the very first time. If he stayed on in his apprenticeship there, the months would turn into years, Tōichirō would take over the business, and as proprietor he would gain confidence, dignity, and honor. And watching from his own low estate as the master's life unfolded,

Ginji would never forget about O-Haru, and he would never forget about the baby. Lurking behind the happy young master, he would always imagine the thin shadow of O-Haru and cradled in its arms a shade of a little baby not yet strong enough to raise its own head. Ginji had watched as O-Haru departed. To have seen this sight at a time when he had not yet come to understand what men were like was his misfortune.

If only they would send him out to run errands again, he would run as fast as he could to the Mannen'ya. There Ginji would tell the old man everything, and the old man would surely tell him just what he should do.

And then one day amid the lingering heat of a harsh late summer, while Ginji was thinking such thoughts as he cleaned up around the storehouse alone, Tōichirō quietly crept up on him. When he called out his name, Ginji jumped up in surprise.

"Sorry, I didn't mean to frighten you," Tōichirō said. "I have a little job for you."

The young master was wearing a fashionable if showy striped kimono decorated with gourd and bat patterns, and his hair was tied in a topknot that suited his small face. Now that Tōichirō was engaged, he tried to put on a more dignified, mature appearance.

"Later today, I'm going to call for you and ask you to go run an errand at Mr. Naitō's place in Shibaguchi. When I do so, I want you to go out with a big, loud 'Yessir.' The job will be to return some books of poetry I borrowed from old man Naitō." All this he said in the space of a single breath, then glancing about to make sure no one else could hear, the young master moved one step closer to Ginji and lowered his voice another octave. "But the real job is something else. I want you to go to Ōshima-mura. To where O-Haru is living."

Ginji's eyes snapped open wide without his realizing it. The young master stared into those eyes and nodded.

"I want you to go and see how she's getting along. I'll give detailed instructions later, but basically I want you to give her a kimono. Tell her for me that it's the most I can do for her to show her how I feel."

Ginji at last found his voice again and said, "Is it . . . all right for me to do something like that?"

Tōichirō smiled weakly. "My father and mother would never allow it. But after all, what I did to her was inexcusable . . ."

The young master crossed his white arms in front of his chest and hung his head. "These days, I dream about her almost every night," he said. "She comes to me with a pale, sickly face and sits at my bedside."

O-Haru wasn't dead, but he was speaking of her as though she were a ghost.

"Maybe it's what they call an *ikiryō*—a hurt, angry soul that goes wandering from its body in the night. She's surely holding a grudge against me. She was used and then thrown away, so it's no wonder. Now that it's come to this, I wish I had never gotten involved with her."

Ginji at last noticed that the young master seemed not so much contrite as . . . frightened. His dark eyes avoided Ginji and simply stared down at the ground near his feet. Then Tōichirō started to speak, and just like water spilling over from a tilted rain barrel, the words came pouring out of him, unstoppable.

"After our relationship grew intimate, she would say the strangest things sometimes. 'Even if we can't live as husband and wife in this life, we can still be together in the next,' she'd say. Or, 'Men and women who'll be united in marriage have matching marks on the soles of their feet from the time they're babies, so you can't keep them apart. And if you force them apart, both will die.' She was a frightening woman to her very core. She told me she had no expectation of becoming my wife—she knew that was above her station—but under the surface . . . I don't know what she was thinking. Now that I think about it, she seemed oddly knowledgeable about a great many things. I don't know where she picked this up, but she told me once about this wholesaler a long time ago that made lots of money selling dyed tea towels that several men and women used to commit shinjū together. The story caught my interest. Just walking the path my dad trained me for is not exactly interesting or enjoyable. I want to try running the business my own way. So thinking we might be able to take a hint from that dyed tea towel story, I went over to Mukōjima to talk about it. Instead, I got chewed out something awful by my grandfather, and it turned into a nasty argument. When I told O-Haru about it, I seem to recall her getting angry too. When I see her in my dreams each night, she has the same angry expression she had back then. So I'm scared. I have a feeling somehow that if I let this alone she'll never forgive me."

So that's what the fight in Mukōjima was about? But even if it is, why is he telling me all this? He didn't have to go out of his way to tell me how scary O-Haru is. I'd run his errand anyway. That was not a story Ginji wanted to hear.

"As you wish, sir," Ginji said with forced politeness. "But I don't know the way to O-Haru's place in Ōshima-mura."

"Ah, that's not a problem. I'll put a map inside the wrappings for the kimono. You've learned to read already, haven't you?"

Since around the beginning of summer, the journeyman directly above Ginji had been teaching him to read, write, and use the abacus.

"Yes, sir. If it's written in *hiragana,* I can usually read it."

"Good. I'm counting on you then."

With that, Tōichirō departed, taking care to quiet his footfalls as he headed off in the direction of the main house. For some time after, Ginji stared as if in a daze at the back of the young master's oddly thin-looking body.

Some time later, Tōichirō summoned him according to their prior arrangement. Ginji took on the job as he had been told, pretended to set off in the direction of Shibaguchi, then turned on his heel along the way. Ōshima-mura was on the other side of the Ōkawa River, on past Fukagawa.

As he walked at a brisk pace, he searched inside the cloth wrapping of the package he had been handed as he left. Inside, he found a scrap of paper with a map sketched on it tucked neatly between the perfectly folded, newly tailored kimono. The kimono was exactly like the one that the young master had been wearing— striped, with gourd and bat patterns. Ginji recalled hearing that the pattern had become all the rage since Danjūrō had made it famous on the kabuki stage. But if O-Haru had a gaudy thing like this, wouldn't everyone know right away that Tōichirō had given it to her? Most of all, who had the young master gone to to have something like this tailored for her?

Truth be told, Ginji had been terribly sleepy that day since early morning. And not on that day only, but for the prior ten days as well. This was for the simple reason that each night before bed, he had been practicing with his abacus. Ginji liked reading and writing, but he was no good with the abacus, and his learning speed was as far from that of the other apprentice being trained on the device as a horse's gallop is from a baby's crawl. The journeyman who taught them was strict and scolded Ginji with blistering criticism. From his own perspective too, it stuck in Ginji's craw to be the one falling behind, so he had been doing extra practices, even late at night at the cost of his sleeping time. On moonlit nights, there was no need for a lantern, and when the moon wasn't out, he could go to the kitchen entrance where a lamp was always burning. No one would disturb him there, and he could bang away at the abacus in peace until he was satisfied.

With Ginji doing this every night, it was only natural that his exhaustion should slowly build. He was fine during the day when he was helping other people with their work, but when he was cleaning by himself or when he was checking the books against the dry goods inventory in the warehouse, his head would often start to nod involuntarily, then as his jaw went slack his eyes would snap open again.

Even now, as he trudged along without anyone else to talk with, he felt as if he was going to fall asleep on his feet. In order to ward that off, he made a point to run for as much of the way as he could. Which was farther: to go from Nihonbashitōri Setomono-chō to Shibaguchi, or to Ōshima-mura? Ginji wasn't very sure. When he looked at the map, he could see that everything was solid white beyond the storehouses for unhusked rice at Fukagawa Sarue-chō, with no buildings of note sketched in beyond that. It was probably mostly rice paddies beyond that point. Moreover, Ōshima-mura lay even farther ahead. They might be calling it "newly opened land," but it was really out in the middle of nowhere. He would need to run to make the trip before sundown.

So run he did. When he finally arrived at Ōshima-mura, he found it much as he had expected: horses and cattle grazed against a view of rice paddy after rice paddy, the odor of night soil wafted to his nostrils, and the ground was soft beneath his sole when he pressed his foot down. The late summer sun burned in a blue sky whose crystal clarity seemed to have taken on entire new degrees of height and transparency.

On the edge of Ōshima-mura, he asked directions of a man who was out weeding and immediately learned the way to O-Haru's rented house. Outsiders were an unusual sight for the people living in the villages around there. The single-story, thatched-roof house that the man pointed out to him stood alone in the midst of a vast expanse of rice paddies, almost as if it had been abandoned there by a receding tide. Like O-Haru when she was driven from the Daikoku'ya, it stood alone and forlorn.

Certainly O-Haru wasn't living there all alone; at the very least, a handmaid should have been sent here with her. When he neared the house, Ginji stopped in front of the brushwood fence and looked all around. The place felt empty and desolate.

Won't someone come out and notice me before I have to call out?

But no one was there. With no other choice, he went inside the fence, conscientiously walking on flat flagstones around to where he could see the kitchen entrance.

The house was deathly quiet.

"Excuse me!"

He heard no answering voice.

"Excuse me! I'm on an errand from Setomono-chō!"

Not a single sound came in response.

Ginji sat down on the step in the earthen kitchen entrance, sighed, and leaned his back against a nearby pillar. He was utterly exhausted. *Ah, what now? Just leave the young master's package here and go back? But if I do that, the person who picks it up won't understand what this is about. And if O-Haru doesn't understand, she'll have no reason to soften up, forgive Tōichirō, and say, "All right, let's stop showing up at his bedside and giving him nightmares."*

And his errand would not be completed. Although Ginji couldn't excuse the young master's behavior, he did sympathize with him just a little, and though he felt sorry for O-Haru as well, he was wise enough to know that nothing good could come of her holding a grudge. What he wanted to do was properly carry out the young master's instructions and set the young master's mind at ease. True, he felt this way in part because he was still a child, but it was also because he was a young man.

"Okay, let's go," he grunted as he got to his feet. He walked back over to where the flagstones were. Amid the wide expanse of rice paddies that spread out around the house, a smattering of people and cows could be seen, but Ginji just didn't have the energy to run all the way over to someone to ask if they knew where the house's occupants had gone.

He went back to the kitchen and sat down in the entryway.

Just wait a little while? Maybe O-Haru is out for a walk with her handmaid or something. In a rural place like this, she probably has to walk all the way to Fukagawa just to buy oil for her hair. If I wait, she's bound to come back eventually. It's not like she has anywhere else to stay.

It was cool in the entryway and felt very nice. Ginji stretched out his road-weary feet and slowly closed his eyes. He let out his breath with a soft blowing sound and relaxed. He had become very sleepy. As though invited by the comfort, exhaustion had crept up on him without his realizing it, and just like a baby that had suckled its fill of milk, he rolled right over into a deep slumber.

And then he had a dream.

Ginji was standing in the darkness of a moonless night, staring down into a deep pool he had never seen before. The pool at his feet was much brighter than the sky overhead; there was a soft luster to the water that gave it a clear, emerald glow. The water was crystal clear and looked cold.

A man and a woman came floating across the surface of the water, facing upward. They drifted from beyond that faraway blackness right up to Ginji's feet.

It was Tōichirō and O-Haru.

Both were clad in matching striped kimono, decorated with gourd and bat designs, and were tightly bound, right arm to left, with a tea towel. The eyes of both were closed, and both wore peaceful expressions on their faces, as though they were sleeping. When the two of them had floated right up in front of Ginji's feet, he saw that O-Haru's submerged chignon had come halfway undone, and her hair was trailing behind her in the water like long strands of black algae.

Ginji looked on, holding his breath, and then right in front of him, O-Haru's eyes snapped open. Somewhere, there was the sound of a splash of water.

His body curled up in surprise, and Ginji awoke. When he realized that he had been sound asleep, he suddenly broke out in a cold sweat. His heart was pounding hard and fast. How long had he been asleep? The sun didn't seem terribly low in the sky, so it had probably just been a short while. Still, he didn't know. His head was all fuzzy, and his back hurt from leaning against the pillar.

"Hello!" he cried in a ridiculously loud voice, eager to conceal his embarrassment if perhaps someone had returned. Ginji's voice echoed off the high kitchen ceiling and disappeared.

"Excuse me! Miss O-Haru, are you in?"

Then, from the other side of a sliding door a little ways down the hall from the kitchen, there arose the sound of a young woman giggling loudly.

Ginji breathed a sigh of relief. Someone was home after all. Most likely she had seen him drowsing on the doorstep looking so happy and peaceful that she had slipped quietly past and let him sleep. That embarrassed him, but he was grateful that he would be able to fulfill his errand. Ginji picked up the cloth-wrapped package that he had set at his side and held it against his chest with both arms as he stepped out of his shoes and up into the kitchen.

"Pardon me," he called out in a loud voice. "I'm letting myself in." He approached the sliding paper door and said, "I'm coming in," just before he set his hand on the door. It slid silently open as though its tracks had been oiled; he hardly had to push at all.

Inside was a six-tatami-mat room. There was a small chest of drawers and a cupboard and by the wall a rack for hanging kimono, a brazier, and an iron kettle.

And in the very center of the room lay the intertwined bodies of a man and a woman.

The woman was lying face up. There was no mistaking the face. It was O-Haru. The man was facing downward, but there was no need for a closer look; his head was turned to the side just slightly, and the sight of his high-bridged nose was enough for Ginji to tell that it was the young master, Tōichirō.

O-Haru's eyes were smiling. Or at the very least, try as he might, Ginji could find no shade of surprise in those eyes suggesting that something unexpected had befallen her.

Young master's left wrist and O-Haru's right wrist were tightly bound together with a tea towel dyed an eccentric purple. There was some kind of pattern on it, like white flowers, that he could glimpse near their sleeves. Because they were bound so tightly, the skin beneath the cloth had changed color on both of their arms.

Were they dead?

Yes, they most certainly were dead.

And yet, how could the young master, who had sent Ginji to this place, have gotten here ahead of him to die here?

The young master was wearing the kimono that he had had on at the shop. O-Haru was also wearing a kimono with the same pattern. That made no sense. Ginji had come all this way here to deliver a kimono with this pattern. How could O-Haru be wearing the striped kimono with the gourd and bat designs without first receiving the cloth-wrapped package that Ginji even now clutched against his chest?

I see, this is a dream, Ginji thought. *I'm still having that same dream. I thought I had woken up, but actually I'm still dozing.*

With the drone of its wings, a single fly came buzzing into the room. It brushed against Ginji's nose in passing, then traced a circle through the air as though lost before at last alighting softly atop O-Haru's still-open eye.

Again, he heard the sound of a young woman bursting into laughter.

At last the spell was broken. Even as Ginji was thinking, *This is a dream! A dream!* he began to tremble all over, and the cloth-wrapped package he was holding fell to his feet. He cried out and fled from the room, tripping and stumbling. He jammed his feet into his shoes and fell all over himself as he staggered outside.

He ran and ran, bound for Setomono-chō. Faster than the wind, never stopping even when he was out of breath, Ginji ran as though some ferocious god were snapping at his heels. Several times along the way, gatekeepers called for him to halt, but he was too terrified to even think of stopping to answer them. Men came running after him, shouting, but Ginji took no notice. At last, someone made a running leap at him from behind, just before he could reach the Eitai Bridge that crosses the Ōkawa River. He fell suddenly to the ground.

"Hey, kid! You all right? What in the world's gotten into you? You running from something? Answer me!"

When he got a good look at the owner of that voice of sanity firing off these questions, he saw a man in his forties, square-jawed and stern of face. Ginji's teeth chattered as he watched the man identify himself as the hired thief-taker responsible for this area. "You run as fast as Skanda," he said with a forced smile. "Shook off two of my men. I was thinking, 'It's gonna be a mess if he runs all the way to the bridge and dives in.' Now what's the matter, kid? A fox or something play a trick on you? There're a lot of foxes around Fukagawa."

One of the onlookers who had gathered teased him, saying, "But, chief, that kind of fox wears face powder, and this kid's a little young for one of those."

Tears fell from Ginji's eyes. His mouth didn't seem to be working right, and at first he was unable to form proper words. Again the tears blurred his vision, his whole body began to shake, and before he realized it, he was weeping openly.

怪

Ginji suffered a terrible fever afterward and was laid up in bed. He did not return to the Daikoku'ya; instead, he was taken in for the time being by the old man at the Mannen'ya. There he spent three days and three nights in a delirium, and even after the fever had broken, reason did not return for some time. It took ten days for him at last to become able to carry on normal conversations. The old man of the Mannen'ya was quite worried.

The kindly thief-taker who had helped him on the east side of the Eitai Bridge was not so careless as to take Ginji's story back to the Daikoku'ya as-is, but neither was he one to take lightly Ginji's mad flight. When he imagined himself in Ginji's shoes, it seemed that there must surely be some extraordinary reason for him to have been running so madly like that. He went and checked out the rented house in Ōshima-mura. He asked around about O-Haru in the neighborhood surrounding the Daikoku'ya. In this way, he investigated the matter, and when at last Ginji was able to be up and about again, he went to the Mannen'ya to have a talk with him.

"The woman named O-Haru wasn't living in that rented house," the thief-taker said. "And certainly, there were no corpses there like you described. It seems that no sooner was she forced into living there than she fled by night and disappeared. The young handmaiden who was sent there by the Daikoku'ya had been sent back to her parents' home right away on O-Haru's instructions. According to that handmaiden, O-Haru had never had any intention of staying quietly in such a place. She'd kept saying, 'I'm getting out of here! I'm getting out of here!'"

Ginji shivered, and the old man of the Mannen'ya helped him into a large, padded kimono.

"Also, the young master of the Daikoku'ya is safe and sound," the thief-taker said with a quiet expression. "He hasn't committed shinjū. Even when I told him about your going crazy— well, he gave me this look like 'What are you talking about?' That might've been because he was in front of his parents, though. Only . . ." Here the thief-taker scratched at his rough jaw and looked at the faces in the Mannen'ya with upturned eyes. Everyone returned that look.

"What is it?" Ginji asked. "Please tell me, sir."

The thief-taker breathed out a sigh before speaking. "When I went to see the Daikoku'ya's young master, there was a bluish, purplish mark on his left wrist . . . almost as if it'd had something tied around it very tightly. It went all the way around, like this."

Ginji shut his eyes.

The old man of the Mannen'ya spoke in a detached, matter-of-fact voice. "Ginji, it would be best if you left the Daikoku'ya," he said in that cold tone of voice. "Nothing good comes of a business where this kind of thing has happened. Don't worry. I'll find you a new apprenticeship."

"Well, kid, like they say, the world's full of all sorts of things," the thief-taker said with a grin.

怪

In the end, Ginji was left having no idea whether what he had seen in the rented house in Ōshima-mura had been a dream or some kind of premonition. Afterward, Tōichirō remained energetic and in good health and took O-Natsu as his wife in early January.

By that time, Ginji was already working in his new apprenticeship. The master of the Mannen'ya had placed him with a drug wholesaler in Lower Surugadai, as Ginji would probably find returning to the old neighborhood too unpleasant. His work in the new shop was difficult but interesting, and—this too was probably part of the old man's calculation—the successor to that business was the family's only daughter, who was already married to a gentle, easy-going groom who had come up from apprenticeship himself. Within the walls of that business, things were quiet and settled, and so comfortable as to be just a little dull. Here Ginji continued to practice his reading, writing, and abacus, though he no longer pushed himself so hard that he stayed up late without sleeping.

He had never forgotten something that the thief-taker had said to him: *That summer at that house in Ōshima-mura, you dozed off and had a bad dream. Decide right now that that's all any of this ever was.*

He wasn't about to let himself nod off, not ever again.

Two years after Ginji moved to Lower Surugadai, when he was home for one of his seasonal visits, he heard from his eldest brother—who had also returned from Kashiwa'ya in Ōdenma-chō—that one month prior to his visit, the young master and mistress of the Daikoku'ya had died. The story was that they'd gone to bed as though nothing was amiss, and the next morning they hadn't gotten up. The maid came in to check on them and found them in their futons covered in blood. It was *aitaijini*. Beside the two of them, a butcher knife that had apparently been brought out of the kitchen lay on the floor. No one had any idea why they had committed shinjū. There was a child in the belly of his young wife. The mistress of the Daikoku'ya was so overcome with grief that she was now apparently laid up in bed.

Inside, Ginji began shaking in terror, though he didn't let it show in front of his mother. Even so, there was one question that he couldn't stop himself from asking his eldest brother.

"The two of them—were their wrists tied together with a tea towel?"

"I don't know. I didn't hear about it in that much detail," his brother said. Then he added, "Right after they committed shinjū, the old master at Mukōjima—he'd been confined to his bed for a long time—died as well. The Daikoku'ya is in a wretched state now. I feel sorry for them."

What happened that summer is over and done with. I don't need to know whether what I saw was a nightmare or some kind of premonition, Ginji thought. *Ah, O-Haru finally went through with it in the end, didn't she?*

Then, feeling such thoughts might actually draw her to him again, Ginji quickly shook his head to drive O-Haru from his mind.

The old man had been right. Nothing good comes of a business where this kind of thing has happened. Half a year afterward, like a mud wall collapsing from one too many storms, the Daikoku'ya went out of business. After the tenants had departed to their homes, the new landlord came to inspect the buildings, and though he found their exteriors in fine condition, the joists under the floors were completely rotted out, and in the end the buildings had to be torn down.

Since that day, Ginji has not gone near Tōri Setomono-chō. He never nods off during the day and has grown into a full-fledged man who hates gaudy, striped patterns, who works hard in his job at the drug wholesaler, and will have nothing to do with monogatari moyō kimono and tea towels.

II
Cage of Shadows

Yes, sir, my name is Matsugorō, as you say—I served as head clerk for the Okada'ya wax wholesaler in Fukagawa Rokkenbori-chō. I do appreciate your coming out to see me in this drizzling rain.

Mr. Isobe, you say? Pardon my rudeness, but you look rather young to be Mr. Isobe. I was told you wanted to ask me some questions about what happened at the Okada'ya, but . . . Oho, twenty-one, you say? Why, that would make you the same age as Mr. Hisaichirō. Born in the year of the Dragon, were you? Did you know Mr. Hisaichirō? Ah, but where would the son of a merchant have the chance to meet such a fine young samurai as yoursel—?

Oh? Ah. Miss O-Chiyo. You knew Miss O-Chiyo?

Mr. Isobe . . . Isobe . . . Isobe—

Ah! I remember now! Forgive me, it takes a bit of an effort when you get to be my age. You're from the Isobe family; your house is among the police barracks of North Hori Block Eight; Miss O-Chiyo was apprenticed in your home for two years for finishing. In that case, your father must be Mr. Isobe Shin'emon, the head detective. Yes, the day Miss O-Chiyo left home to start working for him, I went along with her to pay my respects. That's already seven years in the past now, back when the old master and Mistress O-Tadzu were both still alive and well. I get nostalgic when I think of those times.

I hope your father is in good health. Oh? Is that so? Well, congratulations to him! And in his retirement, it must give him great peace of mind knowing he has such a fine young successor in you. I don't feel even a sliver of regret for the fifty years I served at the Okada'ya, but having resolved to live my whole life at that shop, I never had a home or family of my own, and—quite predictably—was never blessed with children or grandchildren. When you get to be my age, there are times when you suddenly get kind of sad about that. I've only one living relative; I reside at my younger brother's house now. He—and his wife and his children too—have never been anything but good to me, but after all, we're practically strangers. If they make a fuss over me, I feel reticent. It's an embarrassing situation, to be sure.

Even so, if such a sad thing hadn't happened to the Okada'ya, even a dull man like me would have had the option of working in his old age . . .

No, there's nothing to be gained by crying over it now. No, I'll be all right in a moment. Please just smile. I know it must be awkward when an old man sheds tears in front of you. Please forgive my rudeness.

But all that aside, to think it's none other than Mr. Isobe himself who's come to see this old man about the Okada'ya incident! It happened about three months ago, but . . . well, being as it was such a deplorable thing, I'll admit I'm a little terrified of what you're going to ask me.

Yes, it's exactly as you say. The sequence of events is as you have stated, Mr. Isobe. Master Ichibei; his wife Mistress O-Natsu; their eldest son and heir, Mr. Hisaichirō; their second son, Mr. Seijirō; the only daughter of the former master and mistress, Miss O-Chiyo; and their youngest child, Mr. Harujirō—all of them are dead now. The frightened workers have scattered to the winds, until at last no one is left save a worn-out old man like myself.

The Okada'ya is no longer of this world.

怪

Oh? So you went to the house? When was that? Yesterday? Well then, you must've had some terrible dreams last night.

Ha, ha. No, truly; it's an impressive feat. After all, seven people died in that house. All of us who worked there went running out for dear life, not even taking our furniture or tatami mats with us. We don't even think of going near that place anymore. You've inherited your father's pluck, haven't you?

Anyway . . .

Let me say at the outset that I am fully, solemnly aware of the fact that when you hear the words I'm about to speak, you will think me a man who has no pity in his heart and who knows nothing of proper gratitude—a man headed toward damnation. All the same, that house—that house that used to be the Okada'ya—is unbearably frightening to me.

I began working at the Okada'ya just as I turned ten years old. Both of my parents were born way up in Jōshū, and during a food shortage there, they eloped and ran away together. Once they came to Edo, they did odd jobs to make ends meet, but even so, they were a veritable portrait of that old saw about the poor having large families. Starting with me, there were five children all told—four sons and one daughter. My littlest brother was still a baby when I left home for my apprenticeship. When I came home on my first holiday visit, he'd already grown into a little rascal of five. It was awkward though, because he didn't really *feel* like a brother to me. Yet there's an irony in that, since it's that same little brother who's taking care of me now.

As for my other two brothers, one died of smallpox at age fifteen and the other ran away from home as a child. He disappeared and hasn't been heard from since. My younger sister died in a private brothel. Whether she sold herself of her own free will or was sold off by our good-for-nothing parents, I don't really know. I was away at the Okada'ya by that time. Now that I think on it, she'd always seemed a bit listless . . .

But thanks to having apprenticed at the Okada'ya, I've been able to live a decent life. That's something for which I can never be grateful enough. My youngest brother, a fine master carpenter in his own right, also says he was only able to make it in the world thanks to the master carpenter who trained him hard and looked after him from childhood. That's exactly how it is—whether we prosper or whether we fall into poverty, the fortunes of unimportant nobodies like ourselves depend entirely on the fortunes of the shops and the masters we serve. In that sense, both my younger brother and I have been greatly blessed.

This, Mr. Isobe, is why my feelings of gratitude toward the Okada'ya remain unchanged in the slightest. Frightening though that house may be to me now . . .

What's that, you say? I did? Did I really word it like that?

I see, now, you're right. Just a minute ago, I did say that "the Okada'ya is no longer of this world." Normally, one would say, "The *people* of the Okada'ya are no longer of this world." Yes, yes. That must be because I'm harboring the same thoughts you've expressed to me.

Master Ichibei, who lost his life in the recent disturbance, was preceded by Master Jirobei, who built the Okada'ya practically from the ground up in a single generation. This was the same Master Jirobei whom I began serving at age ten. His wife, Mistress O-Tadzu, was like a mother to me. Never for a moment have I ever forgotten the debt of gratitude I owe the both of them.

Even after he had yielded the seat of shopmaster to Master Ichibei, Master Jirobei, the retired master, retained a firm grip on the shop's helm right up until five years ago, when he suddenly caught his death of flu. As retired shopmistress, Mistress O-Tadzu too continued working at her regular brisk pace, holding things together both on the sales floor and in the house. Mistress O-Natsu had grown up in a wealthy family where she'd never known hard labor, so there were many jobs Mistress O-Tadzu wouldn't leave in her hands. To someone like me, whose first job was at the Okada'ya, who, now that I think about it, was practically raised there, this state of affairs inspired confidence, and I was thankful for that.

Only, with everyone in the shop looking up to the retired shopmaster and shopmistress in admiration, it must have been quite a burr in the saddle for Master Ichibei and Mistress O-Natsu. As the days went by and turned into years, relations grew worse and worse between the retired owners and the present ones. True, the proprietorship had been transferred, so my master was now Master Ichibei and my mistress Mistress O-Natsu. I worked every day under that assumption. Still, when things came down to the wire, the Okada'ya's helmsman was the retired shopmaster, and Mistress O-Tadzu was the pin holding the whole fan together, as it were.

Negotiating with our regular clients of many years, making secret loans to favored retainers of the shōgun, attending trade meetings, making suitable offerings of gifts for the shōgun—it was also one-sided that all of these things had been set aside for the acumen of Master Jirobei and Mistress O-Tadzu to deal with.

Master Ichibei was the only son of Master Jirobei and Mistress O-Tadzu, and he was the apple of their eye. Though as husband and wife they had a solid relationship that would make any man envious, they had been blessed with only one child, Master Ichibei. This was why he was so overprotected as a child. I remember being shocked, as a young apprentice, to learn there were children just like me in the world who were doted on like he was. All I could do was just stare at the proceedings with a stupid look on my face. Yes, it was the very year that I started that Master Ichibei was born, so it's something I do know all about.

However . . . it was quite some time after, when I was working as a chief clerk and receiving private instruction from the head clerk, that I heard with my own ears the head clerk say that Master Jirobei had not raised Master Ichibei right. He said that although Master Jirobei certainly loved his son, he should have disciplined him a little more harshly, so as to build in him the bearing and mentality of someone who must lead others. He was so troubled that he even said the future of the Okada'ya would be in doubt if there were a sudden succession.

Generally speaking, people who were spoiled growing up have a tendency to stray from the straight and narrow. Master Ichibei was no exception, even though he was the flesh and blood of Master Jirobei, a true gentleman. Indeed, from where I stood I could see Master Ichibei giving his youth over to a life of prodigality, being cruel to the apprentices around him, saying whatever capricious thing he wanted. I wondered as well what would happen once the proprietorship became his. It was clear to see we had a rocky road ahead of us.

That's why compared to other shops the Okada'ya's succession came quite late. Master Jirobei used to say to me that he was looking forward to retirement and a slow, peaceful life. He would smile when he said that, like it was a favorite phrase of his, but the reality was that he didn't end up retiring until he was almost seventy, and even then, it was only after being worn down by year after year of Master Ichibei's relentless badgering. Even going on forty, Master Ichibei's reputation was still as bad as ever, and Master Jirobei was reluctant to hand him the reins.

And Master Ichibei seemed to carry quite a grudge about that.

Mr. Isobe, I am ultimately a worthless man who knows nothing of marriage or fatherhood, despite having lived this long. I even left my own parents quite early. Naturally, what I don't know about the bonds of parent and child far outweighs what I do. So I'd like to ask you, if I may—is it really possible for a child to be that deeply, obsessively vindictive and spiteful toward his own parents? Can he really hate them that much and burn with such a desire to get even?

He can . . . you think so?

It's as you say. And yet even now, I still can't conceive of it.

怪

If you've been to the house, Mr. Isobe, you've seen it already, haven't you? Yes, a little ways in on the north side—the room they had dug into the ground. Sturdy and well made, isn't it? About three years after the retired master, Master Jirobei, died, Mistress O-Natsu had that cell constructed to imprison Mistress O-Tadzu.

Mistress O-Natsu was the shopmistress now, having hastily married Master Ichibei when he assumed control of the Okada'ya. She was a full twelve years younger than Master Ichibei, and her family home was the Isuzu'ya—a well-off kimono wholesaler—so she had grown up in the lap of luxury.

At the time Master Ichibei and Mistress O-Natsu's engagement was finalized, people thought the match a strange one, and there were a lot of rumors going around. *The Okada'ya's proprietorship's finally gone to that good-for-nothing prodigal of theirs*, they would say. *I guess there's no helping that, but even so, why a woman like Mistress O-Natsu? Could they not make a match with someone wiser . . . more discreet . . . with a sweeter disposition?*

Those of us who knew what was going on in the Okada'ya were well aware at that time how the world outside was scratching its collective head. Every day, we wanted just to curl up and hide.

The Okada'ya was having some hard times in those days. People said it was all thanks to the bills coming due on Master Ichibei's debauchery, but actually, there were other debts mixed in here and there as well. On the surface, Master Jirobei and Mistress O-Tadzu always kept a stiff upper lip, so the only ones who really knew what was going on were those of us who worked in the shop.

As for Mistress O-Natsu, even when she was still a young girl, there were already a lot of nasty rumors circulating about her. She was the youngest of three daughters at the Isuzu'ya—the prettiest of the lot but also the one with the worst reputation. Mistress O-Natsu was crazy about boys before she'd even finished growing into the sleeves of her kimono. She'd go wild over some actor and run away from home, she'd tempt the workers . . . They're indecent tales, and I'll spare you the particulars, but there were even rumors of her getting pregnant—by whom nobody knows— and secretly aborting the child afterward. And not just once or twice, either.

Back then, it was clear to see even for outsiders that Mistress O-Natsu was wild as could be and really too much for the Isuzu'ya to handle. The two older daughters were both young women of upstanding character and had already married. Either of their husbands would be a fine choice to take over the family business someday. But from one day to the next, there was no telling what kind of mischief Mistress O-Natsu would be up to, so the family probably wanted to marry her off as quickly as possible. Even if that wasn't the reason, though, her excesses had become fodder for the rumor mills, and Mistress O-Natsu passed the age of twenty-five still unable to find anyone who would marry her. No matter how beautiful a woman may be, once she passes her prime her prospects grow weaker with every passing year. That, they say, is why the Isuzu'ya made a deal with the Okada'ya. We'll take care of your debts and wipe the slate clean for you . . . if you'll take care of Mistress O-Natsu for us.

You can imagine what a regrettable match this was for Master Jirobei and Mistress O-Tadzu. However, there was no solution to their dilemma without some kind of sacrifice.

Be that as it may, once Mistress O-Natsu had married Master Ichibei and become part of the family, Mistress O-Tadzu wore herself out trying to train her. Also, understanding that it wasn't enough merely to be strict with her, Mistress O-Tadzu made up her mind to treat Mistress O-Natsu—whose own family had given up on her— not just as a daughter-in-law, but with the same kindness that she would show toward a daughter of her own. That part of this tale I saw from beginning to end with my own eyes, and through that,

Mr. Isobe, I learned a fundamental truth: there are some people in the world who cannot comprehend even the most pure-hearted of intentions.

Yes, Mistress O-Natsu disliked Mistress O-Tadzu, first of all, simply for being her mother-in-law. Moreover, she disliked her because Mistress O-Tadzu was still a bewitchingly attractive woman. Also, there was the fact that the workers adored and admired Mistress O-Tadzu so very much more than they ever did her. I said she "disliked" her a moment ago, but truly, "hated" is the more appropriate term. Or should I say it was envy?

That's why the seeds of trouble lay always just beneath the surface, even though Mistress O-Tadzu—as retired shopmistress—did such an admirable job of running things after Master Jirobei passed away. Still, Mistress O-Tadzu was not so foolish as to accidentally provide openings to her daughter-in-law, so in that way, things maintained their own kind of precarious equilibrium, as on sailed the good ship Okada'ya.

At least, until the *incident.*

The look of the sky that day was much as it is today. It was the start of spring, but cold rain was pouring down as though the coldest days of winter had returned. The date was none other than the one-year anniversary of Master Jirobei's death. That day, Mistress O-Tadzu was caught under a falling pile of merchandise that had been stacked for shipping inside the shop. She broke her foot.

You may be aware of this already, but wax—at the stage we wholesalers handle it—is shaped into blocks. One *kan*'s worth is measured out and poured into a mold where it then hardens into a rectangular shape. Because of that, wax can get pretty heavy when it's stacked up for shipping. If a small child were to get trapped under a pile of those blocks, he could even be crushed to death.

All the same, there was something funny about that incident. With the wax being molded in the shape that it is, once it's loaded up and stacked, it hardly ever falls over. But just as Mistress O-Tadzu happened to be standing close by, a pile of wax blocks stacked just as high as her head started to wobble and then collapsed atop her.

Yes . . . It was exactly what you're thinking. Both myself and others in the store believed someone had deliberately taken aim at Mistress O-Tadzu and pushed the stack over on top of her. But just believing this didn't change anything; it carried no more weight than a child's believing it would have. We had no solid evidence to back up what we were thinking, so we hesitated to say anything too loudly.

In any case, Mistress O-Tadzu grew much weaker after that injury and always seemed to be half asleep. The tables had completely turned. And that's when Mistress O-Natsu gleefully had work started on that cell.

Why a cell, you ask? Well, to this day I don't really know. The excuse Mistress O-Natsu gave at the time was, "Mother's become a bit slow in the *head* since the accident. In the daytime she sees things that aren't there, and at night she goes stumbling out of the house half asleep. It's terribly dangerous, so for Mother's own personal safety, we'll be confining her to a locked cell."

And what did I do? Well, I was against it of course. I was vehemently against it. While it was true Mistress O-Tadzu's body was weakened, her mind was still a good sight more sound than Mistress O-Natsu's. The other workers in the shop felt the same way.

But you see, Mr. Isobe, we were there to *serve*, so we were on weak footing. And it's only natural that each person there was clinging to his own job and his own meager allowance. If you don't work you don't eat, and nobody can live without eating. And so the resolution of the young maids, for example, turned into trembling fear when Mistress O-Natsu and Master Ichibei ordered them to say they'd seen Mistress O-Tadzu stumbling around in the corridors late at night . . . when they threatened the maids with what might happen if they didn't obey. With no choice but to do as Mistress O-Natsu and Master Ichibei ordered, they said their lies by ones and twos and hung their heads low, with tears welling up in their eyes. There were two who couldn't take it anymore, and they ran away from the shop. If I'd had their gumption I might've done the same.

Maybe that's what I should've done. But it's too late now. Truly too late. And nothing I say now will change anything.

There's also the fact that those of us who objected to the end, myself included, were ultimately talked into accepting the confinement by none other than Mistress O-Tadzu herself. "I can't bear the sight of you all in torment like this," she said. "If my moving into the cell without a fuss will put an end to all this, then it's no trouble at all." She was smiling when she said it. "But, Matsugorō," she said to me as she bowed her head, "now that you are head clerk, please take good care of the shop."

Nowadays . . . remembering that, I feel such a sense of wasted opportunity that I can't help tearing up.

The last time I would ever see Mistress O-Tadzu's smile was that day, when she moved into the cell with her futons and her personal effects. Afterward, for a space of two years, I neither saw her face nor heard her voice. This was because Mistress O-Natsu had arranged things so that only she would be able to enter Mistress O-Tadzu's cell. If you've seen it you understand, Mr. Isobe. The cell itself was made to be solid and durable, and even in the passageway leading to it, you have to go through two locked doors. Those were put in later, when Mistress O-Natsu called a carpenter to come and build them. The only keys to those doors were always on a string around Mistress O-Natsu's neck, and she never let them out of contact with her own skin. The carpenter was someone Mistress O-Natsu had called in all the way from Kawasaki, so nobody knew who he was or what his business was called.

Now naturally, we workers were worried about how Mistress O-Tadzu was faring. Again and again, we asked Mistress O-Natsu if we might look in on her, but she deflected us at every turn. She said the retired mistress wanted to rest quietly and didn't want to see anyone—in a tone of voice that told us to keep our noses out of it. There was nothing we could do except believe her and trust that Mistress O-Tadzu was well.

It is certain that Master Ichibei had given silent approval to all this. Not once did he ever raise an objection or criticize what she was doing. Instead—and it disgusts me even to say this—it looked to me like he thought it was *funny* seeing Mistress O-Natsu holding the power of life and death over his mother.

Have you heard the story, Mr. Isobe, of what happened after that tragedy three months ago, when a city official finally went into that cell during the cleanup? He came right back out again looking deathly pale, unable to say a single word, and broke out in a high fever. He was laid up in bed for the next three days.

Inside that cell, Mistress O-Tadzu was sitting upright in her bed, completely turned to bone. According to the official who examined her, about a year had passed since she died. They say it was most likely thirst and starvation that killed her. Both of Mistress O-Tadzu's hands were in chains, and the inside of the cell was so messy and filthy it looked like the den of some kind of animal. They say the stench was so bad it was impossible to breathe in there. When I try to imagine the slow horror that tidy, businesslike woman must have experienced in there, I can feel my vision going dark in front of me.

怪

Mr. Isobe . . . I want to ask you one more time. Is there really, truly anyone in this world—no matter how spoiled they might have been growing up—who would really just go along with it when his young bride wants to do such horrible things to the very woman who gave him birth? Who would not even *hesitate* to allow this to be done to his mother?

怪

Mr. Isobe, do you know the sequence of events that led to Miss O-Chiyo's coming to your home for manners training? Did she ever say any— Ah, is that so? Yes, Miss O-Chiyo was truly a sweet, gentle young lady, wasn't she?

Master Ichibei and Mistress O-Natsu's relationship as husband and wife was in its own way an affectionate one. Well, at least it never looked like it wasn't affectionate. But be that as it may, I don't believe this was because of mutual understanding between them so much as the fact that it was somehow easier to backbite against the retired master and Mistress O-Tadzu if they did it together.

Master Ichibei's tempestuous woman troubles and his astonishing debauchery were well known among the other wholesalers in the neighborhood. To illustrate just how wretched things had become, people were saying that no employment agent with a heart should ever place a young housemaid in the Okada'ya of Rokkenbori-chō—especially after the passing of the retired master.

As for Mistress O-Natsu, her promiscuity had not slackened a whit since her younger days, and if anything it was more brazen— and expensive—than ever. Ultimately, it seemed that the Okada'ya's fortune had been eaten out from within by Master Ichibei and Mistress O-Natsu.

Recent events have brought this to light too, but their eldest son, Mr. Hisaichirō, was not even born from Mistress O-Natsu's womb. Their second son, Mr. Seijirō, didn't belong to Master Ichibei. Their youngest, Mr. Harujirō, was the son of both husband and wife, but he was in poor health from the day he was born and was sadly just fifteen when he died. It's doubtful whether he would have lived another year, even if the incident had never occurred . . . For the last two or three years of his life, he hardly left the house. He'd close himself off in a room somewhere, humming to himself all day long as he drew incomprehensible pictures on sheets of paper meant for calligraphy.

The Miss O-Chiyo you knew was a foundling, actually. Nineteen years ago Mistress O-Tadzu met a man who'd happened across an abandoned infant not far from the Rokkenbori Bridge. Initially, the child was to be entrusted to the landlord, but Mistress O-Tadzu took pity on her, went to ask Master Jirobei, and together they took her in to be their adopted daughter. This is why, if I may say so, as a young lady she exhibited such ramrod straight moral fiber, unaffected by Master Ichibei and Mistress O-Natsu's poisonous nature.

This is something I can tell you now, but I couldn't before. Seven years ago, when Miss O-Chiyo was still just twelve, dark circumstances led us to ask your father to take this innocent, helpless child into his home under the pretext of "finishing lessons." To explain, and I feel like I'm defiling my own mouth just by speaking of it, Master Ichibei, in the crowning achievement of his licentiousness, had turned his eye on Miss O-Chiyo . . . Yes. An odious thing to be sure, but true.

This was not something we could simply ignore, so I and one of the older housemaids—she worked near Miss O-Chiyo, took care of her, and was the one who had sensed the danger—agreed to go together and consult with Mistress O-Tadzu and Master Jirobei, who was still healthy and spry at that time.

Now of course it's forbidden for a worker to slander his master. Nevertheless, the situation was what it was. And although I was prepared to lose my head over it, the retired master and Mistress O-Tadzu heeded what I and the maid had to say and took action immediately. I can't imagine how infuriating, how shameful, and how painful that must have been for them. At any rate, the retired master had been an acquaintance of your father's for some time. He talked it over with him, and they agreed to move Miss O-Chiyo temporarily to the Isobe house in North Hori Block Eight for her protection.

The relief I experienced was immense. *Now she'll be safe*, I thought. I only hoped and prayed that Miss O-Chiyo would not have to leave the Isobe house until the time came to do so as a bride, when she could go to some house other than our own. It's too late to say such things now, but—what's that? Is that so? The Isobe family had spoken with you about taking Miss O-Chiyo as your wife? Ah, if only things could have turned out that way! It all could have been so nice.

At any rate, my foolish sense of satisfaction did not last very long. As you well know, as soon as the retired master passed away, Miss O-Chiyo was summoned back to the Okada'ya. But even so, as long as Mistress O-Tadzu was still keeping a watchful eye, things somehow went along without incident. But then Mistress O-Tadzu was at last forced into that cell, with Miss O-Chiyo growing more womanly and beautiful every day.

Ultimately, the day that Miss O-Chiyo was summoned back to the Okada'ya was the beginning of the tragedy of that night three months ago.

怪

It was a snowy day right at the end of the New Year's celebrations this year when Miss O-Chiyo drank rat poison. Mr. Harujirō happened to find her right after she had swallowed it. She was in pain, but he managed to save her life, and the moment of danger passed.

There was no need even to ask why Miss O-Chiyo had attempted suicide. In the end, we had been unable to protect her. It seemed that this had been going on for some time, and even more disgustingly, it wasn't only Master Ichibei.

This is a horrible tale; surely you've heard as much of it now as you want, Mr. Isobe. Do you really want me to continue?

Oh, you will? Well, in that case, I'll dig a moat around my own heart too and tell you.

With Miss O-Chiyo such a lovely young woman, and Mr.

Hisaichirō and Mr. Seijirō both possessed of a nature similar to that of their warped and twisted father, there could be no greater disaster for her than to be trapped under the same roof as them.

Apparently Mistress O-Natsu was aware of these goings-on. Someone heard her laughing once as she said, "We were kind enough to take that girl in when she would've died by the roadside; a girl like that should do whatever the boys want."

Miss O-Chiyo tearfully revealed all of this to me after she'd been pulled back from the brink of death. There was nothing I could do. Nothing except cry with her.

And then—

Suddenly, I heard Mistress O-Tadzu's voice.

Matsugorō, don't worry, she said. *I'll take revenge for what happened to O-Chiyo. I'm a woman too, and I can't ignore her torment any longer. Leave the rest to me.*

As I was just telling you, Mistress O-Tadzu was supposed to have been locked up in that cell all along. At that time, I didn't know that she was already long dead, having wasted away to bone while she still lived. That's why I thought at the time that Mistress O-Tadzu had made a complete recovery and been secretly let out of the cell. That someone had rescued her at some point. That under her guidance the Okada'ya would finally go back to being the upstanding business that it used to be. That's what I thought. I was so happy I wanted to leap for joy. I shouted and started spreading the news all throughout the house. "I heard Mistress O-Tadzu's voice! She's well now and coming back soon! Everything will be all right again!" Master Ichibei and Mistress O-Natsu and even the apprentices stared at me like I was out of my mind, but I didn't back down. This was because I believed what Mistress O-Tadzu had said.

And then, as if to underpin that belief, from that day forward, by day and by night, Mistress O-Tadzu began to frequently appear inside the Okada'ya.

To me? No, my virtue was insufficient; even while the excitement was spreading through the store, I never saw Mistress O-Tadzu with my own eyes. As I just told you, I merely heard her voice—and only that one time—right after Miss O-Chiyo told me what had happened to her.

From the time it began, Master Ichibei and Mistress O-Natsu seemed to be under a considerable threat. Apparently, the Mistress O-Tadzu that they saw would appear with a frightening expression on her face. Well, of course she would. Mr. Hisaichirō and Mr. Seijirō both complained of nightmares where she was slowly, firmly wringing their necks, and it got so they couldn't sleep and would keep a fire burning at night. Eventually, they were jumping at their own shadows even under the light of noon.

It was strange how Mistress O-Tadzu's face began to appear often in Mr. Harujirō's drawings. Usually, he drew her with a smile on her face, but he would say things like, "When Grandmother comes, she stares at me with a face that's as cold and white as snow, not moving at all. This is a picture of what she looks like."

There were other incidents. Oh, yes—the time Mistress O-Natsu was putting up her hair, and Mistress O-Tadzu appeared in the mirror and reached out her hands to grab at it. Sometimes Mistress O-Natsu would cry out in a voice loud enough to turn the whole place upside down, and surprised maids would throw fits. Strange things.

And then there was Miss O-Chiyo. Bit by bit, she was losing her grip on sanity. She began spending her days in intimate conversation with a Mistress O-Tadzu only she could see.

What triggered the incident on that night three months ago, I can't rightly say even now. The one thing that is certain, though, is that Master Ichibei, Mistress O-Natsu, Mr. Hisaichirō, and Mr. Seijirō were all thoroughly drunk.

Who was it who mixed rat poison into the water in the jar by the kitchen? I can't answer that either. Still, when I think about it, I find myself wondering if it might have been Mr. Harujirō. If perhaps the grandmother who appeared in the shattered heart of that lad had told him to do it because it was the only way to purify that house. At least, I heard that just before he died, he mumbled something to that effect himself to the people who rushed over to help him.

Mr. Harujirō had always been bullied and picked on by his parents and both of his brothers, and he'd always felt out of place. When Miss O-Chiyo nearly died drinking rat poison, maybe it had set those dull wheels in his head turning, so that he decided to die and take the family he hated with him. I think that talk about being ordered to do it by Mistress O-Tadzu may have been just an excuse Mr. Harujirō came up with.

That aside, it was a truly fortunate thing that the workers at the shop then were drinking from a different water jar.

Inside the house, the family realized that they had drunk poison, and all began shouting at each other, one saying, "I'll go for a doctor and just save myself!" and another saying, "Just see if I'll let you!" They were holding one another back from going for help. They struck each other and kicked each other until at last it turned into a desperate struggle, and in the end not one of them was saved. It's a sad thing to remember that chain of events. The fact that Miss O-Chiyo alone died in her own room with a peaceful expression on her face is the only consolation I have.

They say that before Mistress O-Natsu stopped breathing, she was crying out Mistress O-Tadzu's name ferociously and cursing it. *"Get out of here!"* she said, *"Don't come near me!"* The way she was waving around her arms and kicking with her feet, they said it looked like she was grappling with someone. The old housemaid saw that insane spectacle, and her hair turned completely white. Mistress O-Natsu's insults and curses were so ferocious that for one brief moment the maid wondered if Mistress O-Tadzu might have come out of her cell and hidden herself in the shadow of the sliding paper doors, looking on as Mistress O-Natsu was dying.

However, she looked around carefully and realized that Mistress O-Tadzu was not there. She couldn't have been of course. Neither the maid nor I knew it at the time, but Mistress O-Tadzu had died a cruel death of hunger and thirst all alone in that cell, a year prior at the very least.

We didn't know that. But Mistress O-Natsu knew it. Master Ichibei may have known it. Mr. Hisaichirō and Mr. Seijirō may have had some vague notion that it had happened. That's why they were able to see Mistress O-Tadzu's ghost. They saw her vengeful apparition. I wonder if it might have been something like that.

怪

Well, well . . . that light drizzle has finally let up, hasn't it? Will you be headed back now? It doesn't change anything to listen to such a sad story all over again, but I hope you've heard what you needed to hear.

Pardon? The carpenter? What happened to the carpenter? From Kawasaki, you mean? The one Mistress O-Natsu hired to build the cell and the locks in the corridor?

You've met with him?

Wh—what did he tell you, that carpenter? Did he perhaps . . .

Did he tell you that he had met with me—with head clerk Matsugorō? That just that one time, right after Mistress O-Tadzu had been forced into the cell, Matsugorō came to see him and begged him to make a duplicate key, bowing so low he pressed his forehead against the tatami floor?

Oh . . . ? And did that carpenter also tell you he accepted Matsugorō's request?

Well then, what do you think Matsugorō intended to do with that key once he had it in hand? What do you think, Mr. Isobe?

Do you think that, even so, Matsugorō's also a strange fellow?

That once he had a duplicate key, he should've gone straight to Mistress O-Tadzu's rescue? That's what a wise man would do.

But by the time Matsugorō finally got hold of a duplicate and snuck into that cell, Mistress O-Tadzu was already in a severely weakened state, having endured every torment Mistress O-Natsu could devise. She was at death's door . . .

Ah, Mr. Isobe, is that what you're thinking?

That Matsugorō was unable to set Mistress O-Tadzu free?

That if Mistress O-Tadzu had been left in there alone, she would have been killed sooner or later by the abuse?

That because of that, Matsugorō thought, *There's only one way I can rescue Mistress O-Tadzu. A simple, easy way for me to give her rest right here and right now.*

That's what you're thinking, isn't it, Mr. Isobe?

But you can also think of it like this too, can you not? That when Matsugorō slipped into her cell, pitiful, half-dead Mistress O-Tadzu begged him to end her misery quickly.

And he did as she asked.

Matsugorō knew that Mistress O-Tadzu's bones were in the cell. Mistress O-Tadzu had been glad to die.

That's why Matsugorō was the only one Mistress O-Tadzu's ghost didn't appear to.

Notwithstanding, Matsugorō will be charged with murder, won't he, Mr. Isobe?

Because when you think about it, ghosts don't use rat poison, do they? Poisoning a water jar must be the work of a human being, after all.

Are you really going back? Then allow me to bid you farewell. I apologize for my rudeness. I'm feeling just a little weak. I don't have much time left myself.

You say you sleep soundly every night, Mr. Isobe. I have dreams. I dream that I am locked in that cell with Mistress O-Tadzu. Mistress O-Tadzu and I are as silent and insubstantial as shadows.

Then we slip right out from between the bars of that sturdy cage and are free to go wherever we want.

That's what a ghost really is.

Please watch your step on your way home, sir. And for the love of mercy, don't ever come here again. Don't even turn to look back.

Consider it Matsugorō's dying wish.

III

The Futon Storeroom

The saké seller known as the Kaneko'ya was located in the Fukagawa district of Edo, Higashi-machi, near the gate of Eitaiji Temple. It was notorious for the fact that its proprietors had, generation after generation, all died young.

Its founder had established it there in 1709—the sixth year of Houei—and one hundred five years had passed since that time. Under normal circumstances, the ownership might have been expected to change hands at most four or five times in that period, but the Kaneko'ya had seen seven different proprietors already.

Even so, there had been nothing particularly ominous or suspicious about the deaths of its previous six owners. Five of them had died peacefully, and one of them . . . had not. They had each passed on with such ease and tranquility that had they been able to fulfill their expected life spans, their lives would have been deemed blessed and full by those who knew them. They would simply climb into bed one night and never wake up. Morning would come and their families would try to wake them, only to realize that they were dead.

Now, rationally speaking, it may be that the men of the Kaneko'ya had had the misfortune of being born with congenitally weak hearts, transmitted from father to son for generation after generation. Indeed, the second and third sons who would not have inherited the proprietorship had died while they were yet in childhood. Only the eldest son ever seemed to make it to adulthood, and then, just as he was reaching the age of sixteen or seventeen, his father would meet with an untimely death. The son would rush to take over the family business, marry as soon as possible, and start a family. Then, once his son somehow managed to reach the age of sixteen or seventeen, the cycle would repeat—it would be the new father's turn to die an easy, if sudden, death.

On the other hand, there were plenty of daughters who had grown up healthy and strong. Every generation had produced hale, energetic young women who left to become wives and mothers. These were blessed with easy births and precious children.

The busybodies of the world would say that the women of the Kaneko'ya were _too_ strong, and that the men of the family died young because they were oppressed by the vigorous spirits of the women. Certainly, that's a simple enough explanation. And actually, the most recent owner—a young man who had only just inherited the family business—had not only a grandmother but also a great-grandmother who was still healthy and spry, and her eyes shone so brightly that perhaps we shouldn't necessarily laugh away the idea as though it came from some penny dreadful. On the other hand, there were also rumors circulating that the women of the Kaneko'ya, mothers and daughters alike, were without exception born in the year of _hinoe'uma_—that once-in-sixty-years annum when the year of the Horse coincided with rising _yang_. Women born in such years were said to be of an unduly passionate temperament that shortened the lives of their husbands. Absurd. In reality, there wasn't a single _hinoe'uma_ in the entire family.

Speaking of rumors, here's another one. I mentioned that in six generations of owners, only one had died differently from the others. That was the fourth owner, Ki'emon, who died of measles at age thirty-three on the morning of New Year's Day. Measles can be a fearsome—and in many cases fatal—disease if you catch it in adulthood.

At that time, however, a rumor went flying around that Ki'emon's death was divine retribution. Which god's retribution? That of the fifth Tokugawa shōgun, Lord Tsunayoshi, they said. Lord Tsunayoshi had died of measles on the morning of New Year's Day in the sixth year of Houei, and the sixth year of Houei had been the same year in which the Kaneko'ya was founded. In other words, the story was that the soul of Lord Tsunayoshi, having achieved divinity, had grown angry with this saké shop called the Kaneko'ya, which had first opened for business in the year of his death, and thus he was punishing it.

These were tall tales and outright fabrications, so in any case they did not spread very far. As fifth Tokugawa shōgun, Lord Tsunayoshi had brandished the authority of his office freely, causing great suffering among the masses; he was the sort of shōgun people wanted to see on the *receiving* end of divine retribution. Furthermore, even if Lord Tsunayoshi's spirit really had become some fussy divinity who was smiting the insolent Kaneko'ya, surely he wouldn't have waited until the fourth generation to get around to it. There were some who did argue that because the first, second, and third generation proprietors had all gotten through the measles safely as children, Tsunayoshi did have to wait, but still, when the quibbling reached that point, it just turned funny, and people would hold their bellies laughing when they heard that sort of thing.

In any case, though, the shop's reputation as a place whose masters died young had taken hold, and every time a master died, annoying rumors took flight. This was a hard thing for a merchant family. Those stories—redolent of Buddhist funerary incense—reeked of death, and the fact that the Kaneko'ya was a seller of saké, a seller of *celebration* if you will, only deepened the sense of incongruity. That was why for generations the Kaneko'ya had maintained the trust of its most loyal clientele by assuming a more humble attitude than that of other stores, by accepting unreasonable orders that the competition would have balked at, and by building a reputation for itself as a place where people worked earnestly and gave their all for the business.

This, naturally, made life quite hard for the workers. But for that reason, the Kaneko'ya had gained a second reputation—one not so colorful as the tales of its owners dying young—as a place where the training and discipline of employees was especially severe. Not severe as in, "It may be severe, but you'll be compensated accordingly." Just severe.

Still, not once in its seven-generation history had it ever had a case of a worker running away or engaging in scandalous behavior. Also, Kaneko'ya's workers truly worked well and never complained or fought amongst themselves. That was something of a wonder to the merchants of Monzen-chō.

Training workers was always the biggest headache for any shopmaster. No matter how you went about it, everyone knew it impossible to do perfectly. If a master hired ten workers, he would train, lodge, and feed them for the next ten years, and if after that as many as one or two had grown into the kind of skilled worker who could be a pillar of the business, it was considered an excellent result indeed. That was how hard it was. Due to the difficulty of the work, many would at some point quit or run away. Also, not a few would become unable to work due to illness or injury.

In the worst cases, workers would sometimes abscond with the shopmaster's money, sink into lives of crime, and even attack the very shop to which they should have owed their gratitude. By law, though, any worker who wounded his master or attempted to set fire to his house, no matter what the reason or explanation, would end up decorating the prison gate with his head—and the reason it had come to that was that there were so many workers doing it.

The workers weren't all adults; apprentices and nursemaids would begin their service while still children. The shop had to train and discipline them in place of their parents, and this wasn't easy either. If they skipped work to go play, if they hid somewhere to eat pilfered food, or if they dozed off during work, they had to be scolded, they had to be lectured, and sometimes they had to be subjected to harsh corporal punishment. A tremendous investment of time and effort was necessary to train them so they could come into their own as seasoned workers. And yet even so, the number of successes was small.

For generations, this difficult feat had been accomplished by the Kaneko'ya with the greatest of ease. Whether it was a young roughneck whose family could do nothing with him or a spineless crybaby of a child, once they went up to work at the Kaneko'ya, ten days would be enough to make a whole new person of them—a serious, devoted worker in the shop. They would also become far less prone to disease and injury.

It was no wonder that the merchants in the neighborhood looked on at this with puzzlement as well as envy. Whenever one of them asked the master, his wife, or the head clerk what the trick to it was, they would just smile and with a tilt of their head say, "Ahh, I don't know . . ." only deepening the mystery. After all, what kind of trick could there be to something like that?

However, that's how things were at the Kaneko'ya at the time one of the young maids died of a sudden, massive hemorrhaging from the nose. That was around mid-October of the eleventh year of Bunka (1814), when the seventh proprietor of the Kaneko'ya, Shichibei, was thirty-five.

怪

O-Sato was her name.

The eldest daughter of a tenant farmer in Ōshima-mura of East Sarue-Gozaimokugura, she had come to the Kaneko'ya at age eleven as a nursemaid. At the time of her death at age sixteen, she had been working in the house as a maid. That meant she had been training at the Kaneko'ya for about five years. Hardworking and gentle of disposition, O-Sato was bony and thin but had a calm, mature face for her age. Her movements were like those of an adult—the kind of girl one might at first glance mistake for a full-fledged housemaid more than twenty years of age.

The Kaneko'ya was not a large operation; at most its scale was on the lower end of average. Among its regular clients were restaurants and samurai households, and they also sold plenty direct from the store. Because it kept its front door open later than any other shop in Fukagawa, it often happened that the workers were unable to reach the public baths before the last bath of the day. The bathhouse employees were familiar with the Kaneko'ya though and well aware of the situation, and they were kind enough to leave their front door open until the Kaneko'ya workers all came running up in a hurry and piled inside.

On the night in question, O-Sato had been all aflutter as she hurried over for the last bath of the evening. She bathed quickly, exchanged greetings with the cashier, and stepped back outside. Until then there had been nothing out of the ordinary in her clipped, efficient movements. But before she had gotten far from the bathhouse, blood suddenly began gushing from her nose. She collapsed by the roadside, stiff as a stick that someone had thrown down, both hands still pressed against her face.

Because she was walking back by herself at the time, the guard at the nearby district gate assisted her, carrying her on his shoulders back to the Kaneko'ya, but by the time they arrived, she had already stopped breathing.

According to the gate guard, however, O-Sato hadn't seemed to be in any pain as he was carrying her on his back down one road after another. All the way back, she kept whispering something in a small, almost singsong voice, like a child playing a hiding game:

> *Oni, oni, come this way,*
> *To where you hear my clapping hands.*

Oni, oni, come this way,
To where you hear my clapping hands.

That voice continued to ring in the gate guard's ears long after he had departed, and he slept for the next three days.

The Kaneko'ya certainly did not sit idle. The thief-taker began an investigation, and town officials launched one of their own as well. Ultimately, however, they were unable to uncover a reason for O-Sato's death. She had been eating the same food as everyone else that night, so it didn't look like poisoning—accidental or deliberate—was a possibility. There were no wounds on her body, and no unusual spotting had appeared on her face as the skin had cooled. Her face had been peaceful in death, and once the blood from her nose was wiped away she looked as though she might be sleeping.

The workers at the Kaneko'ya were stunned by O-Sato's sudden death but could only shake their heads in frustration at the complete absence of any illness, injury, or other explanation they could think of.

The domestic staff was held together by O-Mitsu, the chief housekeeper. She was forty-three years old, strong both in body and will, and not one to get upset over little things, but even O-Mitsu, when questioned by the master and mistress of the house, appeared withdrawn and simply answered that nothing had seemed unusual about O-Sato in the days leading up to her death.

"O-Sato was full of energy right up until she went to the bath," O-Mitsu repeated. "She ate her evening meal late just like always. It didn't look like anything was wrong with her." At last she had broken down in tears and apologized to them, saying, "Whatever was wrong, I failed to see it." O-Mitsu was a model housekeeper, and the master and mistress relied on her to an extraordinary degree. Other shops had expressed envy at the Kaneko'ya having such a competent and hardworking chief housekeeper. The master and mistress were not even thinking of laying any blame on her. Instead, they sought to console her.

In the end, it was decided to hold a very brief wake for O-Sato, then quickly send her body back to her family. In their report to the city officials, they called it a death from illness, tying up the matter neatly. The shops around Monzen-chō buzzed with all manner of rumors about the mysterious sudden death of a Kaneko'ya employee, but when the city clerk approved the report, there was no longer anything to do from the gallery. The most they could do was gaze with even greater curiosity at the Kaneko'ya—in the mornings and evenings, at least, since stores that could afford to stare all day long were few and far between. Naturally, the whispers began to burn down to embers.

Although she had died suddenly while away at her workplace, it was unlikely that O-Sato's parents, having borrowed ahead on her expected pay, would have harsh words for the Kaneko'ya. Far from that, they instead asked whether—in order to fill the gap left by O-Sato's passing—the shop might make use of their youngest daughter, who was soon to be sent out to find a position. The employment agent who stood as go-between with the Kaneko'ya had been well aware of what a hard worker O-Sato was and of the crushing poverty under which her family lived, so he interceded passionately on their behalf with the master and mistress.

And so it was that about two weeks after O-Sato's death, her youngest sister O-Yū came to work at the Kaneko'ya. As might be expected, she was eleven years old. Her parents borrowed ahead on the pay she would receive until she reached the same age at which her older sister had died and sent her out of the house with a small, cloth-wrapped package clutched in her arms.

When O-Yū entered the Kaneko'ya, all of the things that her sister had used were allotted to her as-is. The futon and its covers, the teacup, the chopsticks, the wooden box that doubled as lunch tray and storage container, and even the apron were all O-Sato's hand-me-downs. The same corner of the same maids' chamber where O-Sato had slept was given to O-Yū to sleep in at night as well.

This room was divided among three women, and the other two must have surely known O-Sato well when she was still among the living. They were closer to O-Sato in age than O-Yū was. And yet not even once did they ever share their memories of her. Even though they had to have known that O-Yū was O-Sato's sister, they uttered not a word of condolence. It was as though they had forgotten all about her sister.

O-Yū was not mistreated, but neither was she really paid any mind. When she observed the other maids more closely, it didn't appear that they were particularly close to one another either. A cool, dry wind seemed to be blowing through the place.

At present, there were no children at the Kaneko'ya young enough to need nursemaids, so from the very beginning, the work assigned to O-Yū was of the same type assigned to the older maids: drawing water, cleaning, airing futons, washing, running errands. O-Yū did her utmost, but try as she might, some of these things were too much for the hands of an eleven-year-old girl, and they began slipping through her fingers one after another.

Deep in her little heart, O-Yū understood all too well that she was useless there—a far cry from what her late elder sister had been. But for that reason, she improvised in her own way, thinking up strategies for learning the job as quickly as possible. She knew enough to do that. And the one who had given her that knowledge was none other than O-Sato herself.

As was often the case with poor families, O-Yū came from a large household. There were six children, though O-Sato and O-Yū were the only girls. With her parents ever scrambling just to make ends meet, O-Yū had practically been raised by O-Sato. When O-Sato had left home to go work, O-Yū had gone running after her and cried prodigiously, and when she had come back to visit during New Year's and Obon, she had been happy—so happy!—to see her big sister again that even sleeping at night felt like a waste of precious time.

On such occasions, they would burrow into a single futon together and talk to each other all night long. O-Yū would tell O-Sato everything that had been going on in the family while she was away, and O-Sato would select interesting or pleasant anecdotes from the shop to share with her sister.

That's right. Most of the time, all of O-Sato's stories were about pleasant things. Still, on occasion, her face would grow a little serious and she would say something like this:

"When you get to be my age, you'll go off somewhere and start working too. When that time comes, work hard with all your heart and soul—don't hold anything back. Because in the end, it's the hard workers who win out."

O-Yū had etched those words her sister had spoken into her young heart.

At the Kaneko'ya, there were times when she grew sad, and tears would well up in her eyes. There were times when she missed her home. On nights like that, O-Yū would pull the covers up over her head, curl up into a ball, and lie perfectly still. Whenever she did so, it felt as though she were being enveloped in the warmth of her sister's body—as though her sister's warmth still remained in these covers from when O-Sato was alive. O-Yū would remember those times back home when they had slept side by side in a single futon and almost imagine that she could hear her sister's voice. *She's always right beside me, watching over me*, she would think. And then the tears would dry, and with a soft murmur of "Good night, O-Sato," O-Yū would sleep at last.

怪

After a month in service at the Kaneko'ya, O-Yū gained a general understanding of her work.

Then one morning, she was out doing the wash by the well

when O-Mitsu, the chief housekeeper, strode up to her. O-Yū cringed, expecting to be scolded for something. Usually, the tall, full-bodied chief housekeeper never spoke to her at all. At the Kaneko'ya, there was a clear pecking order even among the housemaids, and those who received their instructions from O-Mitsu directly were limited to those experienced housemaids working directly under her. The experienced housemaids then divided up the work among O-Yū and the young maids with whom she shared her room. Then finally, the other young maids ordered O-Yū around, as she was at the very bottom.

The only time O-Mitsu paid her any mind was to scold her. At those times, O-Mitsu would jump two levels of the hierarchy and suddenly lay right into her.

But this morning was different. O-Yū had set aside her washing, stood up, and lowered her head in meek preparation for whatever sharp words were surely coming, but looking on her O-Mitsu said something most unexpected. She said that the lady of the house had been praising her work.

Just once, when O-Yū had first arrived, the shopmaster and shopmistress had spoken words of greeting to her. In her daily routine, however, O-Yū never even saw their faces. But O-Mitsu was saying that the lady of the house had said to her, "That little sister of O-Sato's who started just recently is quite a good worker."

O-Yū was happy and felt a sense of warmth well up in her chest. It felt like it was not only she being praised, but rather her and the soul of her sister, the silent guardian that was ever by her side.

She bowed her head low and said, "Thank you very much" in a small voice.

O-Mitsu continued to stand beside her, so O-Yū raised her head and fearfully looked up at her. O-Mitsu's eyes had narrowed to mere threads, and she was staring at O-Yū without moving a muscle.

O-Mitsu was not only large-bodied, the features of her face were generally larger than usual. She wasn't beautiful, but she had an unexpected sort of face that could draw people's eyes to it in surprise. When she scolded the maids, her large eyeballs would bulge out and her mouth would open wide as she shouted out her reprimands.

怪

Now, however, she seemed practically a different person. Almost as though she were wearing a mask.

O-Yū suddenly became frightened and wondered frantically whether she should say something or just lower her head and look downward again. Then, as though she had seen right into O-Yū's anxious mind and stepped inside, O-Mitsu stated flatly, "You're afraid of me, aren't you?"

O-Yū's mouth wasn't working. Her tongue had practically retreated into the back of her throat.

Pressing the assault, O-Mitsu continued, "When I call for you tonight, bring your bedding and nightclothes and come with me. Tonight you're to sleep in the main house's futon storeroom."

Saying nothing more, she turned on her heel and departed. When O-Mitsu's broad shoulders had passed out of sight, O-Yū finally broke out in a sudden sweat.

"*. . . you're to sleep in the main house's futon storeroom.*"

It was a strange command, but O-Yū was not all that surprised that it had come. This was because she had some idea of the meaning behind those words.

It had been about ten days from the time O-Yū had first started working when, speaking as though she weren't there, the other two housemaids whose room she shared had begun whispering furiously to one another:

"*O-Mitsu hasn't taken her to the futon storeroom yet, has she?*"

"*How strange! She usually doesn't wait so long.*"

"*She took me three days after I came here.*"

"*For me, it was the very first day.*"

"*Why doesn't she take her?*"

As the days went by, the frequency of the two maids' whisperings had increased, as did the gleam in their eyes at such times and the twisting of their mouths.

So it seemed that being "taken to the futon storeroom" was some kind of terrible punishment for maids or something. That's why those two thought it was suspicious that O-Yū had not yet experienced it, even though they had been taken there right from the start.

If a night in the storeroom was to be a punishment, the maids were right; the delay was a strange thing indeed. After all, O-Yū had already been scolded up, down, left, and right by O-Mitsu. Should her actions be just a little bit too slow, or should she be unable the first time to remember everything she'd been told to do, O-Mitsu would hold nothing back as she laid into O-Yū with words, and sometimes with her hand. If being "taken to the futon storeroom" was some kind of punishment for impressing upon newly arrived housemaids the authority of the chief housekeeper, then, just as the two maids had said, it was bizarre that O-Yū hadn't been taken there long ago.

She had thought one thing and then another, and then one night when the hour had come around for the three of them to lie down side by side for the night, she had tried asking the other two housemaids. Their heads resting against their pillows, both had turned suddenly to look at one another. Their faces had come alive, which for them was a rare sight.

At last they had guardedly answered with a question of their own: "Why do you ask such a thing?"

O-Yū had limited knowledge of what they had been speaking of, but not missing a beat, she told them that she had still not been taken to the futon storeroom and was terribly worried that this meant she was not recognized as a housemaid of the Kaneko'ya and sooner or later would be discharged and sent back to her parents.

The two maids had grown just a little more personable at that and told her that taking newly arrived workers to the futon storeroom was a custom at the shop.

"It's not just the housemaids either. They take the men there too."

O-Yū had already learned where the futon storeroom was. Right at the inauspicious northeast corner of the house was a dim room of four and a half tatami mats' size. It had neither windows nor closet, and though it was empty and not currently being used for anything, long ago it had been used for a time as a storeroom for futons, which was what it was still called.

"I did feel a little uneasy sleeping in a room to the northeast," one of the maids had said a bit precociously. "But it isn't like there are spooks jumping out at you. I slept better there than I do in my own room."

"I wonder if they just make new workers do it to prove they're not afraid," the other had said, nodding in agreement. "That's why on those nights Miss O-Mitsu sits outside the sliding door in the hallway. She's standing watch to make sure the worker sleeping inside doesn't run away."

"It is an odd tradition, but . . . oh well, that's all there is to it."

The two maids had laughed together, but after a brief moment that laugh came to an abrupt halt. Surprised, O-Yū glanced over at the two of them. Both had their eyes opened wide, staring up at the ceiling dazedly, like a pair of marionettes whose strings had been cut.

O-Yū had asked them nothing further and simply crawled under her covers, saying only a word of thanks to them for having answered her question.

And then that night, she had dreamed with remarkable clarity. In pitch-black darkness, without the slightest idea of where she was, she dreamed she was walking hand in hand with O-Sato. O-Sato was gently shaking the hand that she held and whispering to her the same words over and over again:

"It's going to be all right. I'm with you."

Though she tried to ask her sister what was going to be all right, O-Yū was unable to speak in the dream. Before her and behind her, the darkness was utter and complete, and all that came to her was the sensation of the presence of some unknown thing moving through that darkness behind her, following O-Sato and herself, not letting them out of its sight. She felt as though she could hear the sound of its scuffling footsteps, the heaviness of its breathing.

Though she knew she was dreaming, O-Yū's body quaked with terror, and she felt her own hand grow moist with sweat as she held on to her sister's. Although the thing behind them seemed to be walking terribly slowly, there were also times when it seemed to suddenly hasten its footfalls. When at last it seemed to come up right behind them, O-Yū smelled something in the darkness. Perhaps it was the smell of its breath. Its exhalations were terribly hot, and there was a sound like something wheezing or gasping for breath.

"It stinks, doesn't it?" O-Sato said in an icy tone most unlike her. "That thing *is hungry beyond all bearing.*"

She continued walking straight ahead.

For an instant, O-Yū wanted to turn around to see for herself what *that thing* was. Her sister spoke as though spitting something unpleasant from her mouth. But just as she was about to turn, she heard it raise its voice in a growl, and she lost the heart to do so.

The scuffling footsteps began to grow distant. Had the thing behind them slowed its pace? O-Sato had certainly not slowed hers. At that moment it dawned on O-Yū that the thing behind them was not only terribly hungry.

It was also terribly alone.

The next morning when O-Yū awoke, she had felt very sad somehow. Even after the sun had risen higher and the details of the dream had begun to fade from memory, the pungency of that sadness remained with her long afterward—it was like biting into a piece of ginger; she could still smell the raw, open surface of its exposed sorrow.

怪

Between O-Yū's dreams on the one hand and her ruminations about what it would be like to sleep in the futon storeroom on the other, she was not a very enthusiastic worker that day. Three times before midday she made stupid mistakes that got her scolded by O-Mitsu.

That night near midnight, when O-Mitsu came round for her as she had promised, O-Yū felt, oddly enough, just a little bit relieved. It was easier to go ahead and get it over with than sit with her mind playing through one scenario after another. As O-Mitsu had instructed, O-Yū meekly folded up her bedding, set her pillow on top, and carried it all with both hands as she followed behind O-Mitsu until they arrived at the room that was known as the futon storeroom.

O-Mitsu said not a word while they were walking down the corridor. Then, when they arrived and O-Mitsu placed her hand on the sliding door, she suddenly said something most unexpected, though she never turned to look at O-Yū.

"O-Sato's forty-nine days have been fulfilled, correct?"

Indeed, yesterday had been the forty-ninth day. It was often said that the souls of the dead remained in this world until the forty-ninth day after their death and afterward went on to the next world. Because of that, O-Yū had been counting the days until her sister's forty-ninth. She had been terribly worried that once that day passed, her sister's presence might dissipate.

"Yes," she said. "It was yesterday."

O-Mitsu nodded and slid open the paper door.

"Go inside," she said.

Urged on by O-Mitsu, O-Yū stepped into the room. Musty,

humid air enveloped her there. It was going to be hard to breathe in here.

"Now set down your pillow, lie down, and get under your covers." O-Mitsu didn't set foot in the room herself but stood in the doorway holding up a candle as she rattled off instructions. "There's no futon, so you'll sleep directly on the tatami floor."

As O-Yū lay down as she was told, O-Mitsu—still blocking the doorway—spoke again. "Lie there until I wake you tomorrow morning. You mustn't try to leave this room. I'll be standing watch in the hallway all night, so if you try to get out I'll know about it right away."

After underscoring the threat that O-Yū couldn't stay at the shop if she attempted to run away, O-Mitsu shut the sliding paper door. A thick, damp darkness fell across O-Yū from above, as though it had been waiting for her.

At first, she was sure she would be unable to sleep at all. Whether she closed her eyes or opened them, the solid blackness was the same. The quiet room swallowed all sound. She had gotten very used to the two other maids snoring or grinding their teeth in the night, and with the lack of noise unexpectedly keeping her awake, O-Yū tossed and turned again and again in her covers. It was while she was moving her body around in this manner that she had a sudden feeling that the smell of O-Sato's hair was especially strong in her covers tonight.

It's going to be all right. I'm with you.

O-Yū thought, *This must be what O-Sato was talking about in my dream. She was the same age as me when she came here, so they did this to her too. She must've been so frightened. So lonely. But she cheered me up in my dream and said, "My spirit is with you, so you don't have to be afraid."*

Such thoughts comforted her, and she was at last able to close her eyes. In no time at all her breathing grew as peaceful as a baby's, and O-Yū had fallen into slumber.

And then, she dreamed again.

It was the same dream that she had had before. She was holding hands with O-Sato, walking through blackness so dark that she could not tell what was in front of her from what was behind. Her sister held on to her hand tightly and seemed to be walking just a little faster than she had in the earlier dream.

Something was following them. She could feel its presence just as strongly—no, even more strongly—than she had in the prior dream. When she listened closely, she could hear the *scuff, scuff* of its footsteps.

"*You mustn't turn around,*" O-Sato said beside her. There was a smile on her sister's face, but her eyes gleamed with a strong and defiant light, and the corners of her eyes were slightly upturned as though she were just a little angry.

Scuff, scuff. The footsteps followed along behind them. Whether the smell was coming from its mouth or its nose she could not tell, but the stomach-churning stench of its breathing was on the nape of her neck. It reminded O-Yū of when her grandfather had died about three years ago. Her grandfather had died of a disease that caused water to pool in his stomach. From the time he had become bedridden, he had been as kind and as gentle as ever—a model patient who caused little trouble for his caregivers. When he was near death, however, his breath had become so horrible it had made her almost dizzy to smell it. When she had asked her father about that later, he had answered that no matter how pure-hearted a person her grandfather may have been, his insides were rotting now as he neared death, and that was why his breath smelled so bad.

Did that mean the thing that was chasing them was someone who was dying? Was that why its footfalls sounded so leaden?

At that moment, O-Sato suddenly began to sing:

> *Oni, oni, come this way,*
> *To where you hear my clapping hands.*

She sang out loudly. Her voice was lively and strong. She sang as though she knew what the thing chasing them really was, and to get away from it, she was stoking up the fires within herself, daring it to catch up if it could. And so O-Yū joined her own voice with that of her sister.

> *Oni, oni, come this way,*
> *To where you hear my clapping hands.*
> *Oni, oni, come this way,*
> *To where you hear my clapping hands.*

O-Sato marched on steadily, leading O-Yū by the hand. From time to time, she would encourage O-Yū by looking down at her with a gentle smile. O-Yū would look up at her face, and when their eyes met they would smile at one another, thinking of nothing but their earnest forward strides.

She didn't know how far they had walked when at last a faint white light began to appear in the blackness ahead of them.

"Ah, it's dawn at last!" O-Sato said. *"Now run, O-Yū!"*

Pulled along by O-Sato's hand, O-Yū broke into a run. Together, they raced steadily forward, and the white light grew nearer and nearer. It grew stronger and stronger, spreading out in front of them and stretching out overhead, until at last O-Sato let loose with a cry of joy.

"We've gotten away from it now!"

With that single shout, O-Sato leapt into the very heart of that white radiance, pulling O-Yū in along with her. O-Yū was bathed in the dazzling light.

That was when she awakened. O-Yū suddenly sat bolt upright. The inside of the room was still pitch black. But right behind her, O-Yū could sense something moving.

She whirled around to face it. Amid the blackness, something even darker stood crouched by her bedside. O-Yū could feel its body radiating pure malice, so vivid and clear that her eyes could almost see it, her hands almost touch it.

It raised its voice in a moan and, in unfathomable misery and frustration, spat out these words: *"But the forty-ninth day already passed!"*

And then it was gone, leaving only the darkness in its wake.

O-Yū sat unmoving, her covers wrapped all around her. At last, O-Mitsu spoke from the other side of the paper door. She was asking her if she had awakened. O-Yū replied that she had.

The paper door slid open. Morning sunlight was streaming into the hallway. O-Mitsu was sitting there on her calves outside, glaring straight at O-Yū with a steely gaze.

She looked as though she had not slept a wink all night long. Her eyes were so shot through with threads of blood that they were practically crimson.

怪

It was past noon that day when O-Yū was summoned by O-Mitsu once again. "I'm doing some straightening up inside the warehouse, so come and help me," she said.

The housemaids cast doubtful glances at one another. Cleaning inside the warehouse was something O-Mitsu arranged, and it was customary that only the experienced housekeepers worked in there. Many valuable and expensive items were stored in the warehouse, so it was thought to be a matter of course that newcomers should not be allowed inside.

No one was able to defy O-Mitsu, however. With her heart pounding, O-Yū followed her into the warehouse. As soon as they were both inside, O-Mitsu shut the door firmly behind them. Golden beams of sunlight slanted in through skylights that opened high up on the walls above their heads, and specks of dust were dancing in them. They were the only things in the warehouse that were moving.

"Sit there."

O-Mitsu pointed at the floor and sat down first herself. Her movements seemed unusually slow and listless. O-Yū remembered O-Mitsu's bloodshot eyes from that morning and thought, *She really didn't sleep at all last night.*

"I didn't call you here to help with the cleaning," O-Mitsu began, speaking slowly. "There's something I want to talk with you about."

Seeing O-Mitsu from so close, O-Yū noticed that the skin of her cheeks and around her eyes appeared coarse and rough, and her color didn't look all that good either. Only her eyes remained still and placid as they bored into O-Yū.

O-Yū shifted to the floor and sat on her calves, prim and proper. Even so, she kept wriggling her toes around to keep them from going to sleep. She wanted to be able to take off running at any moment if it became necessary.

"You needn't be afraid," O-Mitsu said with a faint smile. It was the first time since she had come to the Kaneko'ya that O-Yū had seen the chief housekeeper smiling. "You really beat me good last night," she said. She raised up her right hand and rubbed her neck wearily. "I was the one who was chasing you. I thought I could pluck the soul right out of your body, but O-Sato's soul interfered, and in the end I wasn't able. Forty-nine days had passed, so I thought that O-Sato's soul was no longer at your side, but she was still close to you, protecting you."

"But the forty-ninth day already passed!"

Remembering those words the malicious thing in the darkness of the futon storeroom had spat at her, O-Yū felt the hair on the nape of her neck stand on end.

So then, is O-Mitsu saying that thing was her?

"Why, of course it was me," O-Mitsu said nodding. "Or perhaps I should say it both was and wasn't me. Now listen well. We're having this conversation because I want you to help me."

O-Mitsu began by telling her that the Kaneko'ya was cursed.

"The current master of the shop is its seventh. This is a fine shop. However, long ago, in order to build it, the first master slew a man and hid his body. For money, most likely; I don't know the details myself."

The soul of the murdered man, she continued, held a grudge and remained in this world, possessing the shop that had been built on his blood. This is why the Kaneko'ya's masters died young generation after generation.

"However, the thing that's possessing and cursing this house eventually grew so much that it could not be pacified by merely shortening the life of the master. So in order to have a form and remain in this world, it must feed on the souls of living people. Just like how we can't survive without eating. So for that purpose it moved into the body of one of the workers, infiltrated the house, and then began plucking out the souls of the other workers."

Generation after generation, there was always one, O-Mitsu said. Some worker whose body was taken over. At times it was the head clerk, and at other times it was the chief housekeeper. The one who was taken over would make the arrangements and bring the workers to that storeroom, over time creating a *custom* of stealing the workers' souls.

"And so presently, that person is me. My body has been taken over by the demon that haunts this house and this shop seeking revenge."

O-Mitsu went on, telling O-Yū that she herself had come here to work at age twelve. She had been twenty when the wicked thing had entered her—just after she became the youngest chief housekeeper in the history of the Kaneko'ya. Proud of her advancement, she had looked down on her fellow workers and her heart had grown brazenly arrogant, creating the opening through which the thing in the dark had taken her. All this she related in a tone of voice like that of someone who had bitten into something bitter.

"Once a worker's soul has been removed, they stop complaining," O-Mitsu said. "They lose their laziness too, and their greed. That childlike nature that wants to go out and play. They don't miss home anymore. At a cursory glance, they look and behave just like a normal human being, but their insides are completely empty. Like a wooden doll. That's why all those employed by the Kaneko'ya turn into the sort of worker that other stores are always on the lookout for. They don't get sick. They don't get injured. But this is because they've become beings that are only half alive."

And so the store prospered. The neighbors were all so impressed because they thought the Kaneko'ya had some incredibly effective method for training workers.

However, for generations the owners were unable to take genuine, heartfelt pleasure in their prosperity and reputation, for they knew that their lives would be plucked from them—that they would depart this world—at only half the age of an ordinary person. If what had happened to the previous master and to the master before him were to continue, it was only natural that the next master too—from about the time that he started pushing thirty—would begin to worry over when the reaper would come for him as well.

The master's wife and children also would spend their days in fear of the sudden death of their husband or father. Living from day to day with the Grim Reaper's scythe pressed against the back of one's neck was by no means a happy thing, no matter how much wealth one might accumulate. It was truly a life without any peace of mind.

That was the true curse that hung over the Kaneko'ya.

"You will be discharged and sent home tomorrow," O-Mitsu said, turning to face O-Yū. There was a slight dampness in her eyes.

"I'll tell both the master and mistress that if you stay here, bad things will happen to the shop. I'll use the same voice I do when giving orders. You'll surely be discharged and sent home. And that's for the best. You mustn't stay here."

But then, leaning forward on her knees, O-Mitsu added that before O-Yū left there was something she wanted her to do. "Behind the water jar in the kitchen, I'm going to hide a bundle of branches from the *sakaki* tree and a package of salt as well. Tonight at the third division of the hour of the ox, two hours after midnight, I want you to sneak over to that futon storeroom, throw those things inside, and then come to see me. Be sure to do it, understand? If you'll just do that, there'll be nothing more to fear."

O-Mitsu grabbed hold of O-Yū's shoulders. "See to it. Understand?"

O-Yū shuddered. The physical power in those hands was as nothing compared to their iciness, which she could feel clearly even through her clothing.

"Yes, ma'am," she answered with a trembling voice. "I promise."

At her answer, O-Mitsu smiled, removed her hands from O-Yū's shoulders, and rose to her feet. "O-Sato's soul is with you, so there's nothing to be afraid of. She beat me." Her tone softened slightly then, and she added, "After all, she was a strong, sure woman who had a lot of grit."

"Last night in that storeroom, I had a dream about my sister," O-Yū said.

"Did you, now?" O-Mitsu nodded her head and tilted it for a moment as though thinking something over. "I'm sorry," she murmured at last. "The truth is, no matter how hard it tried, the evil thing inside me was unable to pry loose your sister's soul either. Even after five years of working in this place . . . after the countless nights I made her sleep in that storeroom . . . it couldn't do it. Surely it was because O-Sato always treasured her little sister and her family living so far away."

Something tightened in O-Yū's chest at the thought of her sister. Without thinking, she said, "It was because my sister was like a mother to me."

"Was she? Then even though you were apart, she must have

never stopped thinking of you for a moment. That's why there was never an opening." O-Mitsu closed her eyes as though accepting this. For a time, she stood like that, unmoving. "But that's also the reason why she died the way she did. She was murdered. And I've had enough of that kind of thing."

So saying, her eyes snapped open with new determination. O-Mitsu put her hand on the warehouse door and pushed it open mightily. She stepped out into the sunshine outside, and her shadow fell across the ground. Trying not to look like she was looking, O-Yū glanced at that shadow and nearly cried out when she saw it.

O-Mitsu's shadow was big and dark, as befitted her large frame, but from its head there grew a pair of horns.

怪

That night at the third division of the hour of the ox, O-Yū did as O-Mitsu had asked. The strong, green scent of the sakaki branches in the storeroom encouraged her in the darkness.

The next morning, she awakened from a light sleep and right away was summoned by O-Mitsu, who took her to see the master and mistress of the house. There she was told that her work was unsatisfactory, and she was to be let go. The master and mistress both looked a little uncertain, and they did not stop glancing over at O-Mitsu's expression the whole time.

O-Yū bowed to the floor obediently, gathered up her belongings into a small cloth wrapper, and departed from the Kaneko'ya. Not one person came out to see her off.

When she came near to Ōshima-mura, O-Yū became frightened for the first time. Her knees went weak and started shaking, and she became unable to take even one more step forward. An old man from the village who happened to be passing by found her and carried her the rest of the way back home on his back.

About ten days afterward, O-Yū heard a rumor that the Kaneko'ya had burned down. It was unclear where the fire started. Word was, the master burned to death, and both the house and the shop burned to the ground, leaving nothing at all behind. A few days before the fire, the chief housekeeper, O-Mitsu, had run away and disappeared, so the town officials and the thief-takers alike, suspicious that she might have had something to do with that mysterious fire, were seeking her for questioning.

O-Mitsu's flight was a strange thing in itself. All of her personal effects had been left behind, and no one had witnessed her leaving the Kaneko'ya. Only . . . the very day on which she disappeared, one of the maids did see an unfamiliar woman of about twenty, casually dressed in a crimson kimono, slipping out of O-Mitsu's bedchamber. When the chief clerk heard the story from her, he said the description of this mysterious woman and the pattern of her kimono closely resembled that of O-Mitsu herself when she was young. However, people don't just suddenly turn young again, so that was as far as the story went.

Some time after the fire, the land where the Kaneko'ya had once stood was excavated, and human bones were discovered beneath the place where the main house's northeast corner once stood. The bones were said to be terribly old and were so changed by their long interment as to retain almost nothing of their original shapes. The story went that it was because of that that the skull appeared to have horns growing out of it.

As for whose bones they were and where that person was from, ultimately nobody knew. Or perhaps the remains weren't even human.

O-Yū found work in another shop. The chief housekeeper there was a frightening woman, and when O-Yū was scolded by her, she could feel her nerve shriveling up inside. However, the shadow of that chief housekeeper was always a *human* shadow, so there was never any need to be afraid of her.

She soon forgot about the Kaneko'ya and no longer dreamed about it. Only—she did remember those futon covers, which O-Sato's scent had permeated. Sometimes when she was feeling nostalgic, a heartfelt thought would flit across her mind: *If I'd known there was going to be a fire, I'd at least have liked to carry those out.*

IV
The Plum Rains Fall

Minokichi stepped out of the Murata'ya service entrance, exchanged his usual parting courtesies with the maid, and was just wiping the oil from his hands with beaten rice straw when a voice came calling out to him from the alleyway.

"Mino! Mino!"

Minokichi turned and saw O-Kō running toward him, her hands waving.

"Oh, thank goodness I've caught you!" she said as she slipped through the wickets at the shop's rear gate. There, breathing hard with her hands on both knees, she said, "O-Ito said you start your rounds with the Murata'ya on days of the Snake, so I came straight over to try and catch you."

"Is something wrong with my wife?" he said. He knew that O-Ito might give birth at any moment now. The housewives at the row house had looked her over, and though they estimated there were still a couple of weeks to go before the start of labor, "when" was certainly not something that they knew for certain. With an uneasy feeling, Minokichi leaned toward O-Kō, who was still bent over and out of breath.

O-Kō put out her palm and waved it around haphazardly in his direction. "No, no, O-Ito's fine. Nothing's wrong with her."

O-Kō had probably run nonstop from the row house in

Daiku-chō to this corner of Saga-chō, but even for that she looked truly pained from the exertion. Seeing her like that, Minokichi suddenly thought, *The years are catching up with her too.* That certainly stood to reason. O-Kō had been a good neighbor to Minokichi's family even in the days when he wore a bib. They had always been together, even when the fire had burned them out of house and home, and even when circumstances beyond his control had forced him to change jobs. Minokichi had always relied on "Auntie O-Kō," and with him soon to become a father himself now, it was only natural that O-Kō wasn't getting around quite like she used to anymore.

With the news that this wasn't about some change in O-Ito's condition, the sudden fear he had felt was draining out of Minokichi. The Murata'ya maid, hearing the sound of voices, poked her head outside the door.

"Can I bring you a cup of water?" Minokichi asked.

Still wheezing, O-Kō nodded. "Please," she said. He disappeared back inside and moments later returned with a large teacup filled with water.

O-Kō drained half of it in a single gulp, then let out a long breath of air. "Ah, I needed that," she said. "I'm sorry, I'm completely useless as a 'messenger palanquin.' Must be going senile too."

After she had said this, she finally looked at Minokichi's face, and that was when he first noticed that her eyes were a little red.

"O-En died last night," said O-Kō. "No sooner had you left this morning than a messenger came from the Kazusa'ya to tell us. They went in to wake her this morning and found her lying cold in her futon."

Tears spilled suddenly from O-Kō's little eyes.

"The poor thing. But she's finally at peace, now, isn't she?"

At first, Minokichi had no words; he merely straightened up slowly, both hands hanging limp at his sides. He trembled around the knees. He'd only just started his sales rounds; there was still plenty of seed oil in his barrel. *If I don't work hard today, I won't be able to lug this thing home*, he'd idly been thinking.

"There'll be a lot of things to take care of, so you should head over to the Kazusa'ya now. If you'll tell me your clients for Serpent Day, we'll divide them up and make your rounds for you. I'm headed over to Matsu's to give him the news."

All of that had spilled out in a single breath. O-Kō wiped her face with the back of her meaty hand. "How old was O-En, again?"

"Twenty-eight," Minokichi answered. His sister had been one year older than he.

"That makes it fifteen years she was ill," O-Kō murmured with renewed feeling. "It's been a long road, hasn't it?"

At this last utterance, Minokichi lifted up his eyes and looked about, because somehow it had sounded as though her words had not been directed at him but at the soul of O-En, now free of the shackles that had been her body, perhaps hovering over them here at this very moment.

Of course, there was no one else present. There was nothing else there at all, save a faint fragrance on the wind hinting at plum trees growing somewhere on the Murata'ya grounds. It reminded Minokichi anew of his sister's love for plum blossoms.

The cherry blossoms and azaleas have nothing but beauty, and I hate them; they're useless once they've fallen. I think plum blossoms are much, much nicer!

As he breathed in that fragrance, even the rhythms of her speech—back when she had been a little girl with an indomitable spirit—came back to him with vivid clarity.

怪

It had been fifteen years ago, right around the same time of the year.

Back then, Minokichi's family lived in a row house along a back alley in North Rokkenbori-chō. It was a family of five: his mother and father, O-En, Minokichi, and the youngest, Matsukichi. His father was a seller of oil who carried his merchandise around with him on his back, and his mother worked as a housekeeper for nigh on twenty years, commuting to the Kazusa'ya, a wholesaler of dried balls of indigo dye in Saga-chō. Minokichi had just turned twelve and had at last become able to help his father sell oil. Feeling himself at the very threshold of manhood, he had also begun to develop a smart mouth.

From age seven or eight, O-En had gradually come to take their busy mother's place in looking after her brothers. By the time she turned ten, she had learned to do a fine job cooking rice and had even gained a reputation in the neighborhood as a serious, hardworking young girl. Around this time, O-Kō and her husband were living across the street. They also came to rely on O-En for some reason and never ceased praising her hard work. It was a pet phrase of O-Kō's to say, "It would sure be a comfort if we had a daughter like O-En too." Her father was proud of her, of course, but in this one matter even her mother—who almost never let an arrogant word cross her lips—embraced that swell of pride she felt when she heard what people thought of O-En, and considered herself a little special.

At times, O-En was even harder on Minokichi than was their own mother. Due to a lack of restraint in the sister-brother relationship, she would not hesitate to give Minokichi a bitingly proper scolding even in front of people, calling him a "slovenly, filthy, blockheaded halfwit." It was spectacularly unfair treatment, since she doted on her younger brother Matsukichi, spoiling him rotten because he was still a small child.

But unfair though it was, it was also clear that no matter how grown-up Minokichi may have fancied himself, when it came down to it he wasn't able to refute even half of O-En's remonstrations.

Girls are usually pretty good with words, and on top of that his opponent was both older and quite bright, making the outcomes of these matches of wits all but predetermined. At that age Minokichi hated O-En through and through, and when he said he wanted to drive her out with a broom or roll her up in a bamboo mat and sink her in the Rokkenbori Moat, he was relating honestly and accurately the true contents of his heart.

But around the time the plum trees were blooming in early spring, misfortune came raining down on the once-unbeatable O-En.

It all began when a job placement agent who had long been a friend of the family approached O-En on behalf of a restaurant near Fukagawa Hachiman Shrine. A girl who had been working there since being swapped in at New Year's had angered the master and his wife and been discharged immediately. The owners were in a rush to find a replacement. According to the agent, the discipline enforced at the restaurant in question was quite strict, and the agent had said that he had lost face himself when the previous maid was fired. A second failure was not to be countenanced, so this time they wanted to be certain the girl they took on was truly the right one. In other words, he was interested in sending O-En to work for them.

This was not the first time O-En had been approached with offers of work. Her mother and father had always turned them down, however, saying that because O-En did such a good job of looking after her brothers and taking care of the house, both of them had been able to focus on earning a living. They were in no position to let someone else have her so easily, they said. This time, however, the agent had come with his head bowed low and said, "It has to be O-En." Also, the restaurant in question was famous, in recent years winning a reputation that put it shoulder-to-shoulder with Hirasei in Ninobashi. Above all, though, the parents' reluctance was no match this time for the enthusiasm of the young girl herself.

Though Minokichi acted as though he had no interest in any of this, in his heart he was hoping mightily that O-En would be sent away. If his nuisance of a sister left home to go work, he wouldn't be scolded anymore. Once she started working, it would be five years before she could come back for a holiday visit, which would leave him free to do as he pleased at home. *Go! Go!* he was thinking. *As soon as you can, even if it's just one day sooner!*

Then, whether because of Minokichi's wish being granted or his parents' being moved by O-En's passion, his mother and father soon gave in and decided to give the agent the answer he was hoping for. The smile that had blossomed on O-En's face at that moment was something Minokichi remembered well even to the present day. O-Kō had been thrilled too and among other things had said she would hurry to make her a new kimono. The plum tree that was at the very front of the Rokkenbori row house was still young and its blossoms right at their peak. Whenever Minokichi saw O-En happily conferring with O-Kō about something under its flowering branches, he would blow out a "hmf!" from his nostrils.

However . . .

When his mother took O-En to the agent to give him their answer, they found his manner toward them suddenly, completely changed. He said that the restaurant opening had already been filled, but if they would be patient a little longer he would bring O-En an even better offer.

Even Minokichi's meek, reserved mother had exploded at that. She tore into the agent, saying, "After *you* came to *us* and went on like that about how it had to be O-En, what do you mean the job went to someone else! Is something wrong with O-En? Is that what you're saying? Explain to us why!" Driven into a corner, the agent had offered excuses left and right, but in the face of a mother and daughter who were having none of it, he was eventually left with no choice but to tell them the real reason.

The reason, he said, that the restaurant had given the previous girl her walking papers was that she had been raised in the country, her movements were heavy and ungraceful, and on top of that she had a pug-nosed face. To hear the shop mistress tell it, a restaurant was a luxury business; therefore it became a problem if the waitresses and women in the back were not befittingly beautiful. A lack of training could be taken care of later, but looks were the one thing that had to be there from the start; nothing could be done about ugly after the fact.

This was why O-En had been rebuffed as well. Determined to avoid repeating her previous mistake with that hayseed from before, the proprietress had quietly checked out the looks of the girl the agent recommended ahead of time. Owing to that, she had leaned toward a girl with a prettier face than O-En's and settled on her instead. That was what had happened.

Minokichi learned about all this when he overheard his weeping, raging mother telling his father about it. O-En was not about to let herself turn into some wilting lily over this; she remained quiet as a stone, with a sort of sharp crease at the edge of each eye that Minokichi had never seen before.

Rumors spread through the row house almost instantly, and by the following day, it was all over Rokkenbori-chō. Minokichi felt sorry for O-En, but at the same time his previously unbeatable sister had been handed her first defeat, and by this he was pleased. When his playmates were making fun of her mercilessly one day, he joined in with the teasing and got an earful afterward from both his mother and O-Kō.

In truth, O-En was by no means a beautiful girl. Perhaps she was even below average in that regard. At that time, though, Minokichi had no idea as yet how terribly worried his sister had become about that as she drew nearer and nearer to marriageable age.

怪

Half a month passed, and no one talked about O-En's missed opportunity anymore. Even the mischievous children no longer said anything; they had forgotten all about it. The young girl herself continued working as swiftly and efficiently as she always had, and to judge by her expression one would think nothing at all had ever happened.

Minokichi was the only one whose circumstances were now slightly altered. Every time his sister scolded him, the words that he and his friends had used to mock her would rise back up all the way to the rear of his throat, and then—fearful of the disaster that would surely befall him should they be uttered—he would somehow manage to gulp them back down. He also had a certain childish cunning that told him, *If you've found the spot where she hurts the most, you should only jab it when you really need to.* In the present day, Minokichi wanted to curl up and hide when he thought of how twisted he had been as a little boy.

The plum blossoms fell, and when a shade of pale crimson began to tint the branches of the cherries, O-Kō took Minokichi and his siblings to a shrine festival. The shrine, located only two blocks east of Rokkenbori-chō, was observing a special day dedicated to the mirror enshrined there, which was believed to house a god. It had long been held that in ancient times, when the area was still beneath the sea, the mirror had drifted there from parts unknown. A tradition had been handed down that this mirror held a mysterious power to unerringly reflect the righteousness or evil in people's hearts, and also to drive out demons.

It was a small shrine but crowded on its festival days, which were held on dates ending with the number five. Minokichi and his siblings occasionally went there to play, with O-Kō leading them by the hand. O-Kō and her husband made their living by lantern-making. Once their day's work was finished, they had nothing else to do, so they lived a rather easy life. They were a harmonious couple but had never had any children, so at such times they made up for it by spoiling Minokichi and his siblings to their heart's content.

O-Kō was a deeply religious person, however, so even though the children raised a fuss when they spotted the festival booths, praying at the shrine always came first. Minokichi accomplished this without a trace of religious passion, clapping his hands together twice while O-Kō held his head down with her hand. Matsukichi, still too young to understand, simply copied what O-Kō did. O-En held her hands together for a little while in some kind of devotional stance, then bowed her head low toward the main shrine until she was apparently satisfied at last. Then she turned and said, "Aunt O-Kō, I'd like to draw a fortune slip."

There was a place where people could draw fortunes under the overhang off to the side of the main shrine. There, it was O-En's custom to draw a fortune slip, tuck it in oh-so-carefully behind her kimono's *obi*, and take it home. Minokichi saw nothing of interest in such things, however.

"All right, let's go!"

O-En set off running with a sound of sandals against the gravel and quickly disappeared among the crowds of people milling through the narrow grounds of the shrine. Minokichi could hear Matsukichi as he was led along by O-Kō, begging her to buy him this and feed him that. His own mind was greatly distracted as well—he was doing his utmost to construct a facial expression that said, *I'm a full-fledged adult now, so really, what's all that special about stuff like shrine festivals?*

O-En didn't return for some time. When at last she poked her head out of the milling crowds ahead, the long, narrow paper of her fortune slip was not tucked into her obi as usual but pinched between her fingertips, as though it were the dangling corpse of a mouse or insect.

"Oh dear, what's the matter?" said O-Kō, whose expression had grown immediately suspicious.

"Auntie," O-En said in a small voice, glancing at her brothers' faces momentarily, "it's *daikyō*."

Daikyō meant extremely bad luck. It was the worst fortune you could draw.

Looking surprised, O-Kō blinked her eyes a few times, then took the paper from O-En's hand and looked it over very closely. "Well, look at that . . . they still give these, eh?"

"I've never gotten one before," O-En said, both eyebrows drawn up together.

"It's nothing to be concerned about. Just like I always tell you— when you hit rock bottom, your luck can only get better. You should tie it to that tree branch over there to give it back to the gods."

O-Kō suddenly looked upward, indicating the plum tree that grew on the grounds. A branch that had already lost its blossoms was conveniently sticking out and almost seemed to be encouraging her, saying, *Here, tie it to me.* A number of fortune slips had already been tied there by other celebrants, dotting the branch with color in place of its fallen flowers.

"That's right, I can do that," said O-En, her knitted brow loosening. Then, as she stretched up to reach the branch, she added with a smile, "Matsukichi's getting fidgety, Auntie, so please, go on ahead with him. He wants to see the candy figures."

O-Kō took both boys by the hand, said, "Well, then, let's go," and started back across the shrine grounds. Minokichi, no longer willing to do something so childish as let Aunt O-Kō lead him by the hand, twisted his body around and managed to get away from her and, in that moment, somehow found himself faced in O-En's direction.

O-En was tying the fortune slip to the plum tree branch. If that had been all, nothing would have seemed out of the ordinary, but Minokichi's eyes were stopped by his sister's lips, which were moving nonstop. *Yikes!* he thought. A strange tension was in her profile as she muttered to herself, and the crease from the corner of her eye was the same as on that day she came home after being turned down for the restaurant job—straight and sharp.

For no particular reason, Minokichi started to have a bad feeling about this.

Then at that moment, Minokichi's gaze suddenly met with O-En's, who had upon finishing the knot lowered her hands and turned her head in his direction.

O-En glared at Minokichi. He felt a twitch of pain, almost as if her gaze had bitten him.

O-En looked away right afterward. In a panic, Minokichi spun around and grabbed hold of O-Kō's hand. At last, his sister caught up with them, but even when they all set out walking together and O-En tried to say something or other to him, Minokichi couldn't raise his head to look at her.

怪

Ten days later, it happened.

Minokichi returned home with his father after making their sales rounds to find that his mother, surprisingly, was already home and engaged in nonstop conversation with O-Kō in the doorway. She looked at them with relief when she saw his father. "Oh, darling! I just heard from O-Kō!" she said, looking back at the other woman. "Remember that restaurant from before? The one that wanted O-En to—"

Minokichi's father set down his bucket and nodded with annoyance, not waiting for her to finish. "What about it?"

"The girl who got that job instead of O-En came down with smallpox," O-Kō said. "She's been sent back to her parents, but since the restaurant served the public, there's a huge uproar."

"Looking back on it now," his mother said with a gesture that looked like she was trying to calm a pounding heart, "we're actually lucky that O-En didn't end up working in that place."

"You can't really call her a beauty now until the smallpox runs its course," said O-Kō rather meanly from between clenched teeth. "This is what they get for going on and on about beauty this and beauty that, being so terrible to a good-natured girl like O-En. It serves them right, doesn't it?"

"Now, O-Kō," said Minokichi's father gently, "it wasn't that young girl's fault, was it? But more importantly, I wonder whereabouts that girl's house is. We need to keep the kids away from there."

"They're in Motomachi. On past Lord Tayasu's mansion."

"Mino and Matsu go there in the fall to gather chestnuts, don't they?" O-Kō said. "They may have playmates there, so they need to be careful."

"That's pretty close," said Minokichi's father, looking suddenly frightened.

"I've never forgotten to pay homage to the god of smallpox," Minokichi's mother said, putting her hands on the boy's shoulders. "I got through it easily, and I'm sure you can too. My children will be fine."

"Where's O-En?"

"She went out on an errand with Matsu," said O-Kō.

The conversation was still going on in earnest when O-En finally came home. Minokichi's mother practically leapt over to her and began to explain what was happening, when O-En suddenly went white as a sheet.

"Oh dear, what's the matter, O-En? You look like the blood's gone right out of you." O-Kō started to put an arm around her, but O-En, in a gesture most unlike her, violently batted the woman's arm away.

"O-En . . . what's the matter?"

At this question, O-En blinked several times, as one who had just returned to lucidity.

"Oh, I'm sorry; it was because I was surprised," she whispered in a trembling voice.

"And right you are to be so," said O-Kō. "I can't blame you for that. O-En, when I think of what might have happened if you'd gone to work there, I just feel weak all over."

"Now, O-Kō, she may not have caught smallpox even if she'd gone there," Minokichi's father said with a conciliatory smile. "When it comes to contagious disease, you've got to be careful wherever you are."

"Well, that's true, but I feel just a little better thinking of it this way," O-Kō said. Flaring her nostrils, she added, "You do too, don't you, O-En?"

O-En didn't answer. Her head was downturned, and she looked as though she were staring intently into some terribly dark place. Minokichi unconsciously glanced down at her feet, but his eyes could discern only one or two cherry petals, blown in from somewhere on the spring wind, forlornly scattered on the dusty floor. The dark place she was staring at was apparently something only O-En could see.

That night O-En jolted awake from restless sleep and screamed so loudly that she frightened not only those in her own flat, but people throughout the entire row house as well. When asked what was the matter she said, "It was nothing. I just had a bad dream. Everything's fine now," and pulled the covers up over her head. Soon afterward, however, she jerked awake again, and in the end morning broke without more than a few minutes' sleep.

On the following day, and in the days after as well, O-En became terribly frightened and unable to sleep when night fell. Her body swiftly weakened. She was unable to eat and unable to speak, and within three or four days she had practically become an invalid. A shudder ran down the spines of people throughout the row house as they watched a heretofore vigorous, energetic girl become unable to rise from her pillow in only a few days. Was this some disease even more frightening than smallpox?

Her mother and father were both so worried they couldn't sleep at night, and her father wouldn't even go out to work. Minokichi and Matsukichi were both sent to stay with O-Kō. An agent arranged for the town doctor to call, but no matter how carefully he examined her, he was unable to find anything specifically wrong with her body and so declared that she was suffering from a mental illness. When asked whether anything had happened to the girl recently that might have caused severe mental distress, the only thing that anyone could think of was the situation with the girl who had contracted smallpox at that restaurant. When the doctor heard about this, he tilted his head in perplexity and said, "Well then, could it be some phobia related to smallpox?" But he had never before seen or heard any example of such a thing.

Several days after O-En became bedridden, the placement agent from before came by to pay her a visit. "How sad!" he said. "What happened? She's a fine girl; I'd been hoping to find her a good job to make up for last time." His concern was evident; it did not appear to be mere lip service.

As he was going out the door, he left them with the news that the girl from that restaurant had died the previous night. "Such a beautiful young lady, but she died with her face covered in pockmarks. A cruel thing to be beautiful in life and then have to look that way in death."

Minokichi heard his mother breathe out a heavy sigh at those words. "Somehow, it seems like that girl and O-En alike have been possessed by something evil."

Minokichi wondered what in the world was at the bottom of that dark hole O-En was staring into—that hole that no one else could see.

The days went past, and O-En did not improve in the slightest.

As a matter of course, her mother and father could no longer stay away from their work, so they started going out again to earn the family's living. When that happened, it fell to Minokichi to stay by O-En's side during the day, keeping a close eye on her condition and doing whatever was needed to care for her.

O-Kō would lend a hand as well, but she wasn't able to stick right by O-En's side all day long; Matsukichi had to be looked after as well. With the supine form of his sister ever in the corner of his eye, Minokichi found himself in the undesirable position of having to do all the chores around the house that had always been entrusted to his elder sister, and by himself.

Minokichi felt in his bones, for the first time, the value of the hard work that O-En had always done. All the things that O-En had done as though they were no trouble at all were more than Minokichi could handle. Minokichi worked all day cleaning the rice, washing the greens, doing the laundry, and drawing water, but couldn't accomplish half of what O-En had been able to.

As for O-En, she would spend the whole day lying on her futon, wasting away to half of what she had weighed when she was well, staring up in silence at the sooty ceiling. If called, she wouldn't answer; if spoken to, she would say nothing. Minokichi, until now having never thought of his sister as anything but an aggravation, had come to think of himself as a thoroughly detestable, dimwitted reprobate, and one time when he carried in to O-En's bedside some thin rice gruel that O-Kō had prepared, he suddenly began to utter squirming apologies for having never listened to her before.

Tears spilled over from O-En's eyes even as she continued to stare up at the ceiling, and at last she raised her voice to weep, drew her hands from her nightclothes, and held them to her face as her shoulders shook from sobbing. Minokichi, having no idea what to do, ran outside to go call O-Kō. When O-Kō came running to her side, O-En was still crying, and even when O-Kō put her arm around her shoulders and helped her sit up, she continued heaving great sobs as she wept. For a while, she wiped her tears with her hands, then asked Minokichi if he would go and bring her a cloth. Minokichi did so, and O-En wiped her face with it. Then, as O-Kō and Minokichi looked on, she used the cloth to cover her face completely.

"What are you doing, O-En?" said O-Kō worriedly. She reached out a hand, but just as she was about to move the cloth away, O-En meekly pulled back from her.

"Leave it, please, Auntie."

"But you—"

"I'm ashamed to have everyone see me like this. Leave it until I'm ready. Please, I'm begging you."

In the end, the cloth stayed where it was. Neither her father nor her mother dared deny her wishes. All they could do now was let her do as she wanted and wait for the passage of time to heal her.

O-En spent the peak of the cherry blossom season that spring wearing the cloth over her head. She would hide her face behind a cloth from morning until night, showing it to no one. The changing of the cloth was accomplished only late at night when everyone was asleep and there was no one to see. She neither bathed nor washed her face. At last, she became able to eat rice, but even then her chopsticks would enter the shadow of a cloth as they carried the food to her mouth.

Eventually, people in the row house began to gossip about O-En having lost her mind.

In this manner, more than a month went past, and then one day something happened.

A light spring rain had been falling since morning. Their parents had already left, and Matsukichi was playing over at O-Kō's. Minokichi had finished up the wash at the side of the well and gotten his hair soaked on the way back to the house. O-En had gotten up from bed and then sat down heavily.

"What's the matter, O-En?" Minokichi asked immediately. Lately, O-En rarely got up from bed without being helped by someone else. "You need to go to the outhouse? Can you stand up by yourself?"

Minokichi came near, and O-En's cloth-covered face tremblingly turned in his direction. She tilted her neck just slightly.

"You there," she said in a voice like a whisper. "Did you pass a young girl as you were coming inside just now?"

Minokichi hadn't seen anyone. *Why is O-En asking something like that?* he wondered, thinking it a rather eerie thing to say. "I didn't pass anybody."

"Oh. I see," O-En said, nodding her trembling head. "You couldn't see her, could you? That's for the best."

"What are you talking about, O-En?"

Minokichi approached the side of his sister's futon. The wrists that protruded from the sleeves of her nightclothes were even thinner than Matsukichi's and had wrinkles like those of an old woman.

"O-Chiyo came here just now," O-En murmured.

"Who's O-Chiyo?"

"The girl who went to work at that restaurant."

Minokichi was surprised; he hadn't thought O-En knew the name of that girl.

"Your big sister knew all about O-Chiyo," O-En continued, as though heading off her younger brother's thoughts. "She was the town belle, after all. I don't know whether she knew anything about me or not, but I knew everything about her."

It had been such a long time since O-En had last spoken that Minokichi didn't want to interrupt her. But at the same time, he had a feeling that he shouldn't just stand there nodding his head as he listened to this. He felt that he shouldn't let his sister speak of such things.

"O-Chiyo was a pretty girl, but lazy," O-En continued. "Also, she had a hard time telling the difference between what was hers and what belonged to others for some reason."

Minokichi wanted to say, *O-En, stop that kind of talk; she's dead now*, but he wasn't able. It was like his tongue was stuck in the back of his throat.

"So you know, when that girl got the job . . . when I was no good . . . it was so frustrating. To lose out on account of how a girl like that looked . . . It was so frustrating it made my stomach churn, and I couldn't sleep at night."

Wrapped in the cloth, O-En's head swayed gently from left to right.

"Hey, remember that time I got that fortune slip and it said daikyō?"

It surprised Minokichi to hear her talking about that all of a sudden, but there was a forceful undertone in O-En's voice, and besides that, Minokichi did remember. "Yeah," he said in a small voice.

"Right. I was sure you would. After all, the look on my face must have been pretty frightening then." She gave a low, chuckling laugh. "I wonder if you remember one other thing? You were still little at the time, so you may not, but do you remember when Aunt O-Kō used to tell us stories about the god of the mountain in her hometown?"

O-Kō and her husband had been born to farmers up in the Jōshū region, but around the time they were both turning twenty they had fled to Edo with little more than the clothes on their backs. From time to time they would tell stories about the village they grew up in, but those were mostly just tales about how hard they had had it, so Minokichi had never taken an active interest in listening to them.

"They say there's a strange tradition at the shrine where they worshipped the village's mountain god, where if you draw a bad fortune, you can go to the plum tree in back of the shrine and, while you're tying it to a branch, ask him to help you by saying these words: 'Please stick this bad luck on so-and-so in my place.'"

Minokichi had no memory of ever having heard such a story.

"They say that when you ask him, you absolutely have to say it out loud. The god of the mountain can't hear you if you don't. But if you don't want to do that, and you just tie the fortune to the plum tree's branch without saying anything, the bad luck will double and come back to you."

Minokichi felt something cold run down his spine. Though the spring rain had been warm, it now felt as though he were chilled all the way to the tips of his toes.

"But that's just some story from Aunt O-Kō's hometown, right?" Minokichi ventured, adding a deliberate gruffness to his tone. "It might just be something somebody made up."

Again, O-En laughed out loud. Minokichi almost shivered at the sound of it. "Yeah . . . that's what your big sister thought too. 'After all, it's not like it'll come true,' I thought. That's why I did it that day."

"You 'did it'—"

"While I was tying the fortune to the plum branch, I asked him out loud, '*Please stick this bad luck on O-Chiyo in my place.*'"

Minokichi fell silent. He could hear the soft whisper of the rain falling outside.

"It's your big sister's fault O-Chiyo got smallpox." O-En spoke in small voice, but one flat with certainty. "So O-Chiyo, she is angry with your big sister."

"Stop it, sis. That's just something they told you."

"She was here just now. Right over there."

O-En moved her shrouded head, motioning toward the doorway with a jerk of her chin. The cloth fluttered, and for an instant he could see her pointy white chin.

"She came because it's her forty-ninth day. Of course she came. To where I am."

Minokichi stood up with sudden violence. He shouted, trying to shake off his own fear. "Stop it, sis! I don't wanna hear any more stories!"

O-En raised her head slowly. Then she said briefly in a voice that cracked, "I'm sorry." O-En raised her hand and in one smooth motion put aside the cloth, revealing her face. He looked straight on at his sister's countenance, which he hadn't seen now in weeks.

The familiar face of the sister he had known wasn't there. It was covered in swollen, blue-black boils and wasted by disease. Her nose and her mouth were both nearly impossible to distinguish. Only her two eyes were clear to see, looking up at Minokichi with sorrowful clarity.

Without a word, Minokichi went stumbling back out of the house in horror. He tripped over his own feet outside and fell face first into mud from the spring rain, and there he finally screamed. O-Kō came running outside wondering what was the matter.

Sitting still on her futon, her cloth-swaddled face swaying up and down, O-En was laughing in a hollow, meaningless voice. Her laughter rang high and low, and like the gentle sound of the steady spring rain, it went on and on without a break.

From that day forward, O-En never again returned to sanity.

怪

When Minokichi returned home to the row house, he found O-Ito sitting down, holding her swollen belly with both hands. Her wicker trunk was open, and she was arranging some socks and undergarments. "The Kazusa'ya has always been so good to us," said O-Ito, a tear in the corner of her eye. "The proprietress asked me to have O-En wear these when she's put in the coffin. She sewed them herself."

"I'll take them with me."

According to O-Kō, the Kazusa-ya was letting them bury O-En's body there. They had taken care of her for so long, they were going to see it through to the end. The offer was much appreciated. Minokichi remembered anew how his late mother used to tell him over and over that he mustn't sleep with his feet pointed toward the Kazusa'ya.

When O-En had completely lost her mind that spring fifteen years ago, there had been nothing that Minokichi or anyone could do for her. From time to time, his mother had cried out that they would die together. But then an offer had been extended from the Kazusa'ya, where Minokichi's mother had worked for many years: they had an empty room in their villa in Mukōjima and were willing to put O-En up there. For the family, this had been like meeting Buddha in the midst of hell.

"She doesn't require a whole lot of care, so you can go see to her whenever you aren't busy. In exchange, you'd become a live-in worker at the villa. Would that be all right?"

Minokichi's mother had wept for joy. The town gossips claimed that long ago the Kazusa'ya's owners also had a daughter who had died of mental illness, and that was probably why they didn't think of O-En as just somebody else's problem. Even that empty room, they often whispered, was the cell in which that daughter had been hidden away. Minokichi's mother, however, cared nothing for such talk.

In the end, she had spent the next thirteen years living and working there, taking care of O-En on the side. During those thirteen years, his father had died unexpectedly of contagious disease, and Minokichi had taken over the oil-selling business in great haste. Matsukichi had started working, been well liked at his workplace, and gotten married. Lots of things had happened, but his mother's life had continued to revolve around O-En. After she had suddenly died the year before last, Minokichi had prepared himself for the need to take in O-En himself, but the Kazusa'ya had been very generous. They said that at this point it would be cruel to turn her out, so they would continue to take care of her as always.

And now at last, O-En's life had come to an end in a small room at the Kazusa'ya.

Leaving O-Ito at the house and carrying only the undergarments that she had packed, Minokichi hurried off toward Mukōjima. The sky had been clear early that morning, but now it was clouding up, and about halfway to Mukōjima a light rain began sprinkling down on him. Because of the rain, the scent of plum blossoms became all the more heady.

At the Kazusa'ya villa, an old man who said he was in charge of the building came out and immediately led him inside. He was taken to a tatami room and, after a short wait, at last introduced to a small woman who was probably in her forties. Placing her hands on the tatami floor, she introduced herself as Miki and said it was a terrible shame about O-En.

"Have you been taking care of my sister?"

"Yes, for these two years, just like the shop mistress told me."

"Thank you so much for that." Minokichi bowed his head deeply. He was searching for words to further express his gratitude, but O-Miki swiftly interrupted him.

"The master and mistress both say that they just couldn't ignore someone in trouble. The world may say all kinds of things, but there really are Buddhalike people in this world."

"I know that very well."

O-Miki stood up when Minokichi asked her to take him to O-En. He followed along behind her and stepped out into the hallway.

Suddenly, he was seized with terror at the sensation of the cold floorboards beneath his feet.

"My sister—" he started to say, but his words broke off.

Would her face still be covered in boils like before? Had she continued to hide them by wearing a cloth over her face to the very end?

As though anticipating his concerns, O-Miki said, "Her face is very lovely in death. You'd almost think she was sleeping."

Minokichi, walking one step behind O-Miki through the corridor, unconsciously came to a halt. "Lovely?"

"Why, yes," O-Miki said, looking at him as if wondering at his surprise. "She had certainly lost a lot of weight, but her face looks very peaceful."

"Her cloth—"

"She wore it till the very end," O-Miki said with a hint of melancholy. "But the face underneath it was lovely."

"She got better, then?" Minokichi asked.

O-Miki's brows narrowed. "Better? What do you mean?"

"Her face's . . . you know."

"Was there something the matter with O-En's face?"

"You're saying there wasn't?"

"There wasn't what?" O-Miki peered at Minokichi. "From beginning to end, O-En never had any kind of illness you could see. I had thought everyone in her family was aware of that."

Minokichi felt himself going lightheaded.

"Back when I had just started helping with her, she had an extended lucid moment. She asked me not to take the cloth away; she wore it as punishment, she said, because she'd done something so wicked she couldn't show her face to other people. I had been told all about that by the mistress as well, so I said all right and agreed to leave it alone. That's why I didn't take it off until I knew she had already stopped breathing. I wonder what kind of bad thing she was talking about. It's not for us to know, of course, but at the sight of that peaceful face, it felt to me like her punishment was already over and done with."

"I see," Minokichi said at last.

But what about those boils on her face? Minokichi had seen that pitiable face himself. Was it something that only he and O-En—as they were at that time—could see?

Had it been that kind of punishment?

"This way, please."

Minokichi followed along behind O-Miki in the dimly lit hallway. Standing in front of him, she was about to open the sliding paper door at the end of the hallway. Just then, however, Minokichi smelled a remarkably strong fragrance of plum blossoms.

He blinked his eyes in surprise. Right beside him, he felt the sensation of a young girl sliding past him with the soft sound of rustling silks.

"Sir?" O-Miki was looking at Minokichi, her hand still on the paper door. Minokichi looked back across the finely polished wood floor of the hallway. No one was there.

"It's nothing," he said. "Pardon me."

He stepped quietly through the doorway.

There O-En was lying with her head facing north, still under most of the covers she had been sleeping in.

Supported by her pillow, her head was lifted up just slightly, with a pure white cloth placed over it.

The strength went out of Minokichi's knees as he bent down and sat beside her futon. O-Miki respectfully put her hands together in prayer and then took away the covering from her face.

The sound of the rain falling outside the window suddenly grew stronger.

"O-En," Minokichi said.

O-En was smiling. It was the same smile that she had had as a diligent worker in her girlhood. Pure and bright. No shadow of misfortune tainted her cheeks. With a feeling as though fifteen long years had without a sound just taken flight, Minokichi smiled in spite of himself.

The fragrance of plum flowers drifted through the room. Out in the hallway, someone's light footfalls were growing steadily more distant. Minokichi could hear the sound clearly, but he knew that if he looked he would see no one. For that reason he simply held his peace, took O-En's hand in his own, and gave it a gentle squeeze.

V

The "Oni" of the Adachi House

On the evening my mother-in-law died, the noise of a chance sudden downpour resounded in the walkway and through the garden, roaring as though everything around us were being hammered by a fall of pebbles. That was why I was unable to catch what she said in the last moments before her eyes closed. To my ears, it sounded as though she had called out a name, but there was no way to be certain. Even so, her death came peacefully, as if she had dozed off to sleep, and there was a faint smile around the corners of her mouth.

Dr. Ryōan, who had not left her bedside for the last hour, tilted his smooth, bald head slightly and spoke in a gentle voice to me and to Tomitarō—the master of the house—who was sitting on his calves at my side.

"The retired mistress has departed," he said.

That day, the two of us had been by Mother's side since morning. Every once in a while, Tomitarō had become motionless and stared intently at her face, saying not a word, a brooding look in his eyes at all times. That expression crumbled at last as grief etched taut lines into his face.

"A good, restful face," the doctor said as he folded Mother's hands on her chest. "Like a young girl looking forward to some pleasant outing, don't you think?"

The doctor was absolutely right. Looking at the expression on Mother's face made me smile unexpectedly as well. And her final words, the words I had just now missed hearing, had surely been the name of Mother's "oni." Tears rose up to sting my eyes as my mind filled with incoherent, regretful thoughts of how at the very end I hadn't been able to learn it.

"It's been a long road," Tomitarō murmured. "But Mum, she seemed satisfied. Don't you think so?"

Tomitarō rested his hand on my arm, seeking solace. I placed my own hand on the back of my husband's, nodded, and said, "Yes, she led a happy life. I'm sure of it."

怪

It was in the spring, three years ago, that I married into the family running the Sasa'ya. In those days Mother had already grown quite weak physically; she had spent about half of the prior year sick in bed. Attending her was a handmaid named O-Tama who had just turned fifteen. Small of body and with a face suggesting an agile mind, the young girl possessed a determined and unyielding spirit, but it was that very outspokenness that seemed to rub my invalid mother-in-law the wrong way, earning her nothing but scoldings and criticism.

Even for a firebrand like O-Tama, caring for an invalid must have been depressing work at times, and to make matters worse she was constantly being fussed at. So about six months after I married into the family, she was overjoyed to hear me say, "Starting today, I'll be taking care of Mother."

"Oh, thank heavens!" O-Tama cried with sincere joy, lifting both hands up over her head.

Naturally, these were not words that a maid in O-Tama's position had any business saying to the shop master's bride. However, I was eighteen years old at that time, close to her age, and moreover

O-Tama was very much aware of the fact that until I got married, I had been working as a maid at the Shōchikudō— a paper whole-saler with deep professional ties to the Sasa'ya. I was a slightly unusual bride, one whose saving grace was the fact that I was a former maid myself. That was probably why O-Tama took a casual, "oh, we're friends here" attitude around me. She was entirely unreserved in how she addressed me. Now that I think about it, even in front of others, O-Tama hardly ever called me "mistress," and certainly never at times when there was no one else around to hear.

"It's just depressing being cooped up all day in a smelly room with no one but an old lady to talk to," O-Tama declared bluntly. "Your life's about to get a lot harder. My sympathies." She gave me the sort of smile that could have been formed by two hooks lifting up the corners of her mouth.

The Sasa'ya was a small shop that sold brushes and ink cakes, but it also had a little bit of land—and a large number of secrets. The mansion was large as well and located on the same plot of land. In addition, there was an annex of about fifteen *tsubo,* separated by a modest courtyard from the main building, which housed the store clerks, the housekeepers, and the live-in workers. This was where my mother-in-law was living. O-Tama and I were speaking there right when it was time for Mother's nap, in the anteroom next door to her bedroom, so no matter how frankly she spoke, and even if she spoke in a loud voice, there was no danger that anyone would overhear and call her to account. And because of that, O-Tama's words were very much unguarded. "Hey, is it true you spent five years taking care of the Shōchikudō's last master when he was sick?"

It certainly was true. The previous master of the Shōchikudō had long been ill with palsy. I had started working there as a nurse-maid at age ten, but when I was released from caring for the babies, I went straight over to caring for the previous master. He was a very selfish patient and more troublesome than the babies, so I really did have a hard time with him.

That previous master died only three months before my wedding. Or to put things in proper sequence, rather, the previous master finally died, so having never done anything up till then except care for children and invalids, a gaping hole opened up with regard to how I could be used. But right at that point, the proposal came from the Sasa'ya.

For a housemaid with no work to do to luck into a marriage proposal instead of being let go—normally it would sound ridiculous. Truth be told, when I first heard about it from the master and mistress of the Shōchikudō, even I had the feeling I was being tricked by a fox. As I was saying just a moment ago, the Sasa'ya was a well-off business, so for someone of my standing, this was quite the proverbial jeweled palanquin. If it had been explained to me that the master of the Sasa'ya was a lover of pretty faces, that would've been one thing, but I knew nothing at all about the man—about his face or character—and above all, I was not the kind of girl blessed with a face that said, "Look at me."

The proposal just hadn't made any sense, and taking note of the increasingly alarmed look on my face, the master of the Shōchikudō stared at me with an awkward smile. Then the mistress promptly revealed to me the truth of what this proposal was all about.

"Master Tomitarō of the Sasa'ya turned thirty this year but has never married. It's not that he dislikes women or anything. Back in his younger days he used to go off carousing in the pleasure quarters something awful, along with my husband."

At that, the awkward smile of the Shōchikudō's master had grown more awkward still.

"There's a retired mistress living at the Sasa'ya. It's Tomitarō's mother, but her health isn't good and—well, her age being what it is, she's practically an invalid. But if nothing else, her mind is sharp, and they say Tomitarō can't do a thing without her. At any rate, the Sasa'ya is the shop that both of Tomitarō's parents built."

The previous master of the Sasa'ya—Tomitarō's father—

had died suddenly when Tomitarō was twenty-five, but they say that when it came to business he had been quite sharp. I don't think there was any doubt of that; Mother said of him, "I never for a moment fell in love with that man, but I swooned over the way he worked." Mother told me such things flatly and not just once or twice.

"The second master, Tomitarō, also has his father's business acumen," said the mistress of the Shōchikudō, "so the Sasa'ya will most likely be able to keep growing. It's impossible for a shop master like that not to have girls wanting to marry him, and in fact, there have been offers enough to bury Tomitarō under. But you know, maybe it's a weakness on his part that he . . ."

The master of the Shōchikudō stroked his chin. "Well, maybe it's better just to say he loves his mother. At any rate, they say that with Master Tomitarō, the better the offer, the less he's interested. As for 'good offers,' now, you've got the ones where the girl's parents run some big business, the ones where her father's a low-ranked vassal to the shōgun—poor but with status—ones where the girl is the daughter of a business partner . . . There's all kinds, right? But Master Tomitarō says he doesn't want anyone like that. He says that if he takes a bride from such a high position, she'll look down on the retired mistress and will never genuinely value her in her heart. He says, 'My parents aren't old money; they worked their fingers to the bone to make that store what it is. Now that she can finally take it easy during her last years, I'd feel sorry for her if she had to spend them deferring to a bride from some higher ranked family. That's why I decided to choose a wife from a no-name family and preferably one from among the working class.'"

"However, at this particular time, he can't really make one of the maids working at the Sasa'ya into the new shop mistress." The mistress of the Shōchikudō shook her head sternly as she spoke. "If he did something like that, it would upset the order of things inside the shop. So no matter what, he needs to find a bride from outside the store. Understand?"

The Shōchikudō's master and mistress both agreed that given these conditions, a girl like me was exactly what he was looking for.

"Not only that, you're also used to taking care of sick people. You've done good work for us. Even at the Sasa'ya, it seems the maids are fairly put out by the retired mistress, so once you start living there, you should take care of your mother-in-law. Master Tomitarō is looking for a bride prepared to do that."

Indeed, that was exactly the kind of proposal it was. "Take a bride from your garden," the saying went. In other words, when bringing a bride into the in-laws' household, it's best to marry low. There was even a saying for this kind of thing, and when I listened closely to what they were saying, I realized that it wasn't such a mysterious invitation after all. At the time, however, I was thinking that this Tomitarō person—while he was obviously respectful of his father and mother—was certainly making a lot of assumptions. Even if a girl had been raised as a pampered young lady, that alone didn't mean she would become a haughty, prideful wife. A lot of that depended on how Tomitarō behaved himself. *Well, anyway,* I thought, *the fact that he has such a serious disposition means he has character . . .*

Also, even if I couldn't exactly nod agreement with this aspect of the Sasa'ya master's way of thinking, there was no path by which I might refuse his proposal. To do so would be to defy the master and mistress of the Shōchikudō, and for someone like me, whose parents had died early, who had been raised by a succession of relatives, and who had been sheltered and nourished by the Shōchikudō for all these long years since I began as a nursemaid, the Shōchikudō was a presence in my life to which I owed an even greater debt of gratitude than I did to my own parents. Also, there was no other man in particular whom I had been thinking of . . . And as women generally marry someone sooner or later, if there was someone out there wanting a bride who'd been raised as a maid, I could hardly object. And then it occurred to me: *What are you thinking? From the outset, this was never about being a bride—you're just changing employers as a maid.* When I looked at it that way, there was really no decision to make at all.

That's how I married into the Sasa'ya.

There was no wedding ceremony. There was not even a private celebration for his family and close friends. Later, I was told by the workers in the house that there had been fierce resistance to such things from his relatives, who argued that showy ceremonies and receptions were out of the question because nothing could be more embarrassing than to go out of one's way to marry a former maidservant after brushing off so many fine offers. I was also informed that, as was to be expected, Tomitarō's more distant relatives did not recognize me as the bride of the master of the Sasa'ya.

Come to think of it, not even once since the day I came here as a bride had I ever made the rounds of exchanging formal greetings with the relatives. For someone like me, with no memory of ever having anyone I could call family or relatives, things like that would completely slip my mind. Then when I remembered, I would get upset and go running to Tomitarō to apologize, but he would say, "What do you mean? I've been ready for this kind of mess from the day I decided to marry you. My association with those people is in name only, and paying courtesy calls would be more of an annoyance to them than anything. Just forget about it. I'm a merchant, so my friends mean more to me than relatives who gather around like parasites trying to benefit themselves."

My husband would say things like that and cheer me up.

As you can see even from words like that, Tomitarō was a gentle, upstanding man, which meant I had married better than I'd ever dreamed. Like many intelligent men who thought things through carefully, he could sometimes be a little unaccommodating, and once he started talking he tended to stop listening, but it was no trouble at all for me to adapt to that. From the outset, I knew nothing about sales, so there was no way I was going to oppose Tomitarō's ideas, and even when in private he expressed an opinion to me, it would always be about some extremely trivial thing. Things like, "Your pillow's too low; the blood in your neck can't flow like that. It's bad for you. Raise it up a little higher," or "You shouldn't use so much soy sauce when you boil winter melons," or "Don't wear thick clothes just because it's cold." For that kind of thing, it was no trouble at all just to say "Yes, dear," and go along with it.

I know it's taken some trouble to set the stage for the story I'm about to tell, but things went on like this for about half a year, and once I had gotten used to keeping the books, I finally set about taking over from O-Tama the job of caring for Mother. Being as I was her son's bride, I had of course been looking in on her daily at the annex even before then to see how she was doing, but because I hadn't been right at her side all that time, I didn't know what to expect. To be honest, my feelings were divided about fifty-fifty between eagerness to work hard and take good care of her . . . and unease over whether or not I'd be up to the job.

As I was saying earlier, the root of O-Tama's lack of reserve toward me was in the circumstances by which I came into the family. O-Tama had heard a surprisingly large amount of the story, which was why even when dealing with me directly, she showed not the slightest trace of deference. The workers are the oars that row a business along, but under no circumstances do they ever take the helm. A ship's captain has to read the current and keep watch on the surroundings in order to choose a safe course through the shoals, but an oar just continues to steadily row and need not worry about such things. Consequently, the oars do know all about the inside of the ship. This is because they have lots of time to look at it. O-Tama was truly, in that respect, an oar that only saw well what was right in front of it.

"I don't understand what the master was thinking. To have spurned engagements to ladies from good places to marry someone like you, and for the sake of an old hag like that!"

Her tongue was sharp, but it was an apt enough comment that

there was nothing I could say for my own part. However, calling Mother an "old hag" could not be allowed to pass unchallenged, so I scolded her for it. O-Tama just smiled the whole time.

"At any rate, I've now finally escaped from that depressing room, so I have to be grateful to you for that. Oh well, work hard and do the best you can, all right?"

After O-Tama had turned down the hallway and disappeared off toward the main building, I rubbed my chest and finally stood up to go to Mother's bedroom. Just then the door slid open with a bang against the wooden frame. My mother-in-law, whom we'd just been discussing, peeked outside.

"Well, well. I guess she told you," she said with a smile. "Leave O-Tama be. What goes around comes around, in time."

That was all she said before banging the door closed again. I was standing there with my mouth open, once again feeling that I had a fox playing tricks on me or perhaps a tanuki making a fool of me.

怪

Mother was by no means a difficult patient, nor was she a hard-to-handle "hag" either. I came to realize this right away when I began to attend her.

The retired master of the Shōchikudō, now . . . *he* had been a lot of trouble to care for. It was true that he was largely paralyzed because of his palsy, and it was true that he was obstinate about accepting that fact. Also, it is most certainly true that in the final year of his life he showed signs, albeit slight ones, of so-called *iro-boke*—a mental preoccupation with the amorous congress of man and woman—and on occasion, I faced situations that left my younger self in tears. Unable to tell anyone, I soldiered on.

Compared to that, Mother was as gentle as the Buddha. Her instructions were clear and easy to understand—"Do it like I show you," "I want you to do this," "Stop doing that"—with no hidden implications in her words. If Mother said, "I'm taking a nap, so leave me be for a while," that was exactly what she meant. If she said, "Let's see your skill at needlework," she was telling me to go to my sewing box and hemming bird.

Mother loved to talk about the good old days—of when Tomitarō was a newborn, of the great pains she and her husband had taken to establish the store. I had never known my own parents' faces and had never been blessed with the chance to sit close to someone and listen to the old tales of their generation, so I was always fascinated by Mother's stories. It seems many complain that they tire of listening to the stories that the elderly tell. They say they repeat the same stories again and again, but I had never heard the stories of an elderly family member repeated enough to tire of them, so for me the experience was truly enjoyable.

One month passed. I smiled widely at her pleasant stories and was on tenterhooks when she spoke of frightening situations from her own past, things that had happened to her or of times when the store had faced make or break situations. This wasn't mere flattery; I really enjoyed spending time with her. Mother was probably aware of this, because one time when the two of us were sewing *yukata*, she suddenly set aside her needle, stared at me with a very earnest expression, and said, "You've lived a very lonely life so far, haven't you?"

After thinking for a moment, I told her that in all honesty, I had always been alone, so loneliness had never even felt lonely.

"That's what I thought." Mother nodded deeply. "You turned eighteen having never done anything outside of caring for children and tending to sick people, so that's certainly understandable. You're not familiar with that thing we call 'the world' at all."

After this, she blinked her eyes a little and asked me very seriously, "But did you never find a man you liked?"

I was shocked. Naturally, I found myself hard-pressed to answer. The reason that Mother was my mother-in-law was because I was Tomitarō's wife. I couldn't just brazenly say to her that before I got married there had been someone else that I loved.

Fortunately or unfortunately, however, I had known absolutely nothing of romantic love. Together with the bedridden previous master of the Shōchikudō, I too had been very constrained in my maidenhood. Back then, even those illustrated chapbooks with the yellow covers that are now so readily available to young maids were not yet easy to come by, so not even from stories could I learn about the workings of the hearts of men and women.

"Ahh, you've never been in love with anyone, have you?" Before I could answer, Mother spoke as though she had somehow looked into my mind. "That's what I thought, but . . ."

It was an odd thing to say. Without thinking, I asked her, "Why is that?"

Mother gave a slight smile and said, "When it comes to Tomitarō, you don't dislike him, but you're not yet in love with him. For a woman, being a wife is a kind of job, so when you married Tomitarō, you were probably thinking of it as a continuation of your work."

As if to console me, she added that she wasn't saying that this attitude was wrong.

"It is, however, a genuinely sad thing. I wish I could help you find love like I did, but that's just something a third party can't do anything about."

From her expression, Mother looked like she was deep in thought about something. What she had said just before that had caught my interest, so stubbornly, I asked one more time. "Mother, how did you know I've never been in love?"

Mother turned her head as though taking a quick look around the interior of the room. After that, she looked toward a place right beside her and gave a little smile at a tatami mat where no one was sitting. "Well, you don't seem able to see anything and you don't seem to sense anything either."

Her answers were growing odder and odder. I was getting ready to ask what she meant yet again, but Mother interrupted, saying she was feeling a little tired, asked if I would put on some tea, and suggested that some sweets would be nice.

And that was all for that day. I had failed to grasp the meaning of what she said, but as it was a trifling matter, I did not remember it for very long.

What happened next occurred several days later. I was asked the following by O-Tama, who now worked in the kitchen: "Hey, you know that funny smell in the retired mistress's room—kind of smelly like an animal? It felt like it was sticking to my body in there! I hated, hated, hated it! Couldn't stand it in there! Doesn't it bother you too?"

I looked at her dubiously. I had never once noticed any such odor. When I quite honestly told her so, O-Tama gave me a sidelong glare.

"Well, well. No sooner do you take over than you start playing the good little girl, don't you? There's no way you haven't noticed. The smell can be strong or weak depending on the day, but on rainy days especially the whole room is just cloying. It has to be coming from the old bat herself. Because no matter how much you try and clean them up, old people smell."

I said to her again that there was no such smell.

"I'm sure you don't," O-Tama shot back hatefully. "Granny must love that one."

It was an outrageous accusation. Not surprisingly, I was angry, I was annoyed, and I was unable to contain it in my heart. This was slander—and although I knew that, I still told Mother about it.

And when I did so, Mother replied in a cheerful voice, "Oh my! Did she now? But it's all right; that horrible, horrible odor is something only O-Tama can smell."

And then, as she had done before, she turned and, looking back over her shoulder at the place right behind her, smiled, and gave a little nod as though seeking agreement, even though no one was in the room except for Mother and me.

That day, I had a vaguely eerie feeling for the first time. In the corner of my heart, a suspicion took root that just maybe, just slightly, Mother's illness might have begun creeping into her mind.

This suspicion created a low but definite wall between me and Mother, or at least from my viewpoint toward her. Perhaps another month went by. It happened that this was at the coldest time of the winter. There was a great deal of snow in Edo that year, and in the Sasa'ya's modest garden the shrubs and oftentimes the standing trees as well were completely cloaked in swathes of white.

Right around this time, a new business associate started visiting Tomitarō regularly. A maker of vermilion and Chinese ink, he had gathered about him a number of his fellow craftsmen and become their leader. He was about the same age as Tomitarō, and he spoke like a very smart and able person, well mannered and careful of his appearance. His name was Sajirō. O-Tama and the others were altogether taken with him, and he would cause a huge stir whenever he came by. I can still remember the sour expression on the chief clerk's face when he found the shape of an umbrella drawn in the new fallen snow with O-Tama and Sajirō's names written side by side beneath it.

You probably know this, but in Edo, the Kobaien in Nihonbashi is famous for its ink cakes and brushes. The ink was particularly famous—so fragrant that even after being washed after use and returned to the writing desk, a brush would continue to smell of it. Naturally, a considerable price tag was attached to it for that reason alone.

Sajirō had come by one day, saying that he and his compatriots had through their own devices created a new kind of ink cake not a whit less fragrant than the best the Kobaien had to offer. They were selling it at a low wholesale price, he said, and hoped that the Sasa'ya would put it out for sale.

Tomitarō seemed interested. As I keep saying, I know little about business, but one time Tomitarō showed it to me, and when I actually ground Sajiro's ink in an inkstone myself, it truly was highly aromatic.

All signs pointed toward smooth negotiations and the swift conclusion of a deal. Even the ever-cautious chief clerk was swept along by Sajirō's fervor and hardly put in a word during the talks, as though charmed by the man's eloquent speech. One day, however, Tomitarō came to me and said, "I'd like to introduce Sajiro to Mum today, so please be ready for that."

"With these past few days of snow and chill, Mother has caught cold and been confined to her bed," I said, explaining that she was entirely unable to receive guests at this time.

But Tomitarō replied, "I know that. It's fine if she does it while lying down in bed. Just slide open the panel door facing the courtyard. For only a short while will be fine. If you'll do that, I can have her look across the garden and see Sajiro's face in my reception room here."

Then Tomitarō added frankly, "I've never done business with anyone without Mum's blessing."

I see, I thought. It dawned on me somewhat belatedly that this was what was meant when people said that Tomitarō "can't do a thing without his mother."

It was after noon when Sajiro arrived, accompanied by an older associate. As had been arranged in advance, Tomitarō conveyed them to a reception room that could be seen across the courtyard from the annex, so at the proper time I opened the sliding panel. Mother, having apparently heard about this from Tomitarō earlier, sat up in bed like one thoroughly used to this procedure and stared off intently toward the room where the guests were sitting.

Viewed from the annex, a camellia tree about as tall as I am appeared to be standing right between Tomitarō and Sajiro, who were engaged in a steady exchange of lighthearted banter. Though the snow had already been brushed off of it once that morning, a steady fall of snowflakes the size of peony blossoms had covered the camellia tree with a second coat of purest white. As if overspread with cotton, the ground in the courtyard was solid white as well, and if you just allowed for the bitter cold, it was a bewitchingly beautiful winter garden scene.

Perhaps by some chance the topic of conversation touched upon the garden. Tomitarō pointed toward the courtyard, and both Sajirō and the companion he had brought turned to face it. At that moment, I looked up from where I was stirring the embers in the brazier next to Mother, having noticed that she was leaning forward.

From across the courtyard, I caught sight of Sajirō's face rapidly going as white as the snow. His eyes were open wide in surprise. He turned his head sharply back toward Tomitarō and the older man who had come with him and said something to them with obvious fervor. Tomitarō drew in his chin a bit as though surprised, and the older man blinked his eyes.

Sajirō leaned forward and suddenly thrust out his arm toward the courtyard. He was pointing toward where we were. At Mother? At me? In any case, I gasped in surprise to see him being so ill mannered as to point fingers at people.

But Sajirō was pointing at the air. His body, his face, his eyes, his arm, and his finger were most certainly angled in our direction, toward this room of Mother's, but they were pointing at nothing— at nothing more than an empty space in the middle of this room. Even so, I stood up quickly and placed a hand on the door, looking down to see if there was something in the garden. But on the sheet of snow that had accumulated there, I saw not even the footprint of a bird. Of course no one was there.

I could hear Sajirō's panicked voice. "That's strange! Are my eyes playing tricks on me? I could've sworn I saw a—"

Tomitarō said something back to him with a smile, and his companion also smiled, so Sajirō grudgingly forced a smile of his own.

Still though, to me he looked as though he were terribly frightened.

"That's enough. Close the screen, please."

At the sound of Mother's voice, I turned around. Mother was nodding her head again and again as though she had come to some sort of realization. "Well, at any rate, it seems that man managed to see something incredible. That will conclude negotiations at this time."

I asked her why that was. I felt the chill run down my spine that wasn't just from the cold and realized that my hand was tightly gripping the frame of the sliding panel. I was very frightened.

Mother observed me in this state for a short while and at last gave a little smile and said, "I'll tell you about it at length later, as soon as I get over this cold." Saying nothing else, she laid her head back on the pillow.

Though the room fell silent and I soon heard the sound of Mother's gentle, steady breathing, I was unable to move from where I sat with my back up against the screen facing the courtyard. Someone I couldn't see was lurking in this room with Mother and me. But why wasn't Mother frightened? Did she know what this "thing" really was? Such thoughts ran around and around in my mind like trapped mice. *It's just my imagination,* I told myself, trying to force a rationalization. *Mother's words just now were just her trying to be a little nasty; there's no deep meaning.* But then my thoughts would return to the question, *What could have caused Sajirō's face to be so convulsed with terror like that?*

Ultimately, I was unable to walk back through that room, so instead I opened the sliding panel at my back, stepped down into the snowy courtyard, and hurriedly ran across it to make my escape to the room on the other side. There in its entryway, I turned to look back, but in the pure, cottony white of the snow, I saw nothing but my own footprints. *There's no one there after all.* I was out of breath from the fright that had hastened my footsteps, and there I let out a deep sigh of relief.

At that moment, a clump of snow fell with a soft *thump* from the camellia tree, baring a branch with leaves of such dark green that they looked almost black. I jumped up in the air and scrambled up into the room without looking back again.

The deal with Sajirō was called off, just as Mother had said it would be. Tomitarō said only that it was because his mother had not given her approval, offering no particular explanation beyond that. Naturally, when O-Tama learned that Sajirō would no longer be visiting the Sasa'ya, she swore all manner of vile oaths in the kitchen against her master, Tomitarō, and, in what was for her quite a slip-up, was overheard by the chief clerk, who took her to task for it. That this was accomplished with the added bonus of a blistering tongue-lashing was for me just a little bit thrilling.

Mother was one to keep her promises. When she got over her cold and was feeling better, she called me to her room so I could hear what she had to say.

During the last few days in which Mother had been bedridden, I had been so terrified during my trips to the annex that I was hardly able to bear it. For this reason, when it was at last time for Mother to explain to me what was going on, I had a feeling as of being rescued. The fear of something you know—no matter how terrifying it might be—was preferable by several degrees to the fear of something you don't clearly understand. That's what I thought, anyway.

Just before Mother started to tell her story, she looked at me with a stern expression I had never before seen on her face and asked, "Do you smell anything, hear anything, or see anything in this room?"

As had always been the case, I could see nothing, hear nothing, and smell nothing.

"I see, then. In that case, I'll tell you," Mother said with her lips very tight. "In this annex, right beside me in this room, there lives an 'oni.'"

怪

Thirty-odd years had already passed, she told me, since the event that occurred when Mother was sixteen.

At that time, Mother was working as a maid for a kimono wholesaler in Nihonbashi-Tōrimachi called the Jōshū'ya.

Actually, Mother was the illegitimate daughter of the master of the Jōshū'ya, born of a live-in maid with whom he had had an affair. Her mother, I'm given to understand, was well known for her conspicuous beauty, but rather than being a blessing to her, it instead awakened evil thoughts in the master of the Jōshū'ya. Mother said with a smile that no matter the roll of the dice women were made for hard lives.

"And my mother was hardly the only one to have such an experience. After all, the master of the Jōshū'ya was indiscriminate in his fondness for women. Aside from myself, he had three other children born to other women, all of them boys. In addition, he had one other son born to the mistress, which meant that later on there was no end of fighting over who would inherit the shop. Things did not end well, and ultimately the family fortune ran dry in the next generation, but, well, that's not directly related to my life story, so let's leave it aside."

Mother's mother, I'm told, died of puerperal fever shortly after giving birth to her. The master of the Jōshū'ya, being the sort of man he was, bore not one sliver of affection for the children of those maids he had laid hands on for sport. Mother was entrusted to the chief housekeeper, by whom she was raised to one day become a worker in the shop. In other words, she lost her mother when she was a baby, was essentially without a father, and from the very beginning was treated as a nuisance. Even so, as a baby she understood none of this herself, so all was as yet well with her. Things didn't get hard until she reached early childhood and became aware of what was going on around her . . .

"The mistress of the Jōshū'ya was a woman harsh in her jealousy, who—in a twisted sort of payback—enjoyed taking her hatred of her philandering husband out on the children he had fathered with other women. When I look back on it now, I feel rather sorry for her on account of that, but be that as it may, as a child, I'd have been less frightened facing Lord Yama in the afterlife than I was facing the mistress of the Jōshū'ya."

The lady of the house often chastised Mother, calling her abusive names like "rice weevil," for eating their rice without contributing anything.

Well, she was a small child at the time; of course she could not work. She was a growing girl; that she got hungry was only natural. Even so, she was stuck on the notion that it was outrageous for anyone in the working class to just eat without doing anything. Mother grew up subjected to all manner of meanness and abuse, delivered in all manner of ways—she was not fed for four or five days, she was left chained like a dog to a peg in the garden beneath a blazing summer sky, she was permitted only an unlined kimono even in the dead of winter, and she was given damp, half-rotted nightclothes.

"You may be wondering why I didn't run away from the Jōshū'ya when I was being treated like that. When I look back on it, I really don't know the answer to that myself. Ah well, I grew up knowing nothing except the inside of that little shop, so it's possible I lacked the wit to even think of running off to someplace else."

Also, although the chief housekeeper who raised Mother was hardly what one would call a kindly second mother to her, she—believing that a social outcast like Mother needed to work, work, work to her very limit to survive in the world—drilled into Mother the training she needed in order to have value as a worker in the shop. Because of that, by the time she turned ten years old, she was already growing into a far more excellent and discreet maidservant than the country girls there who had just arrived.

"By the time I was sixteen, I was already getting a little bit skilled at my work." Mother smiled proudly. "The Jōshū'ya was even starting to rely on what I did for them. All the more so, really, because just at the time I was coming into my own, the chief house-keeper became consumptive and often had to have me fill in for her. It was almost like a changing of the guard. Rather than driving me out, the mistress, as always, seemed more pleased to keep me around to abuse. I was even called in for no reason at all sometimes, only to be struck with fire tongs and the like. But I was a grown woman by this time and as such had grown a little more clever. If you do the same thing year after year, you learn the ways to avoid trouble and the ways to escape it. Yes, indeed, those horrid experiences were growing rarer and rarer."

Around that time, the master of the Jōshū'ya was closing in on his mid-fifties. As people wax in years, they wane in boldness, and from time to time when the mistress wasn't looking, the master would call out to Mother, speaking to her with gentle words.

"As I was saying, he had sons by other women, and the successor the mistress had born him had grown up into a lazy parasite given to terrible debauchery. The master must have been fretting over both of these things. He started saying the strangest things to me, like, 'You're a good, upstanding young girl. I wish I had properly acknowledged you as my own daughter sooner.' Of course, to me it just sounded like nonsense. I thought, 'What's this old man talking about? And why now? He's gotten so timid . . .' But you know what? Before long, I wasn't able to just brush it off and keep ignoring him."

The Jōshū'ya's founder had been the predecessor of the man who had fathered Mother and abandoned her, and that predecessor was originally from a tiny post town called Kuwano in the Jōshū region. It was from there that the shop's name had been derived.

"His predecessor was the second son of a family that provided cheap lodging for merchants in that town of Kuwano. He went broke there and left that place to come here—a common enough thing in Edo. If you're the firstborn, you take over the family business, even if it's a tiny little lodging house, but second sons are third wheels from the day they're born. True, he went to Edo and planted his flag, but Kuwano was still his hometown. They say he was always saying things like, 'Just once, I want to go back,' 'I want to visit my parents' graves,' 'I want to see the big brother I left behind,' but in the end, he died without having once been able to do so."

The master of the Jōshū'ya, who in his old age had come to spend much of his time in reflection on things past, declared his fervent desire to grant the wish that his predecessor had been unable to fulfill.

"The mistress was still speaking coldly to him at that time, in this case accusing him of just wanting to escape because there was nothing but trouble at home. Well, she was probably half right."

In any case, though, the master of the Jōshū'ya had ended up making preparations for the trip. He knew not whether anyone from his family was still living in Kuwano or not, or whether or not the lodging house where his predecessor grew up even still existed, yet he was nonetheless about to set off to find out.

"And then, young lady, he made a shocking announcement: he was going to take me with him."

His rationale had been rather self-serving: "I need a maidservant to wait on me, and as she's my own flesh and blood daughter, she's the only one I can take to Kuwano."

"And I . . ." said Mother, staring intently at my face, "I agreed to go. Why do you think I did?"

Because she thought it would be a perfect chance to get out of the Jōshū'ya.

"Naturally, I had no intention of going all the way to Jōshū. If I were traveling alone with my elderly master, I would be the stronger one. Once we were away from Edo, I was planning to leave the old man behind at some opportune lodging house and run away. I knew he would also be carrying a reasonable amount of money for the trip, so I would take that as well. Really, it was the money I was after. You see, if I had just wanted to run away from the Jōshū'ya, I could've done so at anytime. But something just stuck in my craw about the idea of doing that. On account of my mother being made a plaything of the master's, neither I nor my mother had ever been paid for our work at the Jōshū'ya. So I wanted something to take with me for that. I couldn't have asked for a better chance than this trip."

Looking me in the eye, mother smiled and said, "I am a frightening woman." I tried to return the smile, but it didn't go very well.

"Kuwano was in a region with prosperous silk and sericulture and textile industries, and the lodging house had originally been established there because of the frequent comings and goings of merchants from Edo who came to purchase silks. Even the Jōshū'ya was allowed promissory notes, ostensibly for business purposes, by the lodging house, and in the spring of that year, just as the cherry blossoms were passing their peak, we set out from Edo."

The old man and young woman were traveling on foot, and there were many steep mountain paths along the Jōshuu Road. Even if the way had been flat, it would have normally taken a full ten days to cover the distance. Even so, the master of the Jōshū'ya, in high spirits perhaps, hurried ahead down the road, and moreover . . .

"That dirty old man! He held on tight to the money and wouldn't let it out of his sight. He kept it hidden inside his pillow when he was sleeping, and as a result I failed to make my getaway on the way there . . ."

Eventually, the two of them arrived at the post town of Kuwano after about eight and a half days.

"Kuwano was not in the sort of area where Shinto or Buddhist pilgrims tended to congregate; it was just a little post station in the mountains, frequented exclusively by merchants—a dreary place with nothing in the way of atmosphere. Closed in all around by mountains, and standing in an open space where the reddish-brown mountainside lay exposed, there was just a row of tiny inns, which seemed to be clinging to the bare earth. All day long, the high winds pounded them, and if you opened your mouth widely to talk, you would breathe and swallow the dust. Maybe it was local color, but the people in that place all spoke loudly in their natural voices, and to my eyes, all of the men looked like brigands."

It came as no surprise that the cheap lodging house that had been home to the master's predecessor was no longer there. The family had scattered after a fire or some such thirty years prior. The master and Mother visited a temple and asked its chief priest about the circumstances of the family. He showed them the death register and, with frequent expressions of sympathy, told them many things, but all they truly learned was that there was no longer anyone living in Kuwano connected to the prior master's bloodline.

"The chief priest himself was forty years of age. Being as all this had happened so long ago, he asked us if we weren't just a bit careless, coming all the way from Edo. I felt rather awkward."

Maybe because of the disappointment, all the exhaustion from their travels came upon the master of the Jōshū'ya at once, and he fell ill. The kindly priest suggested that they stay at the temple, and Mother, feeling there was no other choice, availed herself of his hospitality and came to be the caregiver for a sick man in a land whose ways she did not know.

"There was nothing at all in Kuwano. All that place had was wind. The land was poor, with just a smattering of beans, potatoes, and rice grown in the dry earth. Only the mulberry trees and the silkworms were holding together the livelihood of that town."

The strong winds that blew down on them would stop for only brief periods during the day, but at those times the smell of boiling silkworms would come floating through the mountain village.

"In order to spin silk thread, they had to boil the cocoons in seething hot water. When thread was being woven, the worms would come out of their cocoons and give off a raw, fishy smell I can't quite put into words. If you ever smell it once, you'll never forget it. I'd heard the prior master used to always talk about that smell too."

However, the master of the Jōshū'ya hated that smell, saying it was terrible and made him nauseous. "I want to eat good rice," he said, throwing a tantrum like a child. "I want fresh sashimi," "I want to go back to Edo." Mother couldn't help feeling put out with an old man whose selfishness knew no bounds, but oddly, when it came to this, she couldn't abandon him. It was a strange thing, she told me.

"Somehow I had the feeling that the afterlife would not be pleasant for him. I felt a certain degree of pity for him too."

All of the irresponsible things that he—not anyone else—had done had come back to haunt him. Nothing was going well, nothing engaged him—not in his shop in Edo, nor in his family relations either. He had come to visit the birthplace of his father the prior master, hoping that if he could regale his relatives there—relatives just getting by with their cheap lodging house—with boasts of his success in running a pretty good shop in Edo, he could show himself a credit to the family. That was the extent of the self-serving attitude with which he had set out on this journey. Even so, the moment things didn't go his way, he grew homesick for Edo and began saying selfish things as he ordered Mother around. I was getting angry just listening to her story, but Mother was smiling.

Meanwhile, in a bad stroke of luck, the master of the Jōshū'ya really did become sick. Here and there, red rashes appeared on his body, and he broke out in a high fever.

"Maybe when your body gets weak, it isn't good to drink the water and eat the food of an unknown land, which your body isn't used to."

They had the town doctor come and look at him, but the doctor only shook his head, saying there was nothing to do in any case except give him medicated baths and make sure he got lots of rest. Moreover, he looked frightened when he said that this illness was a contagious one.

"The chief priest was standing by at that time, and he said he was very sorry, but because this was not mere exhaustion from travel but a communicable disease, the master could no longer stay at the temple and would have to be moved to the Adachi house. It was a custom in this region, he said, that anyone who became sick or unable to get around due to injury did so."

The Adachi house was located on the outskirts of town and was a fine tile-roofed house with a big wooden front gate. True, it looked rather old, but it was still such a magnificent mansion that Mother could only think it the residence of some great landowner or village headman.

"You mean the sick and the injured are taken into the homes of the local wealthy to be cared for?" Mother had said. "Oh my, you must be so grateful to have a tradition like that."

They arrived there after the considerable effort of carrying a sick man up a terribly steep mountain road, but it turned out that the Adachi house's grandness went no farther than the façade, and within it was simply an empty, deserted house.

Mother was shocked, wondering, *What in the world is this?* The better part of the mansion's interior was falling apart, paper in the sliding doors was torn, and the tatami mats had been pried up from the floor. There was just one corner of the main house that was clean, well taken care of, and ready to be used at a moment's notice, with both bedding for the sick and nightclothes already laid out. The kitchen and outhouse were also both in usable condition. The tools and utensils were of poor manufacture, but for all that none were missing. Indeed, just as the chief priest had said, it appeared that the people of the Kuwano region were regularly going in and out of this place.

"So I tried asking the chief priest, and he told me all about it. The Adachi house, he said, was a place to be thankful for, which assumed the uncleanness of the people who lived in Kuwano."

This was more than fifty years prior to that time, but they said it was the brilliant and long-sighted head of the Adachi family who, as village headman of Kuwano, took charge of the house, managed the land, and gave to that underproductive town a way of making ends meet that involved obtaining thread from silkworms.

"However, they say that in the days of its third head of house, a terrible murderer came out of the Adachi family. It was a big, rich man's house, so there must've been all kinds of squabbles going on inside. After he had claimed nearly ten victims, the killer was taken in ropes and beheaded. The magistrate judged that his property be confiscated, and the Adachi line died out. This mansion, which had become a vacant house, was deemed so unlucky that nobody would live in it and was neglected thereafter."

However, the year after the Adachi family came to its end, the wind that blows down from the mountains came carrying an epidemic disease, and this contagious affliction had raged throughout the entire Kuwano area. People dropped like flies, and the post town was closed off. Without enough doctors, the village headman at the time—hard-pressed to find a solution—came up with the plan to have the sick people gathered into the empty Adachi house, and warned those who were still well to stay away from it. In other words, to push the uncleanness of contagious disease into the Adachi house.

In the end, most of the people who had become ill died, but they succeeded in preventing the disease from spreading any further.

"Since that time, the people of the region of Kuwano have come to take anyone who is seriously ill, has a contagious disease, or has little time left to live due to injury or old age to the Adachi house. Naturally, they wait there to die. While they do that, all of their bad luck and uncleanness is contained within the gates of the Adachi house and can't escape outside. That's how the townspeople think of it."

Because of this, they gradually began to force criminals such as thieves and couples who had tried to commit double suicide into the Adachi house as well. The length of their confinement there was decided in accordance with the greatness or smallness of their offenses: if ten days were determined, ten days they would stay; if half a month was determined, then half a month they would stay. When the period ended, they would be let out. From the beginning, there had been cells in that house—Buddha alone knows what they had been used for—and these were put to use in holding criminals. By doing this, sin was being contained.

It was a very odd tradition, but after hearing its history and cause, the master and Mother were in no position to resist. After all, if they struck a defiant pose, the local people would despise them and they would be refused food, water, and medicinal baths. With little choice, Mother moved into the Adachi house to care for her sick charge.

Mother told me that although it was empty and lifeless, the place wasn't scary.

"Growing up at the Jōshū'ya, I learned painfully well that it was people that were frightening. With no sign of anyone around, I wasn't afraid in the slightest. Though they said the house was a place that removed uncleanness, it wasn't as if there were disgusting things lying about in plain sight, and furthermore, the rooms that the locals used regularly were kept quite clean and comfortably appointed for such a place."

Every day at dusk, you could stand in the highest place in the room at the Adachi house, and the blood-red sunlight sinking behind the rim of the mountains looked close enough to reach out and touch. The view had a kind of magnificence that stole Mother's heart, and she said that she never wearied of gazing off into it dreamily.

The days went by, but the master of the Jōshū'ya didn't improve one bit. His high fever had come down, but the rashes hadn't faded, and day by day he was growing weaker. An express messenger had been dispatched to Edo to give everyone the basic outline of what was going on, but no one had yet come to take them back. Waiting by the side of a sick man drifting in and out of sleep, Mother had no one to talk to and nothing to do but spend the days in idleness. The master's supply of money, too, was shrinking steadily.

In the midst of this, Mother became aware of a very peculiar thing. Although at present no one aside from themselves was supposed to be ensconced in the Adachi house, someone else was there. The shadow of someone would fall across the end of the hallway, the sound of footsteps could be heard late at night, and when Mother was drawing water or doing the wash, she would sometimes feel someone's eyes on her back. When she turned around, shadows within shadows would jump as though surprised . . .

And then one night, Mother saw at last the true face of that shadow.

This happened in the dead of night. As she was brewing medicinal water in a kettle hung above the small brazier, Mother had started to nod off to sleep. Once again, though, she sensed the presence of someone else there, right at the nape of her neck, just as though someone was leaning forward in her direction from behind. She opened her eyes just slightly and saw another shadow cast next to the brazier.

Mother counted silently to three, then raised her head and with a sudden shout whirled around to face the figure.

There before her, an emaciated man about the same age as herself was standing. He was dressed in rags and his hair was wildly unkempt, but his oddly cool eyes were wide open and he was looking Mother right in the face.

Their eyes met, and Mother lost the voice she had just found. In the instant that she moved, the young man, taken aback, disappeared. He had not run away, nor had he hidden himself; he had simply vanished, like a light extinguished by the wind.

"Needless to say, I didn't sleep at all that night."

When morning broke, Mother went running to the temple. She found the chief priest just as he was setting about his morning chores, and with ragged breaths she explained to him what had happened.

The priest furrowed his brow and made a deliberately difficult face. Mother, however, read his expression well and could see that he was not terribly surprised by what she had told him.

"Preceptor, you know something about this, don't you? That man—I don't know if he was a ghost of the dead or some *mononoke*, but I'm not the only one who has seen that strange man, am I?"

Holding on to the fringe of the priest's robe, she kept pressing him until at last, overwhelmed by her insistence, he nodded reluctantly.

"The people in the post town and the people in the village started to complain—about five years ago, I think—that the Adachi house was being haunted by a mysterious figure. Only, the look of him differed according to the witness. Sometimes it was a young man, and sometimes a woman. It's appeared as a child as well. Some say they can't see it at all but can only hear it or smell it."

At this, Mother felt the foreboding in her heart clearing off straightaway.

"Living in that unfamiliar mountain village, I was worried that perhaps I might have been losing my mind."

Mother asked the priest, "Well then, what in the world do you think it is that's haunting the Adachi house?"

Still wearing that difficult face, the chief priest started to say, "I can't tell exactly," but when pressed, said he believed it was an *oni*.

"An oni—you mean one of those ferocious, horned mononoke? It didn't look anything like that, though."

What Mother had seen had in any case been in the form of a weak-looking, sad young man. No horns had been growing out of his head.

"I don't mean an oni like the red and blue ones in storybooks. But clearly, it is something not of this world."

"Well then, where did this 'oni' come from? Did it come down from the mountains and take up residence in the Adachi house?"

"No, no," the chief priest said shaking his head. "Most likely, the uncleanness that the people of Kuwano have been leaving at the Adachi house these many long years has, over time, taken on a form of its own. In other words, it's an incarnation of their uncleanness. Which is exactly why its appearance varies according to who sees it."

After hearing the chief priest's assurances that there was nothing to worry about and that as long as she didn't concern herself with it, the oni would do them no evil, Mother returned to the Adachi house.

Even so, not worrying about it . . . just forgetting about it . . . This was simply not possible for her to do.

If it was just as the priest had said to her, then why did this so-called oni appear to her eyes in the form of a timid young man like that? Mother thought about that. And then she had to admit to herself: there was something in the tint of that man's sad eyes that moved her heart something awful.

"He seemed somehow pitiful . . . you know?"

From that point forward, the "oni" began to periodically appear to Mother. He seemed unimpeded both by day and by night. Mother reached the point where even when she sensed his presence or glimpsed his shadow, she would no longer panic, but instead sit very still and wait for him to appear. Eventually, she started calling out to him.

"Hey, stop hiding and come on out. I'm not here to drive you out or anything."

Such behavior on Mother's part actually seemed to get through to the oni. Gradually, he got to where he would come close to Mother. Speaking not a word, he just kept blinking his eyes at her like some stray dog or cat, but Mother didn't mind. As though talking to herself, she would call out and then provide her own replies. "The winds are even stronger today, aren't they?" "It looks like the money we brought for the trip isn't going to last us, so I'll need to start working." "I wonder if there's an inn somewhere that would hire me."

The oni listened in silence.

When the oni realized how much Mother enjoyed staring off at the sun setting behind the mountains, he began to show himself regularly around that time and eventually began to sit beside her and join her in watching the evening sky. It became such that on days when the oni would for whatever reason not show itself all day long, Mother would actually grow restless and go wandering here and there throughout the crumbling old mansion searching for him.

"That's right. I was starting to enjoy being with the oni." Mother again gave a delicate smile like that of a young virgin. "Don't look so surprised! After all, I'd never spent time with anyone in my life like that before then."

While she was living there, Mother gave the oni a name, since it was inconvenient for him not to have one. Since it remained as silent as ever, there was no way to know whether he liked the name or not, but in time, he came to show himself right away whenever Mother called it out.

I asked her what his name was. Mother only chuckled and pressed her fingertip against her lips.

"Well, that's still a secret," she said. It seemed to me she was acting just as if she'd been asked the name of a beau. "I'll tell you when the time is right. But not today. After all, this is the first time I've ever talked to you about this. It wouldn't do to go over everything right from the very start. Besides, I'm not finished telling the story yet."

This strange but, for Mother, enjoyable life continued for half a month, and then at last some people from the Jōshū'ya in Edo arrived to take the master back.

"Even with the trouble they'd gone to, I wasn't the least bit

happy to see them. Just one thought flashed through my mind—
that I didn't want to give up living there."

Mother was surprised to see that the mistress had come in
person, but when she found herself being suddenly shouted at and
beaten with a walking stick, she thought to herself, *Aha, this is why,
eh?* People from the Jōshū'ya were saying the master had fallen ill
because Mother hadn't been taking good enough care of him.

"We have no more use for you! You should consider yourself lucky we don't hand you over to the authorities for the grudge
you're carrying against your master. I don't care where you go—
just leave!"

And so it was that Mother was all too quickly driven out.

The group from the Jōshū'ya rested one night at the inn in
Kuwano, then, taking the master with them, hurried off back
toward Edo. Left all alone, Mother wondered, *What in the world
am I supposed to do? Can I just keep living here in Kuwano with the
oni?* Without a *mon* to her name, the first thing she needed to do to
survive was find work. No, more important than that—more important than anything—was whether the people of Kuwano might
allow her to stay in the Adachi house alone, even though there was
no sick person with her.

Her fears were well founded. She was summoned to the temple
by the chief priest and a man with a slightly daunting look who said
he was in charge of the post town. They scolded her harshly and told
her to vacate the house immediately. Mother, not wanting to be separated from the oni, was persistent, saying she at least hoped they'd
let her work in the post town until she could save some money for
the road, but the two men, not giving an inch, said, "If it's money
you need, we'll lend you some. Just get out now." Though she bowed
her head low and put her hands on the earth, it was about as effective
as trying to grapple with a boulder-strewn mountain.

The priest, looking at Mother as though he had seen something
unfathomably pitiful in her desperate expression, said, "You're being

bewitched by a mononoke. It may have a human form, but the *thing* in the Adachi house is not something that can coexist with human beings. Leave that place at once. If this goes on, something terrible is sure to happen."

"You're right," Mother fired back. "It's not human. But it's not the least bit frightening either. To me, that oni feels closer than any human being I've ever met! He seems so kind!"

The man who said he was the chief of the post town twisted his lips into a vulgar smile and looked back at the chief priest. "This is quite a story, Your Reverence," he said. "This woman's in league with mononoke. I can't believe such a pretty face just said she likes monsters better than people!"

Mother said in a loud voice that she did; that it was exactly as he had said.

"It's the two of you who look monstrous to me. You force sick people and old folks and criminals into the Adachi house and shut them up in there, all the while wearing know-nothing expressions and living in clear conscience. And while that 'oni' is sucking up everything you vomit out and bearing it in your place, you feel no gratitude, and you're just trying to keep it away. Are you that pure? Are you that righteous?"

The chief fell silent, perhaps cowed by Mother's ferocious on-slaught. The chief priest began to chant a sutra. Mother jumped up from her seat and, giving full rein to her anger, ran, fleeing from the temple. When Mother told me about that day, it was plain to see from her intense manner of speech that even then, the fury she had felt that day remained vivid in her heart. There were swords glinting in her eyes and flames in her mouth.

That evening, as she watched the sun set by the gate of the Adachi house, the oni appeared, just like always.

Mother smiled at him, looked him straight in the face, and asked him, "How about going to Edo with me?

"I've been thinking . . . we're alike in a lot of ways," she said.

Having unpleasant jobs forced on them through no fault of their own, taking on the worst roles, being always alone . . .

"The reason you look so lonely has to be because I'm lonely. But I—until I saw my heart reflected in your face, I didn't even realize I was lonely." Those were the words Mother told me she had said.

The oni nodded in silence. And he went with Mother.

"I was a rash person, though, so when the time came, I suddenly grew worried. If the oni was the embodiment of all the filth that had stagnated in the Adachi house, mightn't he just disappear as soon as he took the first step out of that place?"

In the instant that this occurred to her, the blood in her veins curdled so fast she almost thought she could hear it.

But the oni didn't disappear. When he passed through the gate of the Adachi house, his face lit up for a fleeting instant, and that was all.

"Only—there was just one thing I thought very odd."

It was very, very faint, but once they had traveled some distance from Kuwano, the smell that comes from boiling silkworm cocoons began to float through the air between them.

That odor didn't bother Mother in the least, though.

"Just like a pair of children racing each other, we set off running for the entrance to the highway."

怪

Though she was a woman alone on the road back to Edo, Mother encountered no danger. This was as she had expected. Even when men approached her harboring untoward designs in their hearts, they immediately looked as though they'd seen a ghost and ran away.

"That was only natural. After all, they could see their own inner natures reflected in the oni that was traveling with me. They were so frightened they couldn't help running away."

Mother found a job when she got back to Edo and, for the first time in her life, began working hard for her own sake, to blaze the trail of her own life. The oni always stayed right by Mother's side. If there were times when she could sense only his presence, there were other times when she could see his form, and even occasions when he would not show himself at all for as many as three days in a row. He remained mute as always; even if Mother spoke to him, he would not answer. That's why Mother said, "I've thought in the past that you seem to have two shadows."

The years went by, and at last Mother met the man who would one day become her husband. A journeyman at a brush seller in Lower Kanda Myōjin, he was a quiet but hardworking man. He was not frightened by the oni. He seemed able to sense the oni's presence in his own way and didn't dislike doing so. He was also the first upstanding man in Mother's life to passionately confess to loving her.

"I figured I would be all right if it was him," Mother said, lowering her line of sight a little. "Only, I was very anxious because I thought the oni might not like my being married to a human man."

The oni, however, said nothing and did nothing. Mother wondered if that was only natural, being as it was not a human being. An intangible feeling that was a little like relief and a little like loneliness persisted for a long while after, as though she had just missed grasping something terribly important.

And so in this way, Mother established her family with the journeyman from the brush shop. In time, they became independent and started a store of their own. It was a small shop, only as wide as its one room, but it was *their* shop. That was how the Sasa'ya first started out.

"Even after we'd started our family, the oni continued to live with us. Nothing changed; our relationship has always been just as it was when we were in the Adachi house. I never once told my husband all about him like I'm doing today, but I've also never been less than diligent on the business side of things, always deflecting the kind of people who are frightened by the oni, who feel him as an unsettling presence, or who sense him as a bad odor," Mother said flatly. "That's precisely why the Sasa'ya has been able to come this far in just one generation. It's all thanks to the oni."

Looking around the room in the annex, her eyes fell on a place next to the brazier, and she gave a little smile as if to say, *Why, there he is right now!*

"He's here even now. Although you don't seem able to see him yet.

"Oh, yes!" she added, as though remembering something else. "Right around the time I was pregnant with Tomitarō, the master of the Jōshū'ya passed away after a long illness. Though I never thought of him as my father, he was someone connected to me, so at the height of midsummer, I went to offer incense."

Upon hearing that Mother had arrived, the mistress went out to meet her. Mother was very much on her guard, because it could be harmful to the child in her womb if she were to be beaten again.

"As soon as the mistress saw me, her face went so white it was as if it had been bleached. She cried out and ran away."

Deep in her reminiscence, Mother said she was certain that the mistress had seen the oni right behind her.

"That mistress . . . her whole life had been burnt black by jealousy. I do wonder what in the world the oni looked like to her."

I listened to her long story to the very end and recall myself accepting it. When I asked whether Tomitarō knew about this, Mother shook her head.

"Not in this kind of detail. Only, he's had it drilled into him again and again by his father that I'm an excellent judge of character, so he won't defy what I say."

What kind of oni did Sajirō see, I wondered. *Surely, that man must have deceived a lot of people.* I also thought about that raw, fishy odor that only O-Tama's nose could smell.

"Ah, I'm all tuckered out," Mother said with a sigh as she rubbed her neck. I rushed to assist her in lying back down.

"You can't see the oni, can you? You don't sense anything at all, do you?"

It was as she said. I could neither see nor feel anything.

"You're actually the first person I've ever met like that. And what a strange thing to think that of all people, you happen to be Tomitarō's bride. That interests me. And it's why I felt that I needed to share this long story with you."

I accepted this, thinking, *Was that why? Was Mother worried?*

"You can neither see nor sense the oni, and I want to say that's proof that your heart is pure—but I can't say that's all it is."

Mother's expression grew clouded.

"Anyone who lives an ordinary life will create little grudges, hurts, and bad memories. So normally, people can to some extent see and feel the oni. But you've never had those experiences. Which means you have lived such an exceedingly solitary, closed-off life that you've not yet lived life as a human being. Have you?"

Her voice dropped to a murmur, and she said, *"But starting today . . .*

"Starting today in this house, I want you to weep and to laugh and to fume with anger. Do mean things, do bad things, do compassionate things . . . and see what happens. In time, you'll be able to sense the oni. Just take care not to give it a ferocious appearance."

As I drew the covers up to Mother's collar, I smiled slightly and told her that when I worked at the Shōchikudō, I had wept because the retired master had made lewd advances at me.

Mother's eyes snapped open. "Oh dear, the rumors of that old man's lechery were true, then?" Then in a murmur, she added, "But you didn't see any such oni . . ."

I nodded.

Mother looked up at the ceiling and fell silent for a short while. Then she began to speak slowly: "Good and ill always stand back-to-back. Good luck and ill fortune are two sides of the same coin after all. Someone who has known only hardship might be unable to see the oni. So for you, it's 'starting today' after all. Well, let's end this story here. Let me get a little rest."

I left the room quietly. After that day, Mother never brought up this story again. And because of that, I never got to hear the name she gave the oni either, which Mother had declined to tell me, acting as shy as a demure and sheltered girl.

怪

Three years passed in this manner.

Then, Mother died. Her life had been a very turbulent one, but here at the very end she slept in quiet satisfaction. I was glad for her—and I couldn't help feeling a little jealous of her as well—not just because I was her son's bride, but also because I was a woman who had been born into similar circumstances.

There was just one thing left that bothered me. It was that ultimately, I had never been able to sense the presence of the oni.

I also felt anxious over what had become of the oni after Mother's death. There was nothing I could do, however. After all, I could neither see its form nor sense its presence.

Preparations for the funeral had to be made, and the appropriate places needed to be notified of Mother's passing, so within the Sasa'ya, things suddenly began to get very busy. Though the chief clerk was red-eyed from crying, he began issuing instructions to the journeymen and the maids. My head, too, was full of things that had to be done, but my heart wouldn't cooperate, and I was just staring off into space.

Before doing anything else, I needed to wash the tears from my face, so I headed off toward the entrance, where there was a water jar. The downpour that evening was still coming down hard outside. I slipped into my footwear and stepped down into the entryway, where I noticed that rain was blowing inside through the kitchen door, which had been left open. I drew near to shut it.

At that moment, I became aware of a human shadow falling across it.

I looked up and saw a skinny young man standing out there in the pouring rain. He was dressed in rags and had a slightly dirty appearance. Only his eyes were bright and clear, and they were staring at me intently.

Oh! It's the oni! I thought. There was no doubt about it. This was the "oni," its form unchanged from the time Mother had first met it at the Adachi house in Kuwano.

I stared at that face closely, filled with longing and admiration, just like a child looking up at a rainbow. The oni stared back at me. And then his eyes filled with tears as he curved his lips into a smile.

And I thought, *The oni's little smile—it looks so much like that little grin Mother used to wear! The warmth in its eyes—isn't that just the way Mother's eyes were whenever she looked at me?*

"You—"

But when I called out, the oni shrank back from me and disappeared. Afterward, only the steady sigh of the falling rain remained in my ears.

"Wait!" I said, not realizing I was shouting. "Are you going to leave with Mother?"

My only answer was the sound of rain.

"Starting today!"

The voice of Mother vividly came back to me as though it had been waiting for ages in the back of my ears for just this moment.

"Try living like a human being, and you'll get your first look at the 'oni.'"

For a long while I stood there motionless, as though in a daze, while the rain beat against me. And as I was standing there, Tomitarō's voice came to me from inside, calling my name again and again. It was a voice that sounded worried, that sounded like a plea for help, that was calling out to the closest, dearest one in the whole wide world—an honest voice, without a shred of affectation or pretense.

Tomitarō was calling me.

Tomitarō—with whom I sat watching Mother in her final moments, whose grief for the loss of his mother I shared—was calling me.

I answered and moved back from the kitchen door to the foyer. I went back into my house.

I glanced back abruptly at where the oni had just been standing. Something like a white mist drifted there, but it was lost almost immediately amid the falling rain. I could no longer see it anywhere, neither could I sense its presence.

VI
A Woman's Head

"**Y**ou got awfully nimble fingers for a lad." The adults around Tarō would occasionally touch the boy's hands and say such things. Though he said he was ten years old, his body was gaunt and he was short of stature, and even his bones were slender and delicate, so from a distance he looked only half his age and was often told he looked like a girl. Among children, these words could all too easily slide into derision and intimidation. He was often jeered at, the kids taunting, "Walk around in a girls' kimono" or "I'll bet you sit down to pee." He was often made a laughingstock in this way.

Every time Tarō was mocked like this, his mum would gently cheer him up. "It's all right. When you grow up, I'm sure those nimble fingers of yours will open doors in your life. So you shouldn't worry over this."

Tarō was living alone with his mum. He had been told that his dad had passed away when he was still a little baby. His mother raised him in desperation while doing many odd jobs. Begrudging even the time it took to sleep, she kept working, hardly eating what food they had. She felt that this was bliss.

However, her long years of pushing herself too hard were taking a toll, the overwork building up in her body like mud at the bottom of stagnant waters. For that reason, she had been helpless at the beginning of this summer, when the cholera that had raged through the old working-class neighborhoods of the downtown area had gotten hold of her. Tarō's mum died, not even once opening her eyes or speaking with him from the time that she took to her sickbed.

And so Tarō was left all alone.

During the brief summertime, he had stayed at the home of the row house's landlord. The landlord was as big as a sumo wrestler and had a smooth, shiny face even though he said he'd turned sixty that year. He had large facial features too, which made him look like he was angry year round. Angry while he was eating. Angry while he was soaking in hot bathwater. And when he was out walking, angry.

From the time that Tarō started to stay with the landlord, he had wanted to know if the man wore that same angry face even when he was sleeping, so late one night he got up for a surreptitious peek. Sure enough, he was sleeping with an angry-looking expression. His mouth was downturned in a frown, and his eyelids were halfway open—and what a ferocious snore!

The landlord's frightening face—viewed as a local attraction in the neighborhood—came with a story. Once when the whole row house had been mustered to help clean the well, the sky clouded up unexpectedly, peals of thunder started to sound, and rain began to fall. Everyone was flustered, saying, "This is going to be a problem," when the landlord had lifted up his face to the sky, glared at it, and started to scold it. "Bad timing, rain!" he shouted. "Think about the people down below a little!" And when he did, just like that, the thunder grew distant and departed. Ever since, that landlord had the reputation of being more powerful than the lightning, and for some time afterward there had been a steady stream of visitors wanting him to write "lightning, begone" on talismanic cards meant to ward it off.

Amusingly, the landlord was thoroughly henpecked by his wife, who was only half his size. In the course of looking after Tarō during his stay with them, she often scolded and nagged, and the landlord, too, had many of the same complaints directed his way. And she was truly detail oriented: "Don't scatter your clothes around"; "Don't make noises when you eat your rice"; "Suck the meat off your fish all the way down to the bones"; "When you're cleaning with a rag, wring it out as tightly as you can." Tarō's upbringing had made it a matter of course to do the housework in place of his mother, so he wasn't really bothered by that kind of nagging. Still, every time he saw that giant of a landlord's boarlike neck shrinking back as he was raked across the coals by the little landlady, it was so funny he was hard-pressed to keep from smiling.

By the end of summer, Tarō had become thoroughly acclimated to life as a houseguest. On the other hand, he had noticed the landlord and the landlady putting their heads together—his so large and hers so small—and whispering to one another with serious faces about something. *Most likely, they're talking about what's to become of me from now on.* His guess was right on the money. One morning when a cool wind was blowing, the landlady gave him some chores at the crack of dawn—collecting the wind chimes from under the eaves, taking down the bamboo sunscreens and cleaning them, and the like—and then in the evening, after a busy day of hard work, Tarō was summoned to the landlord and landlady's room.

"Starting tomorrow, you'll be going away to work," the landlord stated flatly. "It's a shop for bags, sacks, coin purses, and the like in Honjo Hitotsume called the Aoi'ya. You may have heard of it. It's on this side of the Ōkawa River and quite well known. You'll be living on-site."

"He says it's well-known, but not on the level of the Marukado'ya in Honjo Block Two." The landlady snorted just slightly when she brought up the name of a shop famous across all Edo. "But that shop is a very rigid environment. I was told that they've placed several boys about your age as apprentices before, but not one of them stayed on. But the shop is managed exclusively by the owners' relatives, and the seamstresses are all women, so there shouldn't be anything frightening about working there."

Tarō nodded obediently.

"You have very nimble fingers," the landlady continued crisply. "Honestly, it's a waste you were born a man. There's no way to avoid putting a gift like that to use, after all. We've done our best to sell them on you, so be diligent and work hard."

It was certainly true that Tarō had taken over all of his landlady's sewing work since coming to stay with them. For that reason, perhaps "selling them" on him was the landlady's way of praising him. She was in fact quite clumsy herself and couldn't even keep a seam straight.

Tarō was not merely dexterous with his fingers; he enjoyed sewing and mending things. Since in any case he would have to go out and work somewhere eventually, he was glad for the offer.

"Normally, ten is about the age when apprentices start walking there to learn the trade," the large landlord said, opening wide his large, bulging eyes. "But you'll be moving in to work. You mustn't hold a grudge over that. People all have their various lots in life. You should be grateful that you'll be able to train at your workplace."

Tarō nodded again, not vaguely this time, but clearly and of his own will.

"By the way," said the landlord, shuffling forward on kneecaps as big as Tarō's head, "don't you want to ask what kind of work you'll be doing?"

Tarō immediately hung his head.

"Oh, leave him alone. This isn't the time for that," said the landlady, scolding as she tried to smooth over her husband's boorishness.

Tarō couldn't talk. For as far back as he could remember, Tarō had never spoken a single word.

He had been that way even as a baby. Even when he cried, it had been without a voice; he had cried only with his tears and his face. He had never spoken in halting baby talk either. For these reasons, his mother and all the adults around him had apparently believed that from birth he was incapable of speech.

However, just three years prior, when he had seen a craftsman who had come to repair the roof of the landlord's house slip and fall straight to the ground, Tarō had cried out, "Ah!" in a loud voice. Tarō's cry had been even more surprising than the craftsman's fall to his mother and the people at the row house, and they had come running to his side. He didn't speak again, however. Not even when they shook him and not even when they yelled at him.

Even so, the adults had learned that his muteness was not due to some physical throat defect. Ever since, the curious gazes directed at Tarō had come to outnumber the sympathetic ones. Regardless of anything anyone said, Tarō's mother would always take his side, comforting him, saying, "If you don't want to say anything, that's all right. You don't have to force yourself." Thanks to her, Tarō didn't experience feelings that were all that terrible; however, it was at that point in time that Tarō started thinking, *I'm not like other people.*

That one time he had cried out, Tarō himself had been more surprised than anyone else. *I made a voice. I have a voice!* For Tarō too, it had been as shocking as if the world had turned upside down, and he had naturally been glad.

And so he had tried to keep on speaking. Of course he would. But it had been no good. It was like there was something— something lurking still and silent, deep in Tarō's heart—telling him, *You mustn't speak . . . speaking is wicked . . . speaking is dangerous.* He had a faint sense that something terrible would happen if he didn't heed these warnings, and he could feel the hairs on both arms stand on end as it welled up from inside him. And so Tarō remained silent and went back into the silence.

He had not spoken again since.

It was not that he hadn't tried. When he was alone, he had opened his mouth to try to say something. However, whenever he did so, that "something" that hid at the bottom of his heart was sure to come clambering up his throat, whispering, *You mustn't! You mustn't!*

Something about that sensation was so raw in its urgency and felt so serious that even the still-young Tarō could sense it clearly, and in the end his mouth would close. Just the same as before.

"Oh well, the Aoi'ya says they prefer a quiet worker to a chatterbox, anyway," said the landlord, flaring the nostrils of his large nose as he exhaled. "As long as you work hard, there shouldn't be any problem. Reading and writing is going to be even more important to you than it is to most people. I understand the Aoi'ya will teach you that, so buckle down and study hard."

Tarō nodded his head up and down in agreement. The landlord and landlady looked at one another briefly, as though they were each trying to cede the floor to the other. At last, the landlady spoke: "Do you want to take your mother's mortuary tablet with you? Or would you rather leave it with us until you come into your own?"

His mother's mortuary tablet was something that the people in the row house had made out of pity for the orphaned Tarō. They had dug all the way down to the lint in the bottoms of their wallets to collect the money for it. He wanted very badly to take it with him, but at the new place where he'd be living, there would be nowhere to safely store the mortuary tablet. Tarō made up his mind and turned his eyes toward the small Buddhist altar of the landlord's family.

The landlady nodded. "I see. Well then, we'll keep it here. In return, I want you to go there wearing the kimono your mother made."

Tarō soon got into bed after a reminder that tomorrow was an early day. Although he was thinking of how this new job meant saying farewell to a lifestyle to which he had grown somewhat accustomed, he didn't feel particularly sad or lonely. The unease he felt about his new workplace was not enough to be worth making any special mention of. Rather, he couldn't sleep well because of a realization that was sinking in—*Aah, I've really turned into a genuine tramp!*

Still wide awake, he shut his eyes and saw foggy images of scenery and people's faces rising up and vanishing behind his eyelids.

It was while he was following after these things that he felt a terrible sadness coming over him. Dragging these feelings along behind him, Tarō slept like one walking into the shadows.

And then, he dreamed a bizarre dream.

Next to the pillow of the sleeping Tarō, a small figure with an oddly yellow head sat. That small person kept wringing its hands, as if terribly worried about something. It was dark, and its face was hard to see. He could, however, see that the figure was wearing a yellow kimono that matched its yellow face. It was a familiar color— just the color of a well-ripened squash.

The color of squash had been his mother's favorite. For some reason, she had decided it was an auspicious color for Tarō and sewed him kimono of that color and made patchwork from pieces of that color of cloth. Because it was one reason he was teased for looking like a girl, Tarō was not terribly happy about this, but he had been fervently taught that just by wearing these things, he could prevent disease and escape disaster, so, reluctantly, he had worn them.

Even when the cholera epidemic had begun, his mother had said that squash yellow was more effective for Tarō than any other cholera-sealing charm or talisman. In the end, perhaps she had been right, but still, were the color so effective a charm, his mother should've worn a squash yellow kimono as well.

It seemed to be the case that his mother had had some kind of reasoning for her beliefs. It wasn't just that she liked squash yellow; since all things had their various gods that resided inside them, there were gods in squash as well. Thinking that she mustn't be disrespectful, his mother had refused to eat squash. Even the auspicious pumpkins that were cooked in saké and soy sauce—of which it was said that if you eat them during the winter solstice you will be healthy all year round—she would not touch with her chopsticks, even when the meal was a gift from someone in the neighborhood. After all, they too were a kind of squash.

—*Why did you do things like that, Mum?*

In his dream, even as he knew it was a dream, Tarō was thinking such things. Presently he fell into a deeper slumber and could no longer see the small person at his bedside.

怪

Asaichirō, the present master of the bag maker known as Aoi'ya, was its second proprietor, but his predecessor had been a seller of tobacco. This man had been a hobbyist who enjoyed working with his hands, and when he himself created a handmade pouch for carrying around shredded tobacco, it became a sensation in the neighborhood and, eventually, a product for sale. For ten years, he sold both tobacco and bags, but in time he shifted to selling bags exclusively. It was very difficult for tobacco dealers to manage their product during the humid parts of the year, and getting out mold and the like was a huge chore, so the industry was a lot of trouble. Also, making bags was in any event work he had started to do because he enjoyed it, so the passion with which he had approached his two products had been unequal.

Asaichirō was, like his father, a man of great craftsmanship, and though he was now the master, he still sometimes took needle in hand to sew a bag. He had warm relations with his wife O-Yū. He was straitlaced and engaged in no debauchery, he didn't drink, and it was said that his only pleasure was to walk around with his wife looking for old clothes and strips of cloth he could use as materials for bag-making. He had a thoroughly one-track mind.

During the brief interval before he went to the Aoi'ya, Tarō had this much breathlessly explained to him by the landlord. Then at last the landlord said to him with a somewhat strange intensity, "The Aoi'ya doesn't have a successor. Ten years ago, Asaichirō and O-Yū lost their newborn baby in a most unfortunate manner. He was kidnapped by a certain outrageous individual. Since then, they've never been blessed with another child. That's why, Tarō, if you do your work like an honest, good lad, I'm sure that they'll name you successor."

Tarō had nodded obediently, but he also had a feeling that these somewhat rude and greedy words of encouragement weren't quite like the landlord he knew. *He doesn't mean it, and besides, he may be feeling uneasy with me going off to work.*

This was probably true, since after all he was a child and couldn't speak a single word. If they had no need for an unsociable, useless lad like him, he might be kicked out right away.

In truth, Tarō was also feeling uneasy, unable to see his way ahead.

Tarō had grown up poor, and until now, when it came to bags, he had never yet seen any except the cheap ones that vendors would fasten to bamboo stalks and come selling. Ornately crafted bags were luxury items. What kind of place was the Aoi'ya, which dealt in such things? What was the inside of the house like? Would he really be able to live there? Wouldn't the rules and ways of doing things be much too different from everything he'd ever known?

However, once he got there and started working, he chided himself for having worried over nothing. The buildings of the Aoi'ya were certainly fine with their tile roofs, but the people who lived there were possessed of the same warm, friendly hearts as the people at the row house. After the passage of only a few days, he understood this well. Everyone used prettier language and more proper manners than the old men and women of the row house, but when they laughed or got angry or ate their meals, they were filled with such a thoroughly natural, rambling quality, it was clear that the people of the Aoi'ya were all hard workers first and foremost. Nor were the master and mistress exceptions; the sight of everyone working energetically, briskly, and well put Tarō in mind of everyday life at that nostalgic row house, where lazy bums couldn't stay as tenants, and the glare of their scary landlord threatened.

The inside of the Aoi'ya, as the landlord had said, was a cozy place operated by relatives. The master and mistress were working in leadership roles. Five years had passed since the death of the previous master, and since then the former mistress—Asaichirō's mother, in other words—had had a small house built in Mukōjima and lived the life of a retiree. However, she was still full of energy both in mind and body, and it was said that she would often come over to the shop.

The chief clerk, to whom was entrusted the details of the business, was an old hand who had worked under the previous master, and indeed this man was also the father of the shop mistress O-Yū. There were two maids, both of them relatives of O-Yū. The journeyman who was learning the business while assisting the chief clerk was the son of Asaichirō's cousin. As products, bags were not difficult items to handle, so it wasn't as if such a large number of people was needed to operate the shop.

On the other hand, many were there to sew. There were five living on-site and another six who commuted. Their ages varied greatly, but all of them were women. The live-in seamstresses were all still young girls, and they also performed chores such as cooking rice, drawing water, and cleaning. The room that was assigned to three of them they cleaned by themselves. Among the seamstresses that commuted, there was one who was raising three children all by herself, and another who said she was caring for her aged parents.

On the first day of his employment, Tarō was brought together with a large number of people all at once, so he couldn't tell who was who. The seamstresses, however, seemed to take a liking to Tarō right away. He was terribly taken aback at the voices saying, "You're the same age as my child, but you're so smart," and "If you have any problems let me know right away."

It wasn't a bad feeling; it was just that with the tension broken he didn't know what to do.

Though it was Tarō's first job, from what he had observed while living at the row house he had a pretty good idea of what apprentice work was like. It was said that there were countless apprentices in the world, that they were made to work from sun up to sun down, that they were scolded and beaten, that the older ones bullied the younger ones, and that they hardly ever got to eat rice—that was the kind of life he had believed would be waiting for him. He would endure this treatment and learn the job little by little. If he could learn the work, he could gradually come to be more recognized, and it would become possible for him to make a place for himself—that, he had believed, was the fate of the shop worker.

However, if you were to ask what Tarō had done on the first day he began working at the Aoi'ya, it had amounted to nothing more than formal introductions beginning with the master and mistress, settling into the three-mat inner room he was given, and eating dinner together with the journeyman and the maids. These three people got on well, and between mouthfuls of rice they frequently spoke to one another or to Tarō. Aware already that Tarō could not speak, they would speak to him, saying things like "You must have been sad when your mother died," and "What do you like to eat?" then provide replies themselves, saying, "You poor thing, to be all alone at your age," and "When I was your age I liked fried egg rolls." Allowing for the fact that they were a little bit noisy, they were enjoyable people to be around.

The next day, too, was exactly the same. After breakfast, he helped the maids dust the hallway, and afterward he had nothing else to do. This only made him more antsy, and when he came near one of the maids, she, probably guessing what the problem was, brought out a mountain of old rags and a small needle box for him and said, "Sew up these dust cloths for us." Tarō took to the task gladly, and before the sunlight had begun to slant he had finished sewing up all of them. He was greatly praised for the job he had done, and again the four of them shared their evening meal. The young journeyman told of how long ago he had once tried to climb and take fruit from a persimmon tree near the row house where Tarō used to live and gotten yelled at by the landlord. The maids both laughed uproariously. "That landlord is probably an ogre even now." "You lived in that scary place for a whole summer, didn't you?" When asked about such things, Tarō tilted his head sideways, and everyone said that was funny and burst out laughing.

The following day, again there was nothing for Tarō to do. Among people who were busily working hard in their jobs, he felt oddly saddened to be standing there with time on his hands; it was as though he were alone and abandoned. So again he went to where the maids were and was asked again to sew up another mountain of dust cloths. This time it wasn't old rags, but rather dusters sewn together from something like strips of cloth, so it took until evening. When he brought the finished items, the maids clapped their hands happily and, impressed, said, "You're really good with your hands. As a reward, I'll ask the mistress and get some sweets for you. Oh, that's right! You can mend socks too, can't you? We have lots of them. Please start on them tomorrow, okay?"

This is an odd shop, thought Tarō. Imagine, letting children who have come up to work apprenticeships have it so easy! Even if this job was for the purpose of becoming a seamster—no, *because* it was for that purpose—shouldn't he have been doing something harder? Could this have been the reason why those boys who were placed here as apprentices before never stayed on? Could it have been because this kind of treatment had the opposite effect and made them feel uncomfortable?

Even so, he spent four or five days obediently doing as he was told as he mended rags, mended socks, and helped with the cleaning. Aside from that, there was nothing for him to do and nowhere for him to go. *I don't like not being worked hard,* he thought; he even wondered if he wasn't being punished.

Nevertheless, strange things are, after all, strange. And when it came to "strange," the master and mistress were the strangest ones of all.

When he had first had his audience with them, Tarō had been nervous, so he had kept his eyes down and hardly seen the master and mistress's faces. Because of this he had little impression of them. Just that they seemed like refined, kind people. However, the speaking voice of the mistress was very, very soft, and so thin that he had thought it seemed to tremble.

After that, however, when Tarō had started to spend his days inside the Aoi'ya, he began to notice that from time to time the master or the mistress would stare at him intently, as though he were under observation. At the very beginning, he had thought, *Ah! They're taking stock of how I'm working*, but somehow amid the relaxed daily routine, he began to think that that wasn't what was going on whenever he noticed them looking at him. The master would stare at Tarō as he dusted the hallway with the maids, and sometimes a thin smile spread out around his mouth. As for the mistress, she would sometimes look as though she were tearing up just slightly when watching him properly washing his rice bowl and storing it away in the wooden box that doubled as his tray.

Unlike large shops such as the Echigo'ya and Kinokuni'ya, the Aoi'ya had only a small number of employees, so it wasn't unusual for even the apprentices to have opportunities to see the master and mistress face to face. However, being stared at by the master and mistress with such intensity was certainly not a matter of course.

When thinking of the strangely relaxed discipline coupled with the easygoing circumstances of the work, it was perhaps fair to say that this scrutiny went beyond awkward and was downright unsettling. The maids, the journeyman, and the seamstresses too, who should've known far better than Tarō what the norms of apprentice service were like, didn't look the least bit bothered by the treatment that he was receiving. That in itself felt terribly frightening.

Mute child though he was, his anxieties apparently did show

on his face. On his tenth day of work, he was cleaning a storage room together with one of the maids, when she said to him, "I get the feeling that somehow you're not comfortable here. Am I wrong?"

The girl's name was O-Aki, and she was the younger of the two maids. She was not beautiful, but she had a cheerful expression and plenty of energy. Her personality was crisp as a pickle.

Tarō was reaching the point at which he could no longer bear the dark uncertainty in his heart, so without hesitation he nodded agreement as an answer. When he did so, O-Aki sat down in the space between a wooden crate and a wicker trunk and, brushing the dust from her apron, said, "Ah, I thought so.

"Listen, before long the master and mistress will probably want to talk to you, so I should probably keep my nose out of this, but your color isn't good and you look like you're worried about something. I feel bad for you, so I'll tell you what's going on now, while nobody can overhear." O-Aki moved her face close to Tarō and whispered, "You were never called here to work as an apprentice in the first place. As you can see, this shop doesn't have an heir to inherit it, so the master and the mistress are thinking about adopting a boy. But of course, that boy can't be just anybody. If he's lazy or has sticky fingers, there'll be trouble. If possible, a boy with nimble fingers who can work for the good of the shop would be best . . . Anyway, that's why they brought you into this house as a worker and are watching how things go with you living under their roof. If you look like a good boy, they say they'll adopt you. That's what they're thinking about."

Tarō felt like the fog had lifted from his eyes. *So that's it. That explains the strange treatment and why the master and mistress stare at me like I'm a rare bird.*

O-Aki put a finger to her lips and smiled a little. "If you come into the house as a worker, they should treat you exactly like one, but both the master and the mistress are very gentle people and from the start could have never worked a small child that hard. Also, from the moment they think they might adopt a young boy as their successor, they become sympathetic to him. But you actually thought it was creepy, didn't you?"

Tarō felt relieved and gave the same little smile as O-Aki had.

"So far, just three have come. In the end, none of them measured up in the master and mistress's eyes, and they were all sent home. You're the fourth. Um, this is just how it looks to me, but I think they really like you. Miss O-Shima and Miss O-Rin—" these were the names of the other maid and a seamstress—"said so too. The journeyman has had a deal from the start to learn the business here and then go start a new store somewhere else, so it doesn't cause any problem for him if they adopt someone. Also, he has a really fine character, so it's all right; you don't need to worry. He's a serious man who doesn't have a wicked, ambitious bone in his body."

At this point, Tarō suddenly remembered how the journeyman and O-Aki were friendly with one other and wondered if perhaps those two had made a promise to get married and settle down. If it were so, they were a well-matched couple. "This is a sad story, so nobody goes out of their way to tell it, but the master and the mistress had a baby that died. This was more than ten years ago, back in the time of the previous master and mistress. At that time, the present master and mistress were called the young master and young mistress. It was barely a year after they married. I wasn't working yet at the time, so I don't know the details. However, they say that when the baby had just had its seventh night celebration, he was kidnapped and murdered. In her grief, the young mistress became bedridden and didn't leave her pillows for half a year."

Tarō hung his head and looked down. He could remember the thin, feeble voice of the mistress.

"It was a boy, so if he had lived, he'd be right at your age now. That's why, if you do get adopted, you should show your respect and be very, very good to the master and mistress. Because they're both really good people. All right?"

Tarō gave a noncommittal response, again showing her a faint smile—it wasn't yet decided whether he would be adopted or not, so nodding his head here felt a bit presumptuous.

O-Aki laughed out loud. Then she added, shrewdly, "Anyway, when you're named successor, please think well of us, all right?" And then she went back to her work. Tarō, feeling like a load had been taken off his shoulders, helped enthusiastically.

The width of the storage room was equal to that of about four tatami mats and looked like it had originally been just an ordinary room; only now its sliding storm shutters were closed, its tatami mats had been pried up, and it was jammed tight with crates for shipping. It even had a closet inside, with two sheets of thick, printed Chinese paper fitted into its door. Until the room had been cleaned, that door had been covered up by boxes and could not be seen, but once several crates had been moved out of the way, Tarō gasped in shock the instant he saw a sheet become fully exposed.

Near the bottom of the Chinese paper door there was a striped pattern. Although the rest of it was yellowed with age, it had originally been a plain white background, without any kind of pattern.

On top of this, a picture had been drawn of a freshly severed woman's head.

It was not a young woman—she was probably about the same age as the mistress of the house. Or no, actually, perhaps she was older. Her hair was made up in a large, gaudy chignon that flared out on both sides, and her eyebrows slanted upward all the way to her temples. Her mouth was closed tightly, and her wide-open eyes were turned straight ahead, but it was hard to read exactly what they were looking—no, glaring—at. Only the head had been drawn, hanging in midair as though it had just been boldly struck off, and the place where the wound appeared to be was tinged with blood.

Her face was repulsive. At just a single glance, Tarō could feel gooseflesh breaking out on every soft part of his body. Unconsciously, he took a step backward and bumped into O-Aki.

"Oh my, what's wrong?" She turned around to face him, dust clinging to the tip of her nose. "Oh dear, you look frightened. And you've broken out in gooseflesh. What did you see? A spider? A gecko?"

Tarō shook his head desperately. He couldn't believe O-Aki's easygoing questions. This was nothing so adorable as a spider or gecko. It was right in front of her, wasn't it? That severed head—

O-Aki, however, glanced around the area, then smiled brightly. "I didn't know you were such a scaredy-cat, Tarō. Bugs won't hurt you. There's nothing to be afraid of."

In utter shock, Tarō looked back and forth between O-Aki and the woman's head on the Chinese paper. Could O-Aki . . . not see it?

Tarō pulled at her sleeve and fighting down his terror drew near to the Chinese paper, pointing at the picture of the woman's head.

"Are you saying something's there? I don't see anything." O-Aki only smiled.

She can't see it. O-Aki couldn't see it. A shudder that Tarō could not suppress went running down his spine.

"It doesn't look like you can do any more cleaning, so you can go on ahead. Can't be helped." As she was speaking, O-Aki gave Tarō a shove, driving him out of the storeroom. They had found a few things that needed to be thrown away, so the inside of the storeroom now had more open space than before. Thanks to that, the woman's head—no longer hidden by crates and wicker trunks—could clearly be seen even from out in the hallway.

Tarō turned on his heel in a hurry, eager to get away from it as quickly as possible.

At that instant, the woman's head—of necessity passing through his peripheral vision—smirked.

Terrified, Tarō whirled around and riveted the paper with his gaze. The woman's head was wearing the same expression that he had seen at the beginning.

However—

Her mouth, which had been shut tight, was now just barely open. Just as if she were about to call out to Tarō.

Tarō ran away.

怪

For the rest of the day Tarō was yet again left empty-handed, so with nothing to distract him, he couldn't stop himself from thinking about the woman's head he had seen in the storeroom. Such a frightening face! What was such a thing doing in a place like that?

And the strangest thing was that the woman's head Tarō had seen was invisible to O-Aki. This was just too strange, and after thinking about it for a while he even started to wonder if it hadn't been that it was invisible to her, but that perhaps somehow his eyes had been playing tricks on him. Like having a nightmare while still awake.

The quickest way to be sure of this was to go and look at it again. This was a frightening thought but still better than being left dangling in uncertainty. Tarō gathered up his courage and headed off toward the storeroom. When he placed his hand on the door, he felt a shiver run not just through his hand but his whole body.

He pulled the sliding door open.

Dimly, the woman's head on the Chinese paper floated up from the darkness in the afternoon sunlight that was shining in the hallway. No matter how many times Tarō blinked and rubbed his eyes, it was still there.

The mouth of the woman, which had earlier appeared to be partly opened, was closed again, as though drawn with a single stroke. No, was it not closed even more tightly this time than it had been the first time he had seen it?

Timidly, Tarō stretched his toes forward and took half a step into the storage room. They struck against the corner of a wicker trunk that was near the tip of his foot, making a tapping sound.

Tarō gasped and looked down at his feet. Then, when he looked up again—

The woman was smiling at him with her mouth wide open. There was a gleam in her eyes, and her bared teeth were pointed like fangs.

Without a cry, Tarō tumbled out of the storeroom, crashing against the sliding door. Someone's footsteps were drawing closer. Perhaps the woman had come out of the Chinese paper. As Tarō was trying to escape down the hallway on all fours, someone grabbed him from behind and stopped him.

"Whoa, there! What's the matter? What are you doing here?"

It was that young journeyman. Concern evident in his face, he lifted up Tarō and looked closely at his face, making certain that he wasn't injured.

"Are you all right?"

Tarō grabbed hold of his arm and started pulling him toward the entrance of the storeroom. Without looking at the Chinese paper, it was all he could do to stretch out his arm and point in the direction of the woman's head.

The journeyman's expression was like that of a victim of some fox's pranks. "What is it? Did you see a mouse or something?"

Tarō wrung out the very last of his meager courage and at last looked in at the Chinese paper from the doorway. The woman's head was there.

The journeyman couldn't see it, however. With a smile, he suggested that Tarō must still be half asleep after an afternoon nap.

"You're really good with a needle and thread. The master's been saying that we should start training you to sew bags pretty soon."

The strength went out of Tarō's knees, and he felt like he was going to collapse right there.

This made no sense. No matter how he thought about it, it made no sense.

That night, Tarō was thinking desperately as he sat on top of his futon with his arms wrapped around his knees. Why was something like that drawn on the Chinese paper door in the storage room? And why could only Tarō see it? Neither O-Aki nor the journeyman had been able to, so it wasn't something that only men could see. Was it something that only children could see? Was it some vengeful ghost or mononoke? Or was it someone with some connection to the Aoi'ya?

That storage room had not been made for storage originally. It was a tatami room whose tatami mats had been taken up in order to use it as a storage room. Could the woman's head on that paper door have had something to do with that? Might that room have been given over to storage in order to hide that picture?

Tarō couldn't sleep at all. He wanted to run away and go back to the row house. He just couldn't stand to be sleeping under the same roof as something like that.

The paper-covered oil lamp on the wooden lamp stand in the corner of the room suddenly went out, trailing a thin tail of light.

There should have still been plenty of oil left. After all, he had planned to leave it burning all night. Squeezing his knees to his chest, Tarō didn't move and sat perfectly still in the darkness.

He could hear nothing but the sound of his own heavy breathing.

How much time had passed? At last Tarō made up his mind and started to get up to go to the lamp. *I'll light the lamp again—*

Just as he was turning toward the lamp, almost as if it had been waiting for him to do so, the Chinese paper door that opened onto the hallway flew open with a bang. Tarō jumped up and turned around.

In the blackness of the hallway stood the slender form of a woman. For some reason he could only see the part of her that was beneath the area of her obi. Everything from her chest upward simply melted into the darkness.

The woman was wearing a kimono the color of wisteria. Above her matching obi was fastened a blood-red sash clip. Her feet were bare and for some reason covered in mud.

Those muddy feet moved and stepped lightly into his room.

In a flash, Tarō jumped up and flew to the window. He slammed himself against the sliding screen in the window and all at once got it open and leaned outside. *Got to get away!*

At that moment, the woman's head suddenly floated up from out of the night air beyond the window. Almost as though it were swimming, it came up right next to Tarō's face. Her crimson lips split apart and exhaled in Tarō's face a breath as cold as the dirt in a graveyard.

In a low moan, the woman's head spoke these words:

"You think you'll get away this time? I'm taking your head!"

Just before losing consciousness, Tarō cried out, "Help!"

怪

By the time he came to, the night had long since departed. Sitting close by on his right-hand side, Mistress O-Yū was watching him with a worried expression and sadness in her eyes. O-Aki was sitting next to her with the same sort of clouded expression. It looked like she had been crying a little.

To his surprise, he heard a familiar voice speaking to him from the left.

"Hey there, you got your head on straight again?"

It was the landlord. And the landlady was there too. His acquaintance with this couple was very deep, but today something seemed slightly different about them. The landlady looked like she was angry, and the landlord seemed somehow terribly gaunt.

I'm being sent back to the row house, Tarō thought. *The landlord is here to take me back.*

"I heard that you spoke once," the landlady said, her unhappy expression unchanged. "If that's the case, try to tell us what happened last night. Why did you faint like that? If you don't tell us anything, we have no way of understanding. Even your mother's worried about you to the point that she won't pass on to the afterlife."

The landlord was scratching the back of his head with his large hand. He seemed to be feeling awkward about something. What was this all about?

"Both of them came to visit us this morning," O-Yū explained. "You had collapsed, so I was planning to send a messenger to inform your landlord as soon as day broke. But before I could do that, they came here themselves . . ."

As if cutting off the soft voice of O-Yū, the landlord's wife quickly said, "Your mother's mortuary tablet—every night it starts shaking around something awful."

Ever since Tarō had left the row house, she said, it had been making a rattling sound all night long from its spot within their household altar.

"We figured she must be worried about you, so every day we offered incense and prayers; we kept telling her, 'With Tarō there'll be nothing to worry about; he's gone to work in a good place and might even be adopted there, so please be at peace and enter Nirvana.' However, Lord Buddha wasn't listening, so finally we got up and came here to see how you were doing." With a bit of a sneer, she added, "Just look how worn out and haggard my husband is. He won a reputation of being stronger than lightning, but he can't sleep a wink with your mother's mortuary tablet rattling around. Turns out he's surprisingly timid, isn't he?"

Again, the landlord scratched at the back of his head. *I see. Is that why he looks so uncomfortable?* Tarō thought.

"When we asked about you, they told us you had taken a fall last night. Just like your mother was afraid of, something *was* happening to you, wasn't it? Now, try and tell us. For the sake of your mother's soul as well, you have to hurry up and do this!"

Tarō sat up and pressed one hand over his pounding heart. Would he be able to speak? He licked his dry lips and took a deep breath.

"A head . . ." he said. "A woman's head . . ."

And then, Tarō began to speak. The words came out with a fluency that surprised even him, and though his spine again felt a chill when he spoke of fearful things, it felt good to get out the things that were in the pit of his stomach.

But as his story continued, the blood began to drain from O-Yū's cheeks. At last her eyes filled with tears that spilled over. She cried out—not in that sad, thin voice, but in a voice that was trembling with joy—and then practically leapt upon him, wrapping Tarō in a tight embrace.

"If you could see that woman's head—if you could really see it, then there's no mistake, Tarō. You are our child! Our flesh and blood child!"

怪

The incident had taken place ten years prior.

The woman who kidnapped the baby born to Asaichirō and O-Yū had worked as a maid at the Aoi'ya and went by the name of O-Kichi.

O-Kichi had been hired through the services of an employment agent, but when she was investigated later, it turned out that everything the agent had said about her was false, and she was assuredly a woman with a dubious background. At that time, she was already in her mid-thirties but was still a coquettish woman and beautiful enough to steal the eyes of men as they passed by. This had apparently clouded the employment agent's judgment as well.

In the beginning, O-Kichi had done her work well. She had been particularly eager to be of help to Asaichirō, who was still unmarried at the time. Being as O-Kichi was so beautiful, even Asaichirō was hardly displeased by this, but in any case she was older than he, and there was something he couldn't quite pin down about this woman, which made it hard for him to let his guard down around her.

However, Asaichirō was from a bloodline whose merits were kind hearts and a sometimes naïve trust of others, and as such he never treated her unkindly. For O-Kichi, who had in any case entered the shop from the very first with eyes set on Asaichirō and the Aoi'ya's fortune, this acted as a spur. After working there for about six months, she had convinced herself that she and Asaichirō would be wed and she would occupy the place of shop mistress, and she began spreading such talk around.

For the Aoi'ya, this was very inconvenient, as Asaichirō and O-Yū's engagement was moving forward. The retired master called O-Kichi in before the marriage had been formally decided and informed her that her services would no longer be required.

O-Kichi had gone pale with rage. Her eyes slanted upward and she said things like "You think you can tear me and the young master apart?" Asaichirō, who could not bear to say nothing with his father at wit's end, told her on the spot to get out. "There is nothing between me and you. It's nothing but assumptions you've made yourself." It was a rather blunt declaration coming from such a gentle man.

O-Kichi went even paler than before.

"Is that so? Well, fine!" she said. "In that case, I have an idea. You won't get away with playing with my feelings and then abandoning me. You'd better realize I'm going to prove that to you before long!"

Spewing curses, O-Kichi departed, leaving something like a bad aftertaste in the Aoi'ya.

Three months later, Asaichirō and O-Yū were wed. There had been no specific signs afterward that O-Kichi's curses were to be fulfilled, and with no suspicious incidents occurring, everyone began to relax, thinking, "Oh well, those must've just been empty threats."

At last a baby was born to the young couple. As firstborn son, he was the designated heir. The Aoi'ya was painted in the colors of celebration. Everyone was filled with a sense of happy expectation.

But then, during a brief moment when no one's eyes were on the baby, the child was taken. He had not yet even been named.

The Aoi'ya immediately appealed to the authorities. The local thief-takers pitched in as well. There was no doubting the one who had taken the baby was O-Kichi. That spiteful woman had been waiting for a baby to be born to the young master and mistress and had managed to pull off this terrible crime. What she planned to do with the baby was something no one wanted to think about, but in any case she had to be found.

O-Kichi was practically the incarnation of selfish greed, but for a greedy person she wasn't very clever. Here and there she had left footprints, and within three days it was known that she was holed up together with the baby in a weather-beaten house on the outskirts of a village called Oshiagemura. However, her pursuers just barely missed her there, and she escaped.

The sun had already set that night. Unfortunately, it was a cloudy night with the new moon, and the stars were only barely visible in the sky. The area was an unbroken swath of fields and rice paddies. Running along paths between the rice fields, leaping across irrigation channels, the pursuers searched for O-Kichi. In the end, they finally caught her fleeing into a barn by a house in the village.

O-Kichi was alone; she had not brought the child along with her. She sneered as she told them she had abandoned him in a field since he had been slowing her down. From the beginning, she said, she had been planning to kill him.

Her pursuers and the people from the Aoi'ya now set about searching for the baby. However, they never found him. The next morning, the baby clothes that the child had been wearing were found caught on the grill of a sluice gate in a channel on the north side of the village. That was all.

Most likely, the baby had fallen into the water and been swept away. He certainly had been killed. Sad and haggard, the search parties gave up. In her heartache, O-Yū took to her futon. Her health was greatly affected, and her womb grew barren. A dark shadow had come and covered over the Aoi'ya, which until then had known no calamity and had been the very essence of happiness.

Under harsh interrogation, O-Kichi admitted that she had stolen money from previous employers. She was sentenced to beheading and the public display of her head. They say that in the moments before they struck it off, she stamped her feet in frustration and through gritted teeth said that she had not abandoned the baby that night—that wanting to hide him just until she could elude her pursuers, she had laid him down in the midst of a squash patch.

"While I was running around, I went back once to pick up the baby, but all of the fields looked alike and all of the still-unripe squashes were lined up in rows and looked like the heads of babies. I couldn't find him," she said. "And that baby—he didn't cry at all. If I had heard him crying I would've known where he was, and then before the search parties could come running, I would've run to him and taken his head. It's true it would have felt good to throw him in the channel and let him be swept away, but after all, I wanted to kill him with my own hands. I wanted to take the head of the child of that hateful Asaichirō and his wife in these two hands and twist, but I failed. Oh, that vexes me!" As she was crying out all these words, O-Kichi's head was lopped off.

Perhaps the evil she had imagined at death's door had remained in this world, and that was why soon afterward stains had begun to appear in the shape of a woman's head on the Chinese paper closet door in what had been Asaichirō's bedroom at the time. After ten days, they had clearly formed a picture of O-Kichi's severed head.

It was curious, however, that this picture of the severed head could only be seen by Asaichirō and O-Yū. Other people didn't see it at all. Furthermore, no matter how many times they changed the paper, held Shinto purification rituals, or had Buddhist sutras recited, the image would always return. There was no end to it.

With no other choice, they closed off Asaichirō's room at the

Aoi'ya and turned it into a storage room. The woman's head had been there ever since.

Hearing this was all too much for Tarō, whose jaw had dropped open. Holding him tight in their arms, Asaichirō and O-Yū were laughing and crying. Off to the side, the landlord and landlady were trading looks with expressions that appeared to be sniping at one another. At last, the landlady gave a sigh and spoke up.

"The reason we've hidden it until now was that we didn't think there was any need to make Tarō listen to this kind of thing. But now it's come to this, he has to be told."

Tarō was not the true child of his late mother, but a child his mother had found when he was a baby. The landlord and landlady had seen through the ruse soon after she had become their tenant and grilled her until they got to the truth.

During the summer ten years prior, Tarō's mother, who had been making her living tending rice paddies south of Oshiagemura, had picked up a baby one night that had been swept down the irrigation channel. His body was very cold, and by the look of him, hardly any time had passed since his birth. Yet somehow the infant had gotten tangled up in some squash leaves, which bore up the baby's body just like a raft, and thanks to that he hadn't drowned.

That year, because of the flooding at the end of the rainy season, Tarō's mother had only just lost both her husband and her one-year-old son. To his mother, who had been living in sadness and sobbing every night, the baby that had drifted to her was a gift from heaven, and she decided to raise him as her own.

She named the baby Tarō, which was also the name of the son she had lost.

There would have been trouble if people found out about the baby, so right away she had left the village. After that, she and Tarō had lived under the pretense that they were truly mother and child.

"Your mother genuinely treasured you. That's why the two of us held our peace—we couldn't bear to separate you by force."

The mistress blinked her eyes. Perhaps she was trying to hide her tears.

Tarō had realized so many things all at once that his head was practically spinning. His mother had so revered squash because it was by their leaves that he had been saved from drowning. *I was the Aoi'ya's child. The master and mistress are my dad and my mum.*

And above all, there's my voice—I was never able to talk. That was because lying still between the furrows of the squash patch without crying or raising a voice had saved my life when O-Kichi came back to look for me. And that was because the "squash spirits" that my mum used to talk about had sealed my voice so that O-Kichi wouldn't find me.

The "squash spirits" are real. Mum was right. They took pity on me and protected me.

He felt such relief that he started to cry. In O-Yū's arms, Tarō cried his eyes out.

"But . . . this isn't a time for rejoicing only," murmured the landlord, whose face had reverted to its rough, oni-like appearance. "When Tarō came back to this house, O-Kichi's spirit returned as well. Last night, she said that you wouldn't get away this time, didn't she? Isn't it a bad idea for you to stay here?"

Everyone looked at one another with uneasy faces. Tarō, however, soothing his chest, which was finally calming down, suddenly remembered the little yellow-faced person that had sat by his pillow on the night before he left the row house. *Oh. That was . . . that had to have been . . .*

"Sir," Tarō said to the landlord, "I've got an idea."

怪

The darkness of the night was so thick and heavy that it was hard to breathe. Tonight not even the voice of a bell cricket could be heard.

Tarō pulled up his covers and curled up in his futon. O-Kichi would come. She would surely come.

The oil lamp he had left burning suddenly went out.

The Chinese paper door to the hallway slowly slid open.

She's here.

"You think you'll get away this time? I'll take your head!"

Raising her voice in a cry—he couldn't tell whether it was a shout or a shriek—the ghost of O-Kichi reached out to take hold of him. There came a sound like that of something being ripped asunder.

At the same time, Tarō knocked aside his covers and leapt to his feet. The eyes of the severed head of O-Kichi snapped wide open, practically coming out of their sockets as they turned toward Tarō. Sharp teeth bared, her mouth was biting into a squash just the size of Tarō's head. Tarō had been hiding under the covers with a squash he had gotten earlier.

" 'You think you'll get away?' " he said. "That's my line!"

With a single cry, the landlord and Asaichirō jumped out of the closet, truncheons in hand. Tarō just managed to throw his bedcovers over O-Kichi's head so that she could not escape and caught her firmly. The landlord and Asaichirō enthusiastically pounded away at the mass under the blanket. Carrying a lantern, the journeyman also came running and stomped on it with his feet.

After some time had passed, breathing heavily, they rolled back the covers to have a look, and underneath it, enveloped in the ruins of a shattered squash, there remained a number of things that looked like incredibly filthy dust balls, all about the size of the palm of someone's hand. The landlord gathered them up and took them out into the garden, where he doused them in oil and burned them all at once. It smelled like the burning of a woman's hair.

"Well, it should be all right now."

The landlord's words were right on the money. The woman's head vanished from the storeroom wall, and it never appeared again.

Tarō began his life as the only son of the Aoi'ya. He still often remembered his dear, departed mother. Asaichirō and O-Yū were both considerate of his feelings and recommended that the mortuary tablet that had been entrusted to the landlord be brought over and given a memorial service.

The Aoi'ya continued to prosper, unchanged except for one thing: the people there stopped eating squash and pumpkins. They offered them on their Shinto altar, but no one ever ate them. The neighbors found this rather odd.

"Why squash?" they sometimes wondered aloud.

VII

The Oni in the Autumn Rain

She had crossed the Shin-Ōhashi Bridge, she had gone over the Saruko Bridge, and she was just reaching South Rokkenbori-chō when the sky, which should have been a crisp autumn blue, grew dark and threatening. When she looked up, the clouds were drifting in from the west to the east. It was clear to see that a late autumn shower was on the way.

O-Nobu broke into a light run. She had told her mistress that the caretaker who had looked after her when she still lived at home had taken to his bed. She had told a groundless lie to get out of the house and had no time to waste. Every day, the autumn colors were deepening, and although the mornings and the evenings had for the past few days been freezing, just a little bit of running brought a sweat to her brow. The thought that even this might be due to her own agitation only made her that much more frantic to hurry onward.

When she turned the corner to enter Mima-chō, her gaze fell immediately on the nostalgic sight of the agency's old sign. There O-Nobu forced herself to stop running and read again and again the vertical line of *kanji* written there, encouraging herself so she might take that next, decisive step forward: EMPLOYMENT AGENCY—MALE AND FEMALE WORKERS.

The sliding paper door in the entrance was closed. If she

didn't open it and go inside, all this trouble would have been for nothing. She could still turn on her heel and go back, and her life as a worker at the Kanō'ya would continue as though nothing had happened.

She felt her body trembling. She felt hot all the way to her earlobes.

O-Nobu closed her eyes for a moment. Then she opened the door and stepped inside, saying, "Excuse me? Is anyone in?"

There was a narrow entryway and, beyond its stoop, a tatami room of about four and a half mats' size. There was a small reception desk enclosed by a low barricade of wooden bars, piled high with account books. It was a sight almost unchanged from five years prior, when the master of this place had found a job for her as a maid at the Kanō'ya. However, that bald proprietor who, insofar as O-Nobu was aware, never left this desk while the office was open during the day was nowhere to be seen just then. There were only a few faded indigo-violet floor cushions, laid out rather forlornly.

Once more, O-Nobu called out, "Excuse me? Is anyone in?" As soon as she did so, a woman's voice called back a long "Yes" from behind the *noren* curtain to the rear of the desk. "Yes, just a moment, please!" she continued briskly.

O-Nobu, urged on by her impatient heart, was unable to keep still and paced about aimlessly in the entryway.

The noren parted and a woman of about forty suddenly appeared, her forelocks cut and her body swathed in a striped kimono of rather garish design. She was wiping off her hands on her apron.

"Why, hello, there!" she said, setting her knees down on the master's floor cushion within the enclosure. "Here to see about job placement, are you?"

O-Nobu had never seen this woman before. Somehow, she managed a nod as, fidgety, she squeezed both her hands into fists.

The woman smiled cheeringly. "That's unfortunate, though. My husband has had a cold and a high fever since yesterday; he's been lying in bed moaning all this time. It's very rare for him to get sick, but we certainly can't take chances, can we?"

Hearing this, the strength went out of O-Nobu's body like air escaping a balloon. Naturally, she was disappointed, but at the same time she felt something like relief. "What with all that, he won't be able to help anyone look for work until he's better, but I've been told to take the requests of anyone who comes in; that's why the front door is open."

"Oh, really . . . ?" O-Nobu said with a meek nod. "Are you, ah, the lady of the establishment then?"

"That's right. Though hardly fancy enough to go calling 'lady.'" The woman laughed, shaking her forelocks. To O-Nobu, she looked about the same age as her mother, but she had a lovely face. Glamorous, even. Five years ago, however, the master of this place, a decently well-off fellow by the auspicious name of Tomizō— "a storehouse of wealth" it meant—had been a bachelor, as she remembered it.

As if sensing O-Nobu's doubts, the woman asked in a pleasant voice, "Have you visited here before?"

"Yes, ma'am. Five years ago, when my last temporary placement ran out."

"In that case, you must not know about me. I and the master here only got together two years ago," she said, showing her teeth a little as she smiled. "We're just an old man and a middle-aged woman; it was a little late in life to be holding a big celebration or anything. There wasn't any reception either, but I'm certainly the wife here, not some suspicious person. Rest assured."

In a dither, O-Nobu shook her head from side to side. "Oh, no . . . it wasn't that I was suspicious."

"Oh, really? Your face got this kind of uneasy look on it. I should have told you this sooner, but my name is Tsuta. I get a little bashful being called mistress, so if you call me O-Tsuta, that'll be fine."

Within the barred enclosure, O-Tsuta adjusted her legs and opened a broad white account book. "As I was just saying," she said, "if you'll just state your business, I'll listen and pass it along to the master. I can't say my brain is exactly reliable, but I'll write it down so I won't forget. It'd be a shame to have come here for nothing. Now, you've come to look for a new job, correct?"

O-Nobu stole a peek at the wide account book O-Tsuta indicated with her finger. Lines of text written in large *hiragana* characters stretched on and on. Most likely, they were requests of customers that O-Tsuta had written down already. It was a sight almost like a child's drill book for writing practice. Her face flushed hot with embarrassment to think of her own words being set down in writing in the same way.

"Oh no, I'll come again some other time," O-Nobu mumbled, naturally shying away.

"Oh my. Well in that case, won't you at least leave your name and where you're staying? You've come here before, so that makes you a valued client. If I give you halfhearted service, the master'll have words for me later!" She laughed at her own little joke.

"Oh, no . . . but even so, I . . ."

"You're in a hurry to find a job, right? But times are hard these days. Did your employer let you go to reduce staff or something? Did this happen at a shop where my husband negotiated your position? You've been working there these five years, yes? And that job was eliminated, you say?"

O-Tsuta's speech was carefree and without malice, but somehow it only pricked O-Nobu's heart all the more for it. O-Nobu's lips were not trained in the telling of lies, and it looked unlikely that she would prove a match for O-Tsuta's rapid-fire questioning.

"I, um," she began, stumbling all over her words. "Five years ago, in February, he found me an opening as a maid at a cleaner and seller of polished white rice in Shimoya called the Kanō'ya."

"The Kanō'ya in Shimoya. Hmmm."

"But then—they let me go."

"Five years of honest work, and they suddenly let you go?" O-Tsuta grimaced. "Did you make some kind of terrible blunder? Though you don't look like the type . . ."

O-Nobu hung her head. O-Tsuta was staring at her, looking her over from top to bottom with great curiosity.

"It looks like you have something you don't want to talk about." She lowered her voice and said, "But no matter; you're a young girl and your looks aren't half bad. By the look of those calloused hands, it's easy to see you give your all on the job."

O-Nobu impulsively hid her hands in her sleeves.

O-Tsuta smiled and went on. "As you can see, I'm a sly little lady, but to the same degree, I'm a good judge of women, so talk straight with me. By any chance, did you get caught up in some sort of trouble regarding a love affair in the shop? Would that be the reason you found yourself suddenly fired?"

There had been no trouble in the shop, but O-Tsuta had hit the bull's-eye with what she had said about a romantic entanglement. O-Nobu felt her heart skip a beat. Completely overwhelmed, she remained silent, eyes still downcast.

"Do you have any family you can turn to? Your dad or your mum?"

"No, ma'am. There's no one . . ."

"So no brothers or sisters either. And that's why you came to an employment agency for help." O-Tsuta leaned forward, placing her hands on top of the barred partition. "The shop master here may have a face like a bearded whale, but you sure do seem to trust him. And not just you either—there've been quite a few other customers coming in here with similar problems. So you have nothing to worry about."

Truly, the master here was a man who took good care of people. Though his face was as frightening as O-Tsuta had said, O-Nobu remembered well how warm, and pleasant, and silly it became when he was smiling.

When she had come to him five years ago, O-Nobu had been a young girl of thirteen who, all alone in the world, hadn't known where else to turn. The previous year, there had been cholera in the summer and flooding in the autumn, and she had lost her father and her mother one after the other. The master here had become like a close relative, thinking carefully about O-Nobu's future in these circumstances. When her employment at the Kanō'ya was decided, he told her to buy a secondhand kimono, wrapped up a small parcel of money, and placed it in her hands.

And it was precisely because his kindness had touched her so deeply that she had decided to come here today seeking help.

"I, um." O-Nobu opened her mouth but couldn't get the words to come out right. She knew she was being terribly rude by so stubbornly refusing to speak but was too embarrassed to open up and tell this woman everything. It felt like she was being rent asunder by these two emotions.

"At the shop—there wasn't any trouble. Everybody at the Kanō'ya has been really good, even to a lackluster maid like me. Even though I didn't know anything about the kitchen, they taught me everything from square one."

"So you were a kitchen maid, were you?" O-Tsuta nodded as though something had just made sense to her. "Polishing rice is hard physical labor. I hear there are a lot of big eaters in places like that. I can just imagine how hard it must be to boil all that rice."

O-Nobu hurriedly shook her head. "It's true that you need tremendous strength to polish rice, but . . . but there aren't such big eaters there. Just ordinary."

"Is that so? So all that about 'a *shō* of rice at dawn and eve' and 'snacking/on rice balls/the size of a baby's head' is just the stuff of workers' *senryū* verse, eh?"

"Yes, ma'am. Yes, ma'am. Absolutely. At the Kanō'ya, Mr. Yasu and Mr. Mino and Mr. Gin all eat pretty neatly."

O-Tsuta burst out laughing at the force with which O-Nobu's words came pouring out. "Oh, that's hilarious!" she said. "But it sounds like you had it pretty good there. And you must have become very familiar with the shop."

Even O-Nobu gave a hint of a smile at being so spoken of. The work of a kitchen maid wasn't easy, but there was no doubting that the Kanō'ya was a fine establishment. Even now, to O-Nobu it was the equal of her own childhood home.

Which was exactly why this hurt so much.

"Still . . ." O-Tsuta's smile lingered only around her mouth as she turned serious again. "Why were you let go by a shop you were so comfortable working in?"

The conversation had come back around to its starting point. It was starting to look like she'd have to run away if she wanted to avoid telling her what was going on.

"As an employee, I gave them no reason for dissatisfaction," O-Nobu said reluctantly. "I had someone tell me I should leave and go somewhere where I could get—a better wage. And he offered to find a place that was perfect for me."

O-Tsuta stared anew at O-Nobu's face. O-Nobu looked down.

"Were you dissatisfied with the Kanō'ya's wages?"

O-Nobu picked her head up. "No, ma'am! Not at all!"

"I should say not. But did you have debts? Relatives dependent on remittances?"

"None . . . but . . ."

"Any other reason why you wanted to earn more?"

O-Nobu nodded silently.

"Let's see if I can guess. There was a man involved."

Even without O-Nobu going to the trouble of nodding, O-Tsuta must have known the answer from looking at her face. Her cheeks were flushed red.

O-Tsuta lowered her eyes to the still-open account book and let out a long breath. Like a song, it had its own subtle melody. *Hmmmmmmmm . . .*

"And if I were to make a further guess," she said, "I'd say that that same man is the one who wants to negotiate that better-paying job opening for you."

"Yes, ma'am," O-Nobu acknowledged in a small voice. "It's the same person."

"In other words, to put it bluntly, that man—your ladies' man—wants you to earn more money. Not for you, but for himself."

"No, ma'am, that isn't true. That isn't true!" O-Nobu put both hands on the partition and leaned forward. She did so with such excessive force that the candle stands between the bars fell off and rolled over to the other side of the desk. O-Tsuta looked on nonchalantly as O-Nobu rushed to pick them up and put them back as before, apologizing and begging forgiveness all the while. And all the while, there was a thin smile on O-Tsuta's face.

O-Nobu continued, breathing as hard as if she were running right then and there. "Mr. Shigetarō was thinking of me when he said it: 'Working as a maid is fine while you're young, but not something you do when you get older. There's a better place for you if you want to earn as much as you can while you're able to work, save for the future, and someday have a little shop on the main street.' He is a much more worldly person than me and knows so much more about the ways of the world. That's how I know he was thinking of me when he said that. Most of all, he's a well-known boatman in Yanagibashi, so he makes a lot of money and wouldn't need to go looking for marks among the likes of me. He's not so pitiful or petty as that."

With eyes that smiled like those of someone teasing a kitten or puppy, O-Tsuta watched O-Nobu's face as she said all of this in one breath, nearly falling forward over the barricade as she did so. Then taking a short breath, she asked gently, "So where is this Mr. Shigetarō recommending you go?"

"It's a place in Asakusa—in Shin-Torigoe-chō—"

"Asakusa, eh?"

"It's a restaurant and tea room called Meigetsu," O-Nobu said, her dry throat swallowing audibly. "He says they're looking for a live-in waitress there."

"A waitress, eh?"

"Yes, ma'am. He says it would just be filling saké cups, but for waiting tables, even an unrefined woman like me would do."

"And he says you'd receive a good wage even so? How much are we talking about?"

According to what Shigetarō had told her, it would be five *ryō* per year. This was big money; the one ryō per year that the Kanō'ya paid didn't even compare.

"Five ryō, eh?" O-Tsuta nodded with an expression that said *There's no such thing!* "Hmmm. That's quite an offer. Enough to make me want to go myself. I wonder if they couldn't use a middle-aged waitress . . ."

She was smiling, but her words were coming out the side of her mouth. O-Nobu realized she was being ridiculed. Her body went rigid.

"So you're saying you *weren't* shown to the exit by the Kanō'ya after that—that it was you who decided to quit? That's right, isn't it?"

"Yes, ma'am."

"If that's what the problem is, why didn't you say so right away? Don't go telling me stupid lies."

O-Nobu tried to object, stumbling over excuses to the effect of, "It was too hard to say," but O-Tsuta was having none of it.

"So what are you here to consult us about? If you've made up your mind to switch to Meigetsu or whatever the place is called, that's not really anything worth picking the wax out of the master's ear to tell him about. You were at the Kanō'ya for five years, and you quit of your own volition. It's not like the master who got you the job loses any face over that. So what was it you ran here all the way from Shimoya to talk about?"

O-Nobu became frightened at the unconcealed sharpness in O-Tsuta's tone of voice, but her steady stream of barbs was also making her angry. She started talking back before she realized it.

"I wasn't thinking of asking anything, especially. But I am obliged to him for finding me work, so I thought I'd take the chance to pay my respects. However, if you're saying such consideration isn't necessary, I suppose I'll be on my way right now."

Ah-ha-ha-ha! O-Tsuta let out a loud burst of laughter, not even bothering to hide her mouth with her hand. "What's that sharp tone about? You're a strange young lady, aren't you?"

Then she leaned forward suddenly, and this time it was O-Tsuta who grabbed the barred enclosure with both hands. She drew so near to O-Nobu's face that it looked almost like they were about to kiss, then said in a confidential tone, "Well then, on your way out, let me make one more guess about you: you came here to ask the master what kind of place this Meigetsu is and if you can really work there as just a waitress, didn't you? You trust in what your darling Shigetarō tells you, but at the same time you just can't quite swallow that story whole. The unease was more than you could take, so you came here to check it out."

She had no response to that. O-Nobu was a lowly earthworm to O-Tsuta's python.

"I've got a question. There's really no need to ask it, and it's a silly one to boot. Also, if you're in love with that Shigetarō fellow, anything I say will probably go in one ear and out the other, but still, I won't be satisfied if I don't ask. Do you—a woman in love—really believe there's a decent man out there who would try to get you to trade the honest work you're doing in a *proper* establishment for a job in some restaurant? It's clear from the outset that any man like that is a good-for-nothing bum who wants his woman to go out and work while he lives a life of leisure."

"That isn't true!" shouted O-Nobu. "Shigetarō is—"

"—nice to you, isn't he?" Though O-Tsuta hadn't spoken in a loud voice, she had upset O-Nobu easily. "Did he even buy you a clip for your obi? And those ornamental hairpins you'll be needing? White powder for your face? When you were all upset on a rainy day because your foot got stuck in the mud and your clog strap snapped, why, he didn't show up and rip apart his hand towel to fix it, did he? And when you were accosted by a gang of roughnecks in an entertainment district on your way back from a long errand for your shop, why, he didn't come to your rescue, did he? You're not falling for that kind of too-good-to-be-true story, are you?"

. . . by roughnecks in an entertainment district. She'd hit the nail on the head with that one. O-Nobu was yet again at a loss for words. Her face flushed red, and she felt a terrible sense of distress; even the insides of her lowered eyelids felt hot.

"Well, well, you're probably wishing you had a hole to jump into about now," said O-Tsuta, clapping her hands in delight. "To think there are still city girls who get duped by that kind of farce! Like they say, 'Edo is yet vast'!"

O-Nobu wanted to cry. At this point, she wished she hadn't come here. Although it was very slight indeed, she had felt some unease about what Shigetarō had told her. Thinking that perhaps the master of this agency might share his wisdom, she had decided to come here. That had been a mistake.

Despite O-Tsuta's gleeful bellowing, there came no sounds of rustling about from inside, nor was there any sensation of a human presence therein. Was Tomizō really in such bad shape? It was said that colds were the root of ten thousand illnesses. And shouldn't O-Tsuta go back to her sick husband's bedside rather than spending forever messing around with O-Nobu out front? What was this relentless *concern* of hers about, anyway? It was absolutely disgusting.

"If you're smart, you'll forget about this Shigetarō fellow right away," O-Tsuta said gently to the tearful O-Nobu. "Once you cool your head a little and think things over calmly, even you should realize that what I'm telling you is right. If he was really thinking of what's best for you, he wouldn't tell you to quit the good job you have now to be a waitress in some tea shop."

Daunted, O-Nobu's heart had been sinking in retreat, but now with a mighty pull she hoisted it back up again and tightened her lips stubbornly. *Her words may be kind on the surface, but this person is making a fool of me. She's selling me short, thinking I'm just a naïve young girl who doesn't know the first thing about the world. She talks about all this like she understands it, but this above all is a subject this woman can't be trusted with.*

"Oh dear, now I've made you mad," O-Tsuta said, looking into O-Nobu's face. "But I don't mind if you get angry with me. It can't be any fun being told that your dear Shigetarō is a good-for-nothing bum."

"You've never even met him!" Without realizing it, O-Nobu lost her temper and snapped at her. "You don't even know Mr. Shigetarō, yet you speak this kind of nonsense about him!"

"It's true I've never met Mr. Shigetarō," O-Tsuta said, not budging in the slightest. "But when it comes to men like him, I know everything. I know them so well I'm sick to death of them. At any rate, any critique of my life would have to start with my listening to a kind, handsome, smooth-talking man just like your Mr. Shigetarō. I followed him around shamelessly and then for my trouble got sold off to a brothel for ten years." O-Tsuta gave a short laugh. This time, she was not laughing at O-Nobu, but at an old story all her own. "I'll mention in passing that I was fifteen at the time. Even younger than you are now. I was a poor judge of men, so my sin was lighter than yours by about three years' worth of age difference. And even with that, I fell as low as a brothel. Once you make a mistake with this kind of thing, it's too late. Women are so weak. They can't resist a man who's looking out for them; they get strung along by them and ultimately end up in a place they can never come back from. I'm a prime example."

O-Tsuta tapped her chest, making a soft sound. *Pon!* She was looking straight at O-Nobu. Many expressions appeared on her face, one melting into the next. Smiling one moment, on the verge of tears the next, then angry . . . It was like she was trying them all out, intent on finding the one that would get through to O-Nobu.

O-Nobu was clutching the sleeves of her kimono, as if trying to hold on to herself. *I'm terrified. But what is it that's so frightening? If I could just get angrier, could it erase this fear?*

O-Tsuta saw right through O-Nobu and charged ahead with her attacks.

"You're frightened. But not of me. You've been frightened from the beginning. You just said so, didn't you? That the reason you came to visit the master was to get confirmation of what kind of restaurant this Meigetsu place is. Because it's you yourself—not anyone else—who's just a little suspicious of your darling Mr. Shigetarō's sweet, sweet story. You should know this better than anyone. And that's certainly not a bad thing; it's a sign that you've got good sense. It's the difference between you and me in my younger days. Maybe the difference three years' worth of living makes; maybe a difference in intelligence. If I had to say one or the other, I'd definitely pick the latter."

O-Nobu remained silent. She was not pleased at all to be complimented in this manner. *You're quick on the uptake; you're good at noticing things; you remember everything right away and work very efficiently*—she got compliments like that all the time at the Kanō'ya. But none of this was really praiseworthy. She was just being told that she was doing well as a maid, which was something anyone else could have done just as easily.

But Mr. Shigetarō was different. He looked at O-Nobu only. He said that he valued O-Nobu more than anything else in the world. Before him, she had never met even one such person in her life.

As O-Tsuta was watching O-Nobu's expressions, she let out a long sigh.

"I still kept getting taken in by men even after I turned thirty. Honestly, I'm not a woman who has any business lecturing you. But still—" Tilting her head, something seemed oddly girlish about her. "—I can't just turn a blind eye to something I know is going to end badly."

O-Nobu retreated a half step. *Ah, enough of this.* Lifting up her chin and making it sound as hateful as she could, O-Nobu said, "I don't need your unasked-for concern. Mr. Shigetarō is fine. I'm quitting the Kanō'ya, but please give my regards to your husband. I'll show myself out." She turned on her heel and was starting for the door when she realized that it was beginning to rain. From a sky now entirely closed off by clouds, the cold rain came falling swiftly.

"Oh dear. An autumn shower's started falling, has it?"

O-Tsuta came down into the entryway and stood next to O-Nobu. When she did so, O-Nobu became aware of a very faint, unpleasant metallic odor coming from her body. *That's quite an odd perfume*, she thought.

"Strange, isn't it," O-Tsuta murmured as if to herself, staring at the long lines traced by the falling raindrops. "Right at a moment like this, an autumn rain starts to fall. Thanks to the rain, I just remembered it . . . an old, old story."

"What old story?"

"Something that happened nearly twenty years ago. Right around the time of the rainy season—I saw something that was just a little . . . *frightening*."

Now anyone's interest would be roused at being told something like that, but O-Nobu, realizing that O-Tsuta's intent was to keep her from going, said nothing.

"In any large group of people," O-Tsuta said, forging ahead, "there are some who are able to put on a kind, gentle face and quite calmly deceive and kill others for the sake of their own greed.

That kind of person is hiding an oni's nature beneath an attractive, perfectly human face."

She was speaking in a near whisper in a detached, quiet tone.

"Back twenty years ago, the Fukagawa area wasn't yet incorporated into the 'crimson circle' on maps marking out the bounds of Edo; this was when it was managed by the local administrator of Shimōsa. Have you ever been out to what they call the hundred thousand and sixty thousand *tsubo* of new rice fields in Sarue and Ōshima? It's very rustic out there, though nowadays there are quite a few samurai homes there. Back then, though, there was much, much less, and as for large estates, there was Lord Hitotsubashi's home and nothing else but a wide expanse of rice paddies. To get from the home of one landowner to that of the next, you'd have to traverse half a *chō*. In the summertime, the hot, still humidity was unbearable, and in the winter you couldn't open your eyes for the dry wind. In exchange, though, the plum groves were splendid. In the spring, it was like they purified your eyes. In the mornings and the evenings, flocks of oystercatchers would form along the blue canals, and they'd fly above plum trees in full bloom. It was enough to make me wonder if this was what people meant by the phrase 'a view of the Pure Land.'"

O-Tsuta half closed her eyes, as if wanting to say she could see that sight behind her eyelids.

"At that time, I couldn't stay in Edo due to a little . . . situation. I'd changed my name, invented a new background, and was working as a live-in housemaid at the home of a landowner in Kameido village. In the countryside, it was possible to move into a place even without proper papers from a guarantor, and that suited me just fine. Although this is an old story, that landowner's family is still prosperous even now, so please excuse me for keeping his name to myself."

O-Tsuta looked at O-Nobu and smiled slightly. When she did so, that faint metallic odor floated through the air again. Maybe it was coming from her breath, O-Nobu decided.

"At that house, there was an old retiree who had celebrated his eighty-eighth birthday. Old age is a fearsome thing. He could hardly get out of bed, and he was quite weak in the head as well. Because of this, he was living alone in an annex, but sometimes I would assist the lady of the house in taking care of this old man.

"He was easy enough to handle, but he had a habit of rambling on and on about odd things every once in a while.

"Such as? Well . . . he said he could see an oni. The window of the annex looked out over a small garden and canal, beyond which you could look across a wide stretch of rice paddies. In one corner of that window, though, you could see a pond surrounded by a lovely grove of plum trees. He'd say that in the middle of that grove, he could see an oni standing all alone."

Her interest quite naturally aroused, O-Nobu asked, "During the daytime?"

O-Tsuta nodded. "During the day. It would be too dark at night, of course. 'There's an oni—standing right out in the sunlight, two horns growing out of its head. You can tell at a glance what it is,' he'd say. Usually, there was only the one oni, but occasionally it would mingle with sharecroppers and the like. However, none of them were aware of the oni. A strange tale, isn't it?"

O-Tsuta had first been told this story in spring, at the height of the plum blossom season. She had entered the master's manor house at the end of the previous year, so she, just getting acclimated to life as a housemaid, had just said, "Yes, that's very nice," to anything he told her, bowing her head obediently.

"The other people living at the landowner's estate hadn't appeared to be taking the old man's words seriously either. They'd just dismiss it as the ravings of an old man, and that would be that. However—"

The summer passed, and autumn came, and around the time you start to feel each day getting shorter, the old man weakened suddenly and quickly died.

"It was decided to clean out the annex, so my days became pretty busy. And then, when the worst of the cleaning was behind us, I started to wonder for some reason—or actually, for no reason at all—about the oni the old man used to talk about. I found myself wondering if he had really been able to see something. I felt an irresistible urge to know and even went out to the plum tree grove to have a look around."

O-Tsuta had sometimes been sent out to run errands on the orders of workers at the mansion, so she had been as far as the sharecroppers' huts and had even walked in the vicinity of that grove before. Even so, this was the first time she had ever felt an urge to go look for something that could support what the old man had said.

"Truth to tell, I was frightened," O-Tsuta said in a small voice. "The way that the old man died had just been too sudden. I was wondering, could the oni, which was visible only to the old man, have perhaps noticed that it was being watched and murdered him?"

Having rounded the garden, O-Tsuta had set off for the footpaths that threaded between rice paddies, and then a refreshing rain had come pouring down.

"The autumn rains had come." Here O-Tsuta looked outside the front door again. There she saw rain falling like pellets of silver. "It was just about like this."

Even as she had walked along the path through the rice fields, the rainfall had grown steadily stronger. She had looked up at the sky and hesitated, wondering if she should turn back, but in the end O-Tsuta had instead run toward the grove as though something was pulling her there.

The rice in the paddies around there was always cut early, and harvest had been entirely finished, leaving her surrounded by nothing but an empty expanse. None of the sharecroppers were out either. It was, of course, not the season for plum groves and flowers, so everything had an emaciated, forlorn look to it, with nothing but the distant cries of birds calling from somewhere.

O-Tsuta had been all alone.

"And it was there that I—" O-Tsuta turned her head, showing O-Nobu her sharp, beautiful profile. "—met the oni."

In the midst of the plum grove, she had suddenly realized that it was there, she said. Soaking wet in the autumn rain, the oni had appeared cold, hungry, and utterly miserable.

"Even for all that, it was an incredibly disgusting thing," continued O-Tsuta, closing her eyes abruptly. "That's why I unconsciously said, 'Oh. You're an oni, aren't you—your human mask must have melted in the rain.'"

Then she had set off running without looking back.

"I did look back when I was on the footpath through the rice fields, but the plum grove was reflected on the surface of the pond, and with everything around fogged white with the rain, I could see neither hide nor hair of oni or human. However, I had without a doubt encountered the oni, and I know that I'd looked him right in the eye." Here O-Tsuta fell silent. She didn't seem to have anything else left to say.

It was a creepy tale, but not one with a very satisfying ending. It hadn't chased her and there hadn't been any uproar over it, nor did the truth about the oni come to light later. It was just an incoherent vignette. O-Nobu felt uncomfortable. She had no idea how to respond.

Perhaps sensing this, O-Tsuta looked back at O-Nobu and smiled, showing her teeth. "I've told a rather boring story, haven't I? The autumn rain makes me remember, though."

"I . . . have to be going."

"I know you do. I'll pass your respects along to my husband. I'm sorry you weren't able to see him."

Autumn rains pass quickly, and in fact, the rain was already turning into a drizzle. O-Tsuta said she would lend her an umbrella, and although O-Nobu refused again and again, O-Tsuta would hear none of it. Then she reminded her, "Take care not to forget one thing about oni: they disguise themselves in human skin." Somehow, she seemed to have lost sight of the thread of their earlier discussion; now all O-Tsuta wanted to talk about was the oni. That was a dangerous thing, and in the end O-Nobu practically fled as she departed the employment agency. She wanted to run, so in the end she never opened the umbrella.

怪

This was what happened two days later.

O-Nobu was in the kitchen boiling some greens when O-Shima, the chief housekeeper, approached her with brows knitted. Something was going on. "A subordinate of Masagorō, a thief-taker in Fukagawa, is here wanting to ask you some questions. Come with me for a moment." She took her by the hand and led her out. O-Nobu's heart skipped a beat when she heard "Fukagawa," but her visit to the employment agency had been a secret from the start, so she obediently followed O-Shima out the kitchen door and stepped outside.

The thief-taker's subordinate was a man as small as a bean and probably no older than twenty at most. The right corner of his mouth was crooked like a nail that had been struck the wrong way, and it was unclear whether this was an affectation or his natural expression. "Sorry to bother you. You're Miss O-Nobu, correct?" he said in an unexpectedly soft voice. "I'd like to speak privately for a bit, so I'm going to borrow Miss O-Nobu."

So saying, the small man sent O-Shima away. The chief housekeeper withdrew looking displeased, then the man lowered his voice, taking a half step toward O-Nobu so she could hear him just the same.

"Just past noon the day before yesterday, you visited an employment agency in Fukagawa Mima-chō, didn't you? Don't make me do extra work; just tell me immediately. We do this for a living, so we've long since determined for a fact that you went there. There was someone there who recognized you."

A shudder ran up from O-Nobu's feet, and she confessed with complete honesty right away. "Yes, sir. I certainly did go there."

"You're already working for the Kanō'ya, so what business did you have there?"

When O-Nobu hesitated, the thief-taker's subordinate clucked his tongue impatiently and said, "In that case, let me ask you something else. Did you meet with the master, Tomizō, at that time?"

"I wasn't able to. He was in bed with a cold or something. I met with the mistress only."

At O-Nobu's reply, the straight corner of the subordinate's mouth curved upward. "The *mistress*?"

"Yes, sir. Mistress O-Tsuta—"

This time, not just the corner of his mouth, but also the corners of both eyes turned upward, and O-Nobu, not understanding why the man looked so surprised, tried her best to explain. A middle-aged, seductive-looking woman right around forty years of age, with disheveled cut forelocks and wearing a striped kimono—

"Whoa, now, wait just a minute!" the subordinate said, abruptly cutting her off. His face remained hard and strained, exaggeratedly so, as if he had a sore spot somewhere. "It really was just past noon the day before yesterday when you went to Mima-chō, wasn't it?" he asked again.

"Yes, sir. There's no mistake. When I came back here, the Sensōji Temple bell was just starting to ring eight, and—oh, yes! The autumn shower that came pouring down as soon as I reached Mima-chō had let up by the time I was crossing the Ōkawa River."

"It's true that two days ago an autumn rain started falling sometime after noon and let up after raining hard for about an hour," the man mumbled under his breath.

"What on earth is all this about?" asked O-Nobu, now jittery.

The thief-taker's subordinate gazed at her very seriously and spoke in a voice that betrayed his own shock. "Well, your surprise looks like the real thing. You really don't know."

He told her then that near sunset on the day before yesterday, a visitor had discovered Tomizō, master of the employment agency in Mima-chō, dead of stab wounds to the neck in the little tatami room in back of his front office.

"Near sunset? Then that means—" O-Nobu put both hands over her mouth, but the subordinate, speaking as soon as she fell silent, said, "It's too early to be surprised. He was found in the evening, but according to the findings of the official who inspected the scene, he was murdered earlier. Even a late estimate can't be any earlier than three nights ago. After all, the body had started to smell. The inside of the house had been ransacked and stripped bare of every last valuable. Somebody did a really cruel thing."

O-Nobu's eyes snapped wide open. *Robbery. Murder.*

Deeds worthy of an oni.

"When you went there, Tomizō's body was lying in the back room. And I'll also mention that he was single. There wasn't a mistress there."

"Then—"

"The woman called O-Tsuta is in league with the thieves. Because what happened in there couldn't have been the handiwork of just one woman. She was keeping watch, saying whatever popped into her head and putting on a show to keep the people in the neighborhood from realizing that Tomizō had been murdered. If she could buy time by doing that, they could take their time searching the house. It was known in the neighborhood that Tomizō kept his savings at home, and perhaps as a precaution, he seems to have divided it up into small amounts and hidden them throughout the house. Though that seems to have been a wasted effort."

O-Nobu at last opened her mouth to speak. "I can't . . . believe such a thing."

"Tell me about it. You were in a dangerous spot yourself. If anything had gone wrong, you could've been dragged to the back and silenced."

"But when I said I was going, it was that Miss O-Tsuta person who was trying to keep me there. Why would she do such a thing? Don't you think it's odd?"

The subordinate hauled the crooked corner of his mouth upward, looking quite proud of himself. "According to your story just now, you were about to leave without ever telling her your name or address, right? That's why she wanted to keep you there."

"Why is that?"

"The reason this O-Tsuta woman was asking and writing down the names and addresses of people who came in was to know exactly who had seen her face. That way, she could feel safer later on."

Had that been it? Had that really been all? Just for that reason alone, had O-Tsuta gone out of her way to keep O-Nobu from leaving, to taunt her about her romantic worries, and to tell her that long story?

It had been something about an oni, hadn't it?

"This is a formidable band of villains," the subordinate said, clucking his tongue again in frustration, though somehow he did not look entirely unexcited either. "The woman O-Tsuta is an important clue. I'm going to leave now and come right back with my boss, so please let us hear more details then. We'll write down a description. Don't go anywhere. Just tell us what you know, and you won't be inconvenienced any further."

Trembling, O-Nobu said, "Yes, sir," and then in a panicked rush, called out to the retreating back of the thief-taker's subordinate, who looked ready to tuck the hem of his kimono into his obi and take off running at any moment.

"Excuse me! I borrowed an umbrella!"

"From Tomizō's place?"

"Yes, sir. Miss O-Tsuta—I mean, that woman called O-Tsuta— lent it to me."

O-Nobu went running to get the umbrella, for the man had said, "Show it to me right away." It was an old, worn-out *bangasa* type, its bamboo frame supporting an oil-paper top; nothing special at all.

"May I open it?"

"Yes, sir. Please do."

When he opened the umbrella, the young man cried out in surprise. O-Nobu gasped.

The inside of the umbrella was dotted with scattered black stains.

"This . . . is from a spray of blood," said the young man, looking more and more engaged. "This is important evidence, so I'm going to hold on to it. I know this is hard on you too, all right? I'm telling you this again and again, but you mustn't do anything like running away because you don't want to be involved. My boss is a bit different from the other crafty thief-takers out there, so there's no need for any excessive worries."

Deeply impressed, O-Nobu could do nothing except lower her head. The subordinate departed at a run, and when she was alone in the kitchen entrance, she felt a wave of something like dizziness come over her and crouched down on the spot, holding her knees.

O-Tsuta had said—

(In any large group of people)

There are oni mingled in that disguise themselves in human skin.

(An oni's nature is hidden beneath an attractive, perfectly human-looking face.)

They quite calmly deceive and kill others.

(I'm a prime example.)

In her terror and sadness, O-Nobu didn't move from the spot where she was curled up. She was afraid even to hear anything more, and the thought of so much as raising up her head made her feel sick. When had the world turned into a place like this?

As she was squeezing her body tightly, the sky outside rapidly grew cloudy again, and soon the rain began to fall. An autumn shower. Those capricious, fleet-footed, cold showers that were part and parcel of a late autumn day.

She remembered O-Tsuta just the day before yesterday, her sharply defined profile facing her, looking all too serious, watching the autumn rain. *Ah, now that I think about it, there was that metallic smell coming from her. Was that not some unusual perfume, but rather the smell of blood from a corpse?*

The sprinkle of falling raindrops bounced cold off O-Nobu's cheeks.

She wiped her face with the back of her hand and withdrew into the kitchen. Though her hair and her face were damp, the shock had made her throat so dry that it hurt. She took off the lid of the water jar that was right inside the kitchen door and took the dipper in hand. When she did so, her face was reflected beautifully on the surface of the water, which came all the way up to the rim of the jar.

As soon as she saw it, she nearly gasped out loud and accidentally dropped the dipper. It struck the edge of the jar, making a light clanging noise.

A pond amid rustic rice paddies and the plum grove surrounding it. And within, blurred by the fall of the autumn rain, O-Tsuta had met the oni, she'd said. Their eyes had met, she said.

But had the true oni perhaps been O-Tsuta's reflection on that pond's surface? Just like the water that was now showing O-Nobu her own reflection? And the oni that the old man said he had seen from afar, had it not perhaps been the form of O-Tsuta herself standing in the grove? Of O-Tsuta herself mingling with the sharecroppers?

In the cold autumn rain, had her mask of human skin perhaps melted, revealing the form of an oni standing out in the open?

"O-Nobu!"

Although she heard herself being called, O-Nobu was too shocked to even speak.

"Mr. Shigetarō . . ."

With one hand on his forehead to keep the rain at bay and the hem of his kimono pulled up and fastened, Shigetarō drew near. "I'll be scolded if Miss O-Shima catches you here," O-Nobu told him.

"I know, but I wanted to see you so badly I just couldn't wait."

As he spoke to her of this and that, he drew O-Nobu near to him. The oil in the hair on both sides of his head gave off a strong fragrance, and O-Nobu felt his firm arms touching her back.

"What's the matter? You're trembling, aren't you? It must be because you got rained on in a place like this."

Shigetarō gazed at O-Nobu's face, stroking the nape of her neck, rubbing her shoulders to try to warm her. As he was doing so, he spoke to her again and again in his lilting tones, and finally gathered her to him and embraced her as he whispered in her ear, "Once you start work at Meigetsu, we won't have to be so discreet. We'll be able to meet whenever we like."

Shigetarō's breath tickled O-Nobu's earlobe.

"They're anxious for you to come. Said 'the sooner the better, even if it's only a single day.' So how about it? Have you made up your mind? I came here so suddenly because I wanted to hear your answer, but the rain and the sun were both so thoughtless. Or no; on second thought, we ended up like this, so maybe they weren't thoughtless at all."

All of a sudden, O-Nobu wanted to raise her voice and burst into tears. She wanted to start flailing her arms, to start hitting Shigetarō. She wanted to rage, to scream, to demand answers. *Is what you're telling me true? Are you lying to me? Are you an oni? Are you not?*

What should I believe?

"What's the matter, O-Nobu darling? Why are you crying?"

Shigetarō spoke soothingly enough for the moment, and when

he drew away slightly, he pulled out a small, cloth-wrapped object from the inside breast pocket of his kimono.

"Here, have a look at this. I found it during booth setup last night. It's by no means an expensive gift, but it's pretty, isn't it? And if you make it into a decorative pin, it'll look really nice in your hair."

What he put before her eyes was a jewel that was crimson like blood and about the size of a candy drop. It was polished, smooth and slick. O-Nobu didn't reach out to take it but instead merely stared at it. She could see a tiny reflection of her own face on its surface.

O-Nobu's face. A human face.

Still human.

"If you work at Meigetsu, even a waitress needs to wear stylish hairpins."

As she listened to Shigetarō's voice, O-Nobu was thinking. She wondered if Masagorō, the thief-taker whom that little subordinate had mentioned just now, was really someone wise in the ways of the world, who could listen to her story and tell her what to do. If he was . . . if she revealed everything about her reason for visiting Tomizō's place—about Shigetarō and about Meigetsu in Shin-Torigoe-chō—and asked for help, would he offer it? Would even Boss Masagorō, who knew how things worked, tell her that there were no good men who would try to make her quit a job in a reputable shop?

She didn't know. She didn't know anything. Because, after all, O-Nobu loved Shigetarō.

Even so, the words of O-Tsuta lingered in her heart. They wouldn't go away. She couldn't erase them. After all, they were words left to her by an oni. Change the path you're on before it's too late, or you will become an oni like me.

O-Nobu watched the autumn rain over Shigetarō's shoulder. After it had been falling for a long time, after yet more had fallen and puddles had formed on the ground, might the two of them step up to one together and look at their reflections, side by side?

Amidst the refreshing, steady fall of the drizzling rain, something misshapen, inhuman, was oh-so-quietly standing. The illusion shown her by the autumn rain faced O-Nobu and slowly shook its head.

O-Nobu covered her face with both her hands.

VIII
Ash Kagura

To Masagorō of Honjo Motomachi, from the Taira'ya of Kiryū-chō Block Five: One of our workers has attacked and wounded someone with a knife in the shop. Can you come over right away?

It was the very morning of the winter solstice, and the messenger had arrived while it was yet predawn.

Awakened by an apprentice, Masagorō got up right away and went to the kitchen entrance, still in his bedclothes. There he found a little old man standing in the cold, wearing nothing but a padded robe over his nightclothes. With both his hands, he was holding on to the handle of a lit paper lantern.

The Taira'ya, a maker of wooden clogs, was an offshoot of its main store in Kanda Kaji-chō. At the Kiryū-chō location there lived surely no more than ten people all told, including the master's family and the workers. However, it was hardly a shop with such deep connections to Masagorō that he could recognize its people at a glance. When he asked his visitor if he was chief clerk there, the old man bowed his head, shivered as though he were frightfully cold, and finally said in a faint, halting voice, "I am chief clerk Minosuke. I'm terribly sorry to call so early."

"There's no need for that. What about the worker who's caused this uproar? Has he been subdued?"

"Yes, sir. We've subdued the scoundrel and locked *her* up."

"How about the person she stabbed? Have you managed to scare up a doctor?"

"A maid was sent to fetch the doctor treating the mistress's lower abdominal troubles."

"In Honjo?"

"No, sir; in Kanda. The main shop's—"

"I see," said Masagorō, not letting him finish. No matter what kind of a knifing had unfolded there, if they called the local doctor in Kanda—who had a long history with their main shop—it would ultimately be no trouble at all to have certain details omitted from the official report. Masagorō was relieved. For the time being at least, all he need do was hurry over.

He dressed quickly and wiped his face with a towel, finishing just in time to hear the ringing of the six o'clock bell. It had a muffled sort of tone. Perhaps the weather would require he carry an umbrella.

When he finished his preparations and emerged from the kitchen, the elderly chief clerk was sitting on the stoop in the entrance, both hands wrapped around a large earthenware cup, the lantern lying extinguished and folded by his side. Hot steam was rising from the cup.

This was according to the system employed by Masagorō's wife. Since the current guest was an old man, his cup contained plain hot water. But when it was a woman or a child who came running over, she'd dissolve a little starch syrup in their water because sweets had a calming effect on easily upset women and children. However, when men in the prime of their working years rushed over, even at midsummer or midwinter, they got nothing at all. Saké, of course, was out of the question. Masagorō's wife was well versed in such tricks of the trade. From the start of autumn and all through the winter, she would get up again and again during the night, never letting the coals die, making sure she could serve hot water at any time of day or night, even if she had to go to the trouble of refilling the iron kettle. Her meticulousness was such that some even considered it a little bit obnoxious.

"Well now, are you warming up a little? You seem to have your color back. Shall we go?" Masagorō said, trying to urge Minosuke along. "Things may have calmed down, but I'm sure everyone at the shop must be very worried. Let's hurry up and be on our way. Now, now, you mustn't still be upset. Just leave everything to me."

Once the sun came up, there would be people watching. If someone who knew Minosuke's face were to see such a sight as the old chief clerk, white as a sheet, running along beside a thief-taker, like it or not, there would rumors. As might be expected of such a tried-and-true shop man, though, Minosuke apparently caught the meaning behind Masagorō's words. He gave an obedient bow of the head, said "Yes, sir," and followed along behind Masagorō.

The distance between Motomachi and the fifth block of Kiryū-chō was such that an adult could cover it in a single unbroken run. Since voices carried a surprising distance in the late night and early morning hours, it was careless to speak while walking the streets. Masagorō walked swiftly, headed for the Taira'ya. The Tatekawa River reflected the sky—leaden, gloomy, and stagnant. There was no sign yet of any cormorants out this morning. A cold wind that stung at the tips of Masagorō's and the old man's noses came blowing in from across the water.

Just two months prior, the Taira'ya in Kiryū-chō had been licked by the flames from a small blaze at the Soba'ya next door, and the entire kitchen, from the door to the far walls, had just recently been rebuilt.

Masagorō entered through that kitchen door and could faintly make out the scent of fresh new wood. The handmaid who had been waiting for him there showed him immediately to the reception room. The house wasn't all that large, and he could clearly hear the noisy footfalls of the master and mistress as they approached.

Masagorō was surprised when he met with them face to face.

They were very young. Neither of them appeared to have yet reached thirty. The master looked pale, and it was clear that the mistress had been crying. After an exchange of greetings, Masagorō said that he wanted to see the wounded immediately.

"Right this way, sir. We carried him to our bedroom. I must apologize for the unseemlines of it all."

When they reached the bedroom, a young man was lying on his back with soft covers drawn up to his chin. His face was as white as if it had been bleached, but his eyes were open, and when he saw Masagorō, he tried to sit up, found himself unable, and quickly gave up trying.

"This is my younger brother, Zenkichi," said the young master of the Taira'ya. With a strained expression, he edged toward the face sticking out of the futon. "He works in the main shop in Kanda, but he's been staying with us since the day before yesterday."

"How are his injuries? May I examine them?"

The mistress turned the covers back until Zenkichi's chest was revealed. She undid the collar of his nightshirt, and underneath, towels and bleached cotton cloth were wrapped around and around his neck. Masagorō discerned blood-tinged spots here and there, but he could tell that these wounds weren't all that severe. The cuts were all shallow, and there didn't appear to be any lacerations or stab wounds.

"His chest as well," said the master, slowly lifting up his younger brother's arms. It was also covered in cuts.

"You tried to dodge the knife, didn't you?"

"Yes, sir," Zenkichi said weakly. "But since I was sleeping when she started carving me up all of a sudden, I was just in utter shock."

Masagorō flashed him a reassuring smile, though that didn't mean he was buying Zenkichi's story wholesale. If someone really had started cutting him all of a sudden while he was sound asleep, there was no way he would have gotten off with wounds as light as the ones he had.

"I'm told the assailant is locked up? It's one of your employees?"

"Yes, sir," said the young master, who exchanged looks with his wife and breathed out a heavy sigh. "For heaven's sake, why did she go and do such a thing?"

"It was a housemaid named O-Koma," the mistress said in a halting voice, still teary-eyed. "When I came here to marry, she came along with me from my hometown."

"So when the Taira'ya opened this branch here, was it for the two of you to establish your home?"

Husband and wife both nodded. "Yes, sir."

"And how many years ago was that?"

"It was two years ago."

"Does your family also operate a business, ma'am?"

"Yes, sir. A wholesaler of medicines in my hometown."

"How old is O-Koma?"

"Twenty, sir. She's two years younger than me, so I always thought of her like a younger sister. In any case, she's been right at my side since as far back as I can remember."

"Before I ask this, I need to request that you please don't get angry. Mr. Zenkichi, do you have any memory of O-Koma at your bedside with her knife?"

Zenkichi looked up at his elder brother uneasily. The master of the Taira'ya gazed back at the face of his younger brother. The mistress looked from one to the other. The two brothers looked quite similar when they did this. In the mistress's face as well, there somehow seemed to be something shared with the faces of the other two.

"I have no recollection whatsoever." He grimaced as he answered, perhaps from the pain of his wounds. When he at last began to speak again, there was no strength in his voice; he was lying on his back and, moreover, taking care not to move suddenly. "I acknowledge the fact that a man may sound like he's lying if he says he can't remember a woman stabbing him. However, when I came here the day before yesterday, it was my first time to see O-Koma's face up close, to talk to her, or even to learn her name."

Masagorō smiled faintly. "No need to be so defensive. People do get stabbed through no fault of their own all the time."

Zenkichi smiled weakly. Perhaps feeling relief at that, the master and mistress both smiled as well, some of the tension draining out of their faces.

"Only—forgive me—why did you say again that you came from the home branch to stay here? Given the distance between Kanda and Honjo, I don't think it's because you got roaring drunk and couldn't find your way home."

Zenkichi blinked his eyes, looking put upon. The master of the Taira'ya, just like a helpful brother, stepped in for him. "I'm the second son of the Taira'ya's originating household. Zenkichi is the third. The firstborn son, who will succeed to the ownership, is a hard man—even though Zenkichi helps in the business, in terms of his social standing, he 'eats cold rice'—you know, he always comes in last. In many ways, staying there was like sleeping on a bed of nails for him. So—this was the day before yesterday—he finally reached the point where he couldn't take it anymore and got into a fight with my elder brother. Because of that, he came here."

"I see. Is that what happened, then?" Masagorō said smiling. "I understand perfectly. Well, I wonder if the local doctor is here? If so, there's nothing more for you to worry about. Just listen to what he tells you and don't overdo it. You'll be fine. Wounds like those should heal right up, cleanly and quickly."

Masagorō stood up to go.

"Well then, may I see O-Koma now?"

怪

O-Koma was locked up in the shed.

Her hands and legs were bound with tea towels. She was gagged with another towel that was tied behind her head. In the shed were many stacks of wooden crates and wicker trunks, and O-Koma's body had been squeezed into a gap between some of them; moreover, she was lying on her side, so that unless someone brought a lamp and stared closely at her, her face was obscured.

Though Masagorō called out to her, O-Koma did not reply. Even when he put a little strength into his voice to threaten her a little—"I'm carrying an iron truncheon," "Do you know what you've done?" and the like—she answered not a word. Thinking that maybe the towel had blocked her airway, Masagorō pulled her upright, but as he began to loosen the gag, her eyes suddenly flashed brightly, and she tried to bite his fingers right off, just like a rabid dog.

Masagorō laid O-Koma back down and left the shed for just a moment. His fingers were splattered with her saliva. Masagorō wiped them off with a paper napkin.

Standing guard in the entrance of the shed was a grim-looking man about the same age as Masagorō. He introduced himself as Seiji the clog maker. Although he was a family man who lived in a row house in Aioi-chō, he sometimes stayed overnight when there were rush orders. That was why he had been staying here last night as well. He said that he had worked late. "Good thing I was here too," he said, mincing no words. "The chief clerk's an old man, and Little Master doesn't have the guts."

"Did you ever work at the main shop?"

"Yeah, I did. When Little Master started up the new branch, the retired master asked me to go along, so I came here with him."

"This probably goes without saying, but this 'Little Master' of yours is the shop master here, correct?"

"That's right. 'Cause he's the second son."

"And the firstborn is at the main shop?"

"Right. He's the present shop master. The retired master is the father of my master, the young master, and Zenkichi." Seiji made a face that looked just a little bit proud. "By the time the old master took over the store from his predecessor, I was already a full-fledged craftsman, you see."

"Do you know much about O-Koma? I've heard that she works for the mistress and came here with her when the mistress married."

"Not a very friendly woman," Seiji spat back. "She comes from a family of medicine sellers. That bunch was always putting on airs. Even the maids there made fun of clog makers."

"But the Little Master and his wife seem to get along quite well, don't they?"

Seiji harrumphed. "They're just playing house."

"So besides them, who else is in this house?"

Seiji told him that the live-in workers consisted of another maid and one apprentice. There were also two craftsmen, albeit young ones, who lived off-grounds and would be arriving presently.

"Thank you very much. Would you mind continuing to stand guard here while I go and try to get the gist of what went on from them?"

"I'll do it, and it's an easy request." Seiji laughed confidently. "Even in the one-in-a-million case where O-Koma lashes out again, she won't catch me napping like Zenkichi. Leave it to me, boss!"

怪

It took only half an hour for Masagorō to make the rounds and listen to everyone else's versions of the story. He also inspected the knife that O-Koma had used on Zenkichi. It was a vegetable knife, taken from the kitchen, and it was said that just last night O-Koma had been using it to slice onions. Indeed, the fact that it was a vegetable knife might well be why Zenkichi's wounds were as light as they were.

However, that didn't mean Masagorō had actually figured anything out.

O-Koma, everyone said, was a serious, hardworking woman.

They said she was a chaste woman who had never once been involved in any kind of man trouble. Zenkichi had made social calls twice before, but the night before last had been the first time he had ever come over to stay the night. Given that, there shouldn't have been any chance that he and O-Koma were romantically involved. This case had everyone's head turned.

Masagorō knew enough to understand that when listening to people living under the same roof and working together to make ends meet, one had to take what they said with a pinch of salt. It was possible that they all might be covering for Zenkichi. Perhaps he had laid salacious hands on O-Koma, hurt her, angered her, and been recompensed by her. That was the most obvious scenario.

But Masagorō had been doing this for twenty years now, and his thief-taker's intuition was whispering in his ear. *No, the Taira'ya people aren't lying, nobody's covering for Zenkichi, and everyone really is wide-eyed in shock and dismay over what O-Koma did.* Even things that didn't appear to be true sometimes turned out to be, and it was the way of the world that even events that didn't fit a narrative happened when they happened.

The doctor who had come running over from Kanda Ta-chō carefully dressed Zenkichi's wounds and gave assurances that there was nothing to worry about. Masagorō waited for him to finish, then approached him saying that he had something he needed to talk about.

The doctor was of about the same age and build as Minosuke the chief clerk but had a natural speaking voice that was most unsuited to the discussion of confidential matters—it was as loud as the crack of a horsewhip.

Masagorō explained that something had seemed wrong with O-Koma, who was shut away in the shed, and that she had tried to bite his fingers.

"Doctor, I was wondering if we might be able to have you take a quick look at O-Koma."

"Thief-taker Masagorō, you called yourself? What do you think it might be? Hydrophobia?"

Masagorō cringed at the loud voice. He'd be lucky if the entire Taira'ya household hadn't leapt up in astonishment—they had no doubt pricked up their ears at the doctor and thief-taker's whisperings to each other.

"That's just what I was thinking, Doctor. You get hydrophobia from dog bites, right? Then you froth at the mouth like a dog and start trying to bite everyone yourself. It's called 'hydrophobia' because you become frightened of water, right?"

The doctor tilted his unshaven head, full of salt-and-pepper hair, and said again in a loud voice, "At any rate, I'll examine O-Koma. If there are any bite marks left, that's a warning sign. If I find any, I'll show her a pail of water and see how she reacts."

Masagorō walked with the doctor to the shed, when in a state of utter distress, the master, the mistress, Minosuke, and the others came and grabbed hold of them, asking with faces on the verge of tears if O-Koma had been stricken by some terrible disease, if it had been transmitted to Zenichi, and if they were safe themselves.

The loud-voiced doctor, perhaps accustomed to such confusion being spread by his habitual bellowing, was not the least bit perturbed. He gave O-Koma a leisurely examination. To be on the safe side, he left the gag in place, but so as to give her a thorough once over, he undid the bindings on her hands and feet. O-Koma was surprisingly easy to handle and didn't become violent at all. Now that Masagorō looked closer, weren't her eyes looking a lot calmer now than when she had tried to bite him earlier?

"There are no marks on her body," the doctor said, glancing across the crowd of Taira'ya people hanging on to the sliding door in the entrance of the shed. "During the last ten or twenty days, have any of you noticed a stray dog roaming around the neighborhood? Or a sick dog? Or a dead dog? Nobody's spotted a dog behaving unusually, have they?"

No one had. Everyone was looking at one another and shaking their heads.

The doctor put his hands on his knees, made a grave face as though he were about to preach a sermon, then looked down at O-Koma. At last he spoke to her in his thunderous voice, "Now, see here. You promise to be good?"

O-Koma stared up at the doctor with huge eyes, the gag still in her mouth.

"You may be ill, so I want to examine you further. Do you understand?"

"Mmm-mmm," O-Koma said as best she could, nodding. A single thread of saliva dangled from the corner of her mouth, which was stretched tightly to the right and left because of the towel.

"All right, then. I'm going to remove the gag now."

The doctor put his hand around to the back of O-Koma's head and untied the knot.

Masagorō braced himself. Even back by the sliding door, everyone swallowed.

O-Koma spat the towel out of her mouth and coughed violently. Then she looked up and looked around.

And then she started crying feebly.

The doctor, his stern expression unchanged, turned slightly back toward Masagorō. "We can't take this young lady out of here, can we?"

Masagorō looked at the doctor's expression, then leaned forward toward O-Koma. "O-Koma," he said, "do you know what you did?"

O-Koma kept on crying. Tears ran down her plump cheeks. Seeing her like this, she actually appeared quite beautiful.

"You attacked and wounded Zenkichi, of your master's family. Given your station of housemaid, you won't get off with anything less than the public display of your head on the prison gate. But be that as it may, you might have your own side of this story to tell. And because of that, the master and mistress of the Taira'ya sent for me, Masagorō the private thief-taker, in great haste, asking if there was some way to hide this from the authorities—asking if it was somehow possible to avoid sending you out of the Taira'ya with a noose around your neck. Your master and mistress love you like parents do their children. Do you understand that?"

O-Koma ceased from sobbing and wiped her face with her hands. But she didn't say anything.

"The doctor here thinks you might have a serious disease and is going to examine you further. If you're ill, we can't exactly hand you over to the constable. So he says he'll check you over now. Understand? Do as he tells you, humbly and without resistance. If you don't, you'll be tied up again and, this time, dragged off to the constable for real."

O-Koma looked up at him with a long, smooth motion of her head. Although she wasn't an especially long-necked girl, at just that moment, it somehow looked to Masagorō as though a serpent had raised its head.

"Thief-taker," O-Koma said in a flat tone of voice.

Masagorō looked into her eyes and for an instant was nearly pulled into them. Those black eyes flashed like shallow pools reflecting the sun.

"Masagorō," O-Koma called once more. Then, in a voice as crisp and clear as if she were reading it aloud, she said, *"You killed somebody once, didn't you?"*

Everyone present froze.

O-Koma burst out in a cackling laugh. It was a distant kind of laugh, though, and as smoke rises to the ceiling, its pitch rapidly grew higher and higher until it became like a screeching shriek.

"Kyaaa!"

Along with that single cry, she exhaled what looked like some sort of white ash, opened her eyes wide, and collapsed to the floor with a heavy thump.

The doctor rushed forward and lifted her up, searching for a pulse. Then, with that same angry-looking expression on his face, he wordlessly shook his head. O-Koma had breathed her last.

怪

In the end, Masagorō decided to close the case as follows: O-Koma had died suddenly of hydrophobia, but before her death the disease got into her head and drove her mad, causing her to injure Zenkichi. Such an explanation would be unlikely to arouse suspicion among Edo's city administrators, but just to be on the safe side, it would probably be a good idea to make the rounds of the local constables' stations as well, urging them to greater strictness in the hunting of stray dogs. That way would appear most natural.

But though the case was closed, questions still lingered.

Had O-Koma . . . been sane?

And that white ash she had expelled just before she died—what on earth could that have been?

Was it a sign that O-Koma was infected with some mysterious disease?

And why had O-Koma said, "You killed somebody once," to Masagorō?

Of course, she was correct. Masagorō had killed somebody once. It happened when he was still young, long before anyone ever called him a thief-taker, back when he had lived his life in dissipation. If he had continued walking down that path, he would have surely long since vanished with the dew on the executioner's block. Among those who lived by their truncheons, there were people—besides Masagorō—who had pasts they couldn't speak of. Those who were trying to make up for their old transgressions with their lives since becoming thief-takers were desperate workers.

Masagorō himself had been like that. That was why, for a long time, he had forgotten that he was a murderer.

Once the people at the Taira'ya were satisfied that the incident was safely concluded, they seemed to care little about getting to the truth. Masagorō could hardly blame them. The doctor who had the loud voice and energy to spare considering his age said to Masagorō, "There's one thing *only* that bothers me: that white exhalation that O-Koma breathed out on the point of death—as pure a white as the ashes from a brazier." When he said this, he placed a special emphasis on the word *only*, as if to tacitly signal to Masagorō the pretense he was adopting: *I didn't hear anything about any murders.*

So Masagorō went along with him.

"Doctor, have you ever heard of a disease like that where you exhale such a breath right before you die?"

The doctor shook his head, tugging at a long eyebrow with his fingers. "Never," he said. "I have no idea what that was. How about you?"

"If you don't know, there's no way I would."

"That white breath, it looked like brazier ashes, didn't it?"

"Yes, I thought so too. I wonder if you can get sick in the lungs from breathing in ashes from a brazier?"

Sullenly, the doctor said that he'd never heard of such a thing, but he ended up calling for the maid who had been living in the same room as O-Koma and asking her whether a brazier had been in use in that room.

The maid was younger than O-Koma and clearly grieving for one who had been like an elder sister to her. With an expression that might collapse back into tears at any moment, her answers were vague and incoherent.

Seeing this avenue lead nowhere, the doctor and Masagorō tried asking the lady of the house if she had permitted O-Koma's use of a brazier in the maids' room.

Leaping to the wrong conclusion, the mistress became upset and asked if she had been wrong to do so.

"No, it's not a bad thing. It's just that usually merchants don't let their workers use braziers in the house."

"I . . . that's true, but . . . still, the maids must get cold this time of year too, I think."

She explained that she had been allowing fire in the maids' room only during midwinter, provided they bought the braziers themselves and paid for the cost of charcoal from their wages.

"Would it be possible for us to take a quick look at O-Koma's brazier?"

The brazier that the mistress brought out of the maids' room was a small porcelain hand-warmer about a foot in diameter, which, given the fine cracks in its surface here and there, had seen many years of service. The white ashes had been neatly leveled out, burying the cinders.

"Now that you mention it . . ." the younger maid said suddenly, watching Masagorō and the doctor as they examined the brazier, "Miss O-Koma had recently started pouring water into it to make the ashes dance, then she'd sit watching them . . ."

Masagorō exchanged a glance with the doctor.

"What did you say?" he asked.

The young maid shrunk back in terror.

"Don't be afraid," he said. "I'm not scolding you. You're saying O-Koma was making ash *kaguras*—little dancing tendrils of smoke—in this brazier and staring into them?"

"She'd start a fire and stir the coals until they were piping hot, then go to the kitchen to fill a cup with water," the maid said. "Then she'd bring it back to the room and pour it into the brazier."

And then a cloud of steam and ashes would erupt from the bowl, dancing in the air as though before a Shinto shrine . . . dancing a serpentine *kagura* dance.

"Then she would stare into it, not moving a muscle." The young maid fell silent briefly, then perhaps feeling that her words had been inadequate, added, "It looked just like she was in a staring contest with somebody."

Masagorō remembered his own sight of O-Koma's face up close. *Like she was in a staring contest.*

He felt an icy shiver, as though cold water had suddenly been poured over him.

"That's quite a waste of charcoal, isn't it?" the doctor said. "Did you ever ask her why she did that?"

"No, sir."

"But you must have thought it was a strange thing to do."

"I did . . . but I only saw her doing it twice, and both times were at night." Yet again, the maid looked like she was on the verge of tears. "I was thinking, 'We only just got permission to have a fire, so we can't afford even the slightest chance of an accident. So maybe that's why she's pouring in water—to put out the coals.'"

But wouldn't it ruin the charcoal to pour water on it every time?

Masagorō slowly drew near to the brazier and peered inside. It smelled of ashes. They tickled his nose.

"About these ashes . . . ?"

"They're the same as what we use throughout the house," replied the mistress, twisting her fingers with unease. "Should we not use these ashes? Did they make her sick?"

"No, it isn't that at all," the doctor said right away. "Please don't worry over that."

"But . . . shouldn't we use a different kind? Even if only in Zenkichi's room? An injured man's body might be affected by things that wouldn't normally bother him."

"This brazier, did O-Koma buy it and bring it here?"

"Yes, I'm certain she did."

Most likely, she had bought it from a secondhand shop somewhere.

"When did she start using it? Do you have any idea?"

"I don't really know." The mistress looked over at the young maid. The maid just looked down at the floor.

"Is that so? Ah, me! Honestly, this has been a truly terrible tragedy." Masagorō decided it was time to bring this interview to a close. "I promise not to worry you any further over this matter. However, Mistress, if it's all right with you, might I hold on to this brazier for a short while?"

The mistress of the house practically leapt at the chance to get rid of it. "Yes! Please do! Please do! You'd be more than welcome to!"

Masagorō borrowed a cloth wrap, carefully folded it around the brazier, and took it with him. He promised the doctor that he would use it at his house for a while to see if anything happened.

"I don't think this had anything to do with the brazier or the ashes; at any rate, I've never seen or heard of any disease like that. Still—"

Pulling at his long eyebrow, the doctor gave him a rather frightening look. "Use it in a place where the ventilation is as good as possible. All right?"

怪

It happened that night.

Masagorō told his wife all about what had happened, and when all his subordinates in the house were fast asleep, he set the brazier in a room and lit a fire inside it.

By day, this was the room Masagorō used to receive visitors in his role as a thief-taker. It had a porch facing a tidy garden, as well as a finely made family Shinto altar. His wife being a woman of considerably strong nerve—were she not, she could never have made a home with Masagorō—did not wear a frightened expression, exactly, but she did light a bright votive candle on the Shinto altar and brought in a paper-covered lamp stand as well as other lamps that had been in use elsewhere, lighting three of them and making the room just a little *too* bright. Then she opened wide the sliding screens facing the porch, causing Masagorō to sneeze. The ventilation was now *too* good.

Once he had a fire going in the brazier, Masagorō picked up an iron kettle that he had started heating in the larger, rectangular brazier used to warm the room.

"All right now, cover your nose and mouth so you don't breathe in any ashes."

His wife covered half of her face with her sleeve and nodded. "You do the same," she said. "Hold your breath."

Masagorō said, "All right," and then spilled a torrent of hot water from the spout into O-Koma's brazier. The water sizzled on the coals as the ash kagura surged upward.

Masagorō watched intently. His wife watched intently. In Masagorō's mind, O-Koma's voice came back vividly, echoing as it said,

"*You killed somebody once, didn't you?*"

The ash kagura, a vaguely rounded shape, like the head of the fabled sea monster *umibōzu*, unraveling and losing its shape right away, drifted toward the night air that lay beyond the porch and disappeared.

"Is that all?" Masagorō's wife murmured. There was a hint of disappointment in her voice. "That's just an ordinary ash kagura, isn't it? What's going on here?"

"I don't know," said Masagorō. Even so, he continued to grip the handle of the iron kettle for a little while longer, in the same frame of mind as when he brandished his truncheon. At last, feeling as though he had awakened from a drunken haze, he set it back down on the room's main brazier.

His wife burst out laughing.

Carried along with her, Masagorō also laughed out loud.

All this buildup over nothing. It was just an ordinary brazier. Masagorō had been overthinking things a bit, it seemed.

"I'm not sure I understand, but I don't think this brazier's to blame."

Masagorō nodded in agreement.

Come to think of it, even the doctor had said it wasn't the brazier or the ashes that were to blame, hadn't he? It wasn't even clear how much truth there had been to the story about O-Koma's staring into the ash kagura—it might well have been the observer's imagination running away with her. That maid was still just a child, after all.

"Shall I warm up a bottle of saké, dear?"

"Yeah, that sounds really nice."

Masagorō was in a gentle mood now. His wife of many years wasn't as young as she used to be, but she was a good woman. From girlhood, she had had a highly virtuous nature, such that Masagorō, had he not mended the mistaken ways of his youth, could have never had a home with her like this—far from that, they might never have even passed on the street.

"It just so happens that I got some good *shiokara* from the Kazusa'ya." Masagorō's wife stood up hurriedly. "It's the kind you like, with *kōji* in it—"

And that was when it happened.

Masagorō's wife was turning toward the cupboard and had her back facing the porch, so she didn't notice anything at all. She couldn't have seen. Masagorō believed and prayed that it was so. *It was only for an instant, so I have to have been the only one who saw it.*

It.

Along the porch beyond the still-open screens, along the boundary of the light from the lamps shining brightly in the room and the darkness of a pitch-black winter's night, a barefoot woman with wild hair stormed past the entrance, moving swiftly from the side on which Masagorō sat to the other side. Her white kimono, too small for her, bared her skinny shins. He knew not where she had come from on his side of the entrance, nor where she had gone to on the far side. He hadn't the slightest idea. And yet, Masagorō was certain that she had walked past this room along his porch, a confidence evident in her footsteps that she knew exactly where she was going. She had been walking fast, not sparing even a sidelong glance, so he had only gotten a glimpse of her. He hadn't seen her face. In this, he was fortunate.

Still, she had been dreadfully thin. Emaciated . . . almost skeletal. Yet even so, her footsteps had been so terribly swift.

And for some reason, after she passed by, a dry, grainy scent like that of brazier ashes hung in the air.

"Dear? Is something the matter?"

But even when his wife spoke to him, Masagorō couldn't answer.

"What's the matter, dear? You look like you've seen a—"

怪

Making his way in the world as a thief-taker, Masagorō found that on occasion items would fall into his hands that were difficult to dispose of properly. A knife that had been used to stab someone. A rope someone had hanged himself with.

At such times, Masagorō made it a point to remember Shōhōji Temple in Oshiagemura, where he shared a long acquaintance with the chief priest. This man, almost big enough to be a sumo wrestler, actually had some old tattoos on his body, which nobody knew about save the man himself and Masagorō.

Masagorō took O-Koma's brazier to him.

The chief priest didn't bat an eyelash while listening to Masagorō's story. With a sleepy-looking countenance, he just said, "Well, that kind of thing does happen.

"We'll give the brazier a proper memorial service, and then you won't need to worry, no matter what it was that got into it."

What was it that had taken hold of O-Koma? And how had the thing possessing her known that Masagorō was a murderer?

The chief priest gave Masagorō a vicious smile when he asked these questions. "A murderer looks like a murderer," the chief priest said, only pretending to know nothing. "And that's just what you look like. That's all it was."

Because the Taira'ya wanted the case surrounding O-Koma to stay within the family, they seemed to feel a great debt of gratitude toward Masagorō. In the box of sweets that had arrived several days afterward, a sum of money had been concealed inside that was more than double what Masagorō was expecting. Of course, much of it had passed right through his hands to go to Shōhōji Temple instead, but still.

As for Zenkichi's injuries, they healed in no time. He was a truly honest and sincere man, and the story that he had quarreled with his eldest brother that day, fled the main shop, ended up in Kiryū-chō, and made no salacious advances whatsoever on the maid was proven to be true.

O-Koma had been without family, so the Taira'ya buried her quickly. Afterward, there were no further disturbances there, and the young master and mistress, Minosuke, Seiji, and the young maid all went back to their work as before.

About ten days passed, and a message arrived from Shōhōji, informing Masagorō that the disposal of the brazier had been completed. It was written in a fine, dignified script, and at the end of this letter, set down in writing by the chief priest himself, was a postscript saying that the young monks had been in an uproar after observing white puffs of some substance flying up from that brazier just after nightfall and floating around the main temple building and the kitchen.

Also, this had happened only once, but late one night, the chief priest himself had apparently spied the figure of a woman standing perfectly still by the side of that brazier, her back turned toward him. Bedraggled hair, a kimono that was too small for her, all skin and bones, as thin as a scarecrow. He had seen her, but he hadn't seen her face. It didn't really matter, though, he said, and ended the letter.

Masagorō burned the letter in the big brazier in his reception room. Its ashes he ground into powder and threw down the hole in the outhouse. If it was dealt with, then that was enough for him. There was no need ever to think about it again.

In any case, it was still midwinter, and for a while yet, he couldn't do without a brazier.

IX
The Mussel Mound

Before heading over to the Ogawa'ya workers' villa in Mukōjima, Yonesuke made first for Asakusa-Okura, where he stopped in at the establishment of a certain fishmonger with whom he was familiar. The day before yesterday, he had asked the fishmonger to purchase Okura mussels for him to pick up today.

True to his word, the fishmonger showed him a basket of woven bamboo filled with freshwater mussels. These he then transferred to a small pot and told him there was fresh water inside, which would make them spit out the sand in their shells as he carried them along.

"You better watch your step, 'Mr. Rice,'" he added, using a nickname based on the first kanji of Yonesuke's name. "If you fall down and they spill out all over the road, you'll be out quite a bit of money."

"Yeah, I know," Yonesuke assured him as he handed over the money.

Okura mussels were harvested from a row of eight berths dug into the banks of the Sumida River at Asakusa-Okura. Every day, ships loaded with sacks of rice bound for the shogunate's Okura storage facility would dock there, and as these sacks were being off-loaded and carried away to Okura, grains of rice would often spill out and fall into the water. Because the mussels below the waterline grew to maturity eating that rice, they had a better flavor than those found elsewhere.

For that reason alone their price was high—usually about five times the price of ordinary mussels. That was how much Yonesuke paid to the fishmonger. Being as there was a limit on how many could be taken in a single day, it was possible for the price to climb even higher at times when customers wanted them badly enough. So today, it seemed that Yonesuke was in luck.

"A pleasure as always," the stern-faced fishmonger said pleasantly. "But today isn't the anniversary of your father's passing, is it? Are you headed off on an errand somewhere?"

Yonesuke nodded. "There's an old man who played *go* with my father for many years, but about six months back he got sick and is now bedridden. His age being what it is, his mind's getting a little weak too. So I thought I'd go check on him in my father's place."

"Is that so? Checking on your father's go partner, eh? You're a loyal son after all, aren't you, Mr. Rice!"

"Oh no, not at all," Yonesuke said with a laugh, thinking, *No, if I'd truly been some paragon of filial piety, I would've been there when my mother died too, and I would've taken over the employment agency like I was supposed to before my old man collapsed and became an invalid.* "The kanji for 'filial piety' do not describe the likes of me. It's just that, according to the property manager, the old man was a tremendous help to my father. He didn't have any other pastime, but if nothing else, he was uncommonly good at go. A very patient opponent whenever he'd get serious about winning. Given his current state, I think even my dad must be worried about him from the other world."

"Is that so? Well, take care of yourself, then," the fishmonger repeated once more as he saw Yonesuke out of the store. The weather outside was nice, but a cold wind was blowing from across the river. Yonesuke sneezed twice as he was walking.

It had been just five years since the sudden death of his father, when he had inherited the business license and office of the employment agency, located on land out past Yanagibashi, which the government had provided in exchange for previously confiscated property. Yonesuke was nearly forty years of age, and like his father he generally made a good impression on people. When he wasn't careful, he could even be mistaken for a man in his fifties.

Yonesuke's late father had been a stubborn old coot who was skilled at finding fault in others and giving them a piece of his mind. He was also an excellent judge of character, exact in his finances, and good at remembering things—just the sort of man suited to running an employment agency. Yonesuke, however, had never gotten on well with him and had run away from home at fifteen. He had lived by hiring himself out as a day laborer and as a footman to various samurai, and bouncing around from job to job. While living as he pleased, he had slipped into his thirties. Five years ago, his father had collapsed. Had it not been for the efforts of his good friend the caretaker in Yanagibashi to somehow to locate his only son and get him to see his father before the end, Yonesuke would have probably not even known of his father's passing.

Once the caretaker had talked him into it, he had returned home to find his mother already dead and his father no longer able to even speak. Yonesuke, now old enough to know better, had of course been ashamed of his past selfishness. And then five days after his return—after his father had breathed his last without having once opened his eyes or spoken with him—Yonesuke had approached the caretaker himself wondering if it might be possible for him to succeed to his father's agency.

Yonesuke learned by watching others, though early on, he was frequently bewildered. His father had been a trusted and well-liked employment agent, but Yonesuke had, after all, been away from home for a very long time and was an unknown quantity to the people around him. When going out to meet his father's clients, he would show up out of the blue and declare, "I'm his son, and I'll be taking over for him." "Oh, is that so?" the people at these shops would say, hardly acknowledging him as such.

Yonesuke was generally lacking in perseverance, and if the caretaker—his late father's equal when it came to pointing out his mistakes and keeping a sharp eye on him—hadn't stuck to him like glue, he might have just given it all up and run away.

Yonesuke had learned from the caretaker of his late father's taste for mussel soup. The only luxury he'd allowed himself had been Okura mussels a few times each year. He had learned as well that Matsubei, the head clerk of the West Nihonbashi kimono-maker Ogawa'ya, had become his friend through playing go. In the space of about two years, Yonesuke at last became settled in the employee-placement business, so during the equinoctial weeks, during Obon, and on the anniversary of his father's death, Yonesuke would offer his father's spirit a bowl of soup—soup containing a lavish serving of Okura mussels. Even the caretaker, however, couldn't remember what his mother's favorite food had been. She had died of cholera ten years before his father, so this was hardly surprising. Not knowing what else to do, Yonesuke merely offered her flowers on the family altar.

Yonesuke had first met Matsubei, the head clerk of the Ogawa'ya, on the occasion of his father's modest funeral. The man hadn't spoken of their go matches himself, but Yonesuke heard about them from the caretaker afterward, and after his father's forty-nine days were completed, he went to visit the old man and tried to interest him in a game. Matsubei, however, just shook his head sadly and made a weak-willed excuse. "I don't think I'll ever meet a go player as good as your dad again, so I think I'll just give up playing." This was dreary to excess. Yonesuke found himself wondering if his father really had gotten along all that well with the man.

It had been ten days ago that he heard that Matsubei had

become bedridden. O-Mon, the chief housekeeper who nearly thirty years ago had gone to work at the Ogawa'ya thanks to the good offices of Yonesuke's father, came on an errand to the office in Yanagibashi and told him about it.

"The doctor says that it's dropsy, you see. It's no wonder his breathing is so difficult."

"Did it just recently get bad?"

"This past year he's stopped climbing up and down staircases. Said his chest hurts. Even before he was bedridden, he'd complain of chest pains, like he was being crushed under a giant boulder."

"Ah, that won't do . . ."

"The master was also worried, so right away he moved him to the villa in Mukōjima. But, Mr. Rice, it's not time yet for the seasonal shift change, and no matter who comes, he won't be able to do everything that the chief clerk did. At any rate we've always been shorthanded, so we're really in a bind. If you would, we'd like you to find us one new worker as quickly as you can."

"That shouldn't be a problem, but can no one come over from your parent shop?"

He asked this because the Ogawa'ya had been created as a branch house of the Kawadzu'ya, a kimono wholesaler in Tōri Block Two, from which it had split off. That was where the shop's name came from as well.

"Well . . . the chief clerks at the main house weren't on good terms with Matsu. Competiton and all that." O-Mon's mouth twisted a bit, as though amused. "So the master says if we were to call someone from the parent shop house over to fill the gap, Matsu wouldn't be able to settle down enough to sleep."

"Is that so? Well in that case, I'll see what I can do right away," Yonesuke assured her. He had two or three ideas already.

As she was leaving, O-Mon said a rather kind thing, belying her stern-looking facial features. "Matsu seems awfully lonely, so if you wouldn't mind, could you go over and pay him a visit?"

"If I wouldn't be getting in the way of his treatment, of course I'll go."

"You won't be in the way at all," O-Mon said with a shake of her large head. "Things don't look very good for him, so please see him while you can. I can feel the years too. It's somehow depressing, isn't it? I've known Matsu for a long, long time."

Yonesuke had no words with which to cheer O-Mon. All he could do was say he'd be sure to go and pay the man a visit.

Fortunately, a worker was found right away to fill the gap. His name was Rokutarō, a young man in his early twenties living in a row house in Kaya-chō. At the end of the prior month, a fire had broken out at the clothing reseller in Lower Ushigome where he had worked since the age of ten. The master and mistress had both died, and the shop had burned to the ground. Though he was presently staying with an acquaintance at the Fukagawa row house, he was in truly dire straits. He had lost his working papers in the fire, and it was thanks to the row house caretaker's introduction that he came to see Yonesuke at his office. He was interested and enthusiastic right from the start, saying, "If it's a kimono shop, then I definitely want to work there." He was clear and lucid, tactful, and carried himself gracefully—a young man well suited to the merchant's trade. Upon their first meeting, the people at the Ogawa'ya also seemed to take to him right away, so the talks progressed rapidly and an agreement was soon reached.

Yonesuke felt greatly relieved. He had spent several days stewing in his impatience to set aside some time to go and visit Matsubei. And now today, he was at last able to set out.

The villa in Mukōjima, strictly speaking, did not belong to the Ogawa'ya. Its parent shop, the Kawadzu'ya, had built it in order to house workers. Because the Kawadzu'ya was the third largest shop in Nihonbashi after the Shiroki'ya and the Echigo'ya, the dormitory was a splendid building. Although it was located in the middle of Edo, Mukōjima had a rustic atmosphere. It was a very quiet, relaxed area with many plots of land containing rice paddies or temples. Nothing crossed Yonesuke's path on the way there except the songs of nightingales that could occasionally be heard from the forest.

When he arrived at the villa, a handmaid came out immediately. Once she learned who Yonesuke was, she said, "Oh, I heard from O-Mon you'd be coming."

"How is Matsubei doing?"

"He's gotten very weak, but this morning he finished his rice gruel. He's awake now, so I'll show you right in."

"I'm sorry for the trouble. Oh, these are for him . . ." Yonesuke said, getting a bit tongue-tied. He held out the mussels, container and all.

The handmaid received them gladly. "They say mussel soup is good for dropsy, don't they?"

Matsubei was resting in a bright six-mat room facing a wide field. Although he had lost a lot of weight and his color was not good at all, he recognized Yonesuke right away and conscientiously tried to get up. Yonesuke tried to stop him, but he wouldn't settle down until the girl finally helped him to sit up in his futon and draped a padded robe around his shoulders.

"Looks like I can't even get out of bed by myself. It's all over now." He smiled painfully as he said this; his cheeks were sunken from loss of weight and his breathing sounded hurried and painful.

"You always hope you'll go before it drags out and you become a nuisance to everyone."

Yonesuke, trying to make him feel better, moved on to other topics and tried talking about them, but none of his stories would last very long, and silence alone would dominate the room. At such times, there was only the echo of water from the field's irrigation channel outside.

"Quiet around here, isn't it?"

Despite the quiet, Yonesuke was doing his best, trying hard

to lighten the conversation. "If my old man had been able to re-cuperate in a quiet place with clear water like this, I'm sure he would've gotten better."

Matsubei, who thus far had been frowning as though lost in thought, glanced up suddenly at the corners of the room and out the window, like someone sneaking a look at his surroundings. The girl who had shown Yonesuke in was long gone by this point, and insofar as it was possible to see, not even a plowman's shadow could be discerned out in the field. Matsubei had a look in his eyes as though he were confirming that.

"Listen, Mr. Rice. What you were saying just now reminded me of your father's last moments."

Yonesuke interrupted, saying, "Please don't remember such sad times."

"No, no, I'm not trying to cheer you up by telling gloomy stories." Matsubei waved around an arm that had lost its flesh and become little more than bone. "However, there is something I'd like to confirm. It was after your father became bedridden that you came back, so in the end you didn't get to have a single word of conversation with him—is that right?"

Yonesuke shrugged his shoulders. "That's right. We didn't get to talk at all. He was asleep the whole time, it seemed . . . And that's how he died."

Matsubei folded arms like dried trees in front of his thin chest and rumbled out a long *hmmmm*. "In that case, you didn't hear a thing from your old man, did you? And naturally, he wouldn't have known that you would come back. So since he died having no idea that you were going to take over his office, he wouldn't have had any reason to tell you." He was mumbling to himself.

Yonesuke hadn't the faintest idea what he was going on about, but it sounded like something mysterious. "Matsubei, was there something that I should've heard about from my father?"

Matsubei, by way of answer, let out another long *hmmmmm*.

"If there's something I need to know, would you know what it is?"

Blinking his eyes slowly, Matsubei looked at Yonesuke's face. In the corners of his eyes was a very slight wetness, but one probably due to his illness. Being stuck in bed all the time was enough to make anyone's eyes a bit bleary.

"I haven't gone around Edo asking all the fathers at placement agencies," Matsubei muttered, "and I haven't checked with all the head clerks in Edo either."

"Um . . ." Yonesuke said, not sure how to respond to this declaration.

"But even so," said Matsubei, pulling at his chin with bony fingers, "there's still that business with Rokutarō . . ."

Yonesuke leaned forward on his knees. "Rokutarō? You mean that workman I found to fill in for you?"

Matsubei nodded his emaciated head. "That's right. That Rokutarō."

"Has there been some sort of problem with him?"

"Nah, he's a fine man. Even came here to pay his respects. He made a big fuss over me."

Although he was praising the man, Matsubei spoke like somebody forcing himself to swallow something nasty.

"He'll be a great help in the shop," he continued. "It's the Ogawa'ya's policy—and the main store's too—not to be feeding extra mouths, so the workers always need to bear that in mind and give it their all. But Rokutarō'll be all right."

"To be talking about him like that, Matsubei, you sure don't sound very happy." So saying, Yonesuke was thinking in the back of his mind, *Matsubei must really be down about this.* Compared with Matsubei's own weakening, disease-ravaged body, Rokutarō was young, full of energy, his whole life still ahead of him. The very thought of the man must have put Matsubei in mind of a boil or abscess, and moreover, the old man likely thought his replacement cheeky to boot. The truth of his feelings seeped into the tone of his voice.

Rokutarō shouldn't have come here to pay respects. That was a mistake. Yonesuke was wondering when he had come and who had brought him here, when Matsubei spoke. "It's not that I really have anything against him," he said, rubbing at the corner of his eye sadly. "So maybe it's best if I don't tell you."

Again, Yonesuke had no idea what the old man was talking about. "What's this all about, Matsubei?"

Matsubei let out a heavy sigh that whistled in his lungs like a cold winter wind in the trees. "But why don't I tell you anyway? If your old man had had the chance, I'm sure he would've told you."

Matsubei straightened his back as well as he was able and turned to look at Yonesuke. "Mr. Rice, you're the proprietor of the agency. You are the agent." His formal tone of voice was unintentionally funny, but Yonesuke just answered "yes" and didn't crack a smile.

"How long has it been since you took over?"

"It's been five years, but—"

"Five years? Well then, you probably haven't had a chance to notice yet."

Matsubei put one hand to his forehead. Yonesuke resisted the urge to hurry him by saying, *Notice what?*

"At the outset, I came to the main store as an apprentice, and then came here with the head clerk at the time of the split. It's been thirty years, and I've served this shop all along," Matsubei said, still holding his forehead. "I also got to know your dad exactly thirty years ago, just after the founding of the Ogawa'ya. Because they needed to increase the number of workers, you see?"

"Was this also the time when you two started playing go together?" Yonesuke asked with a hint of a smile. He wanted to relax Matsubei's strained expression.

Matsubei didn't smile, however. "That's right. That was actually the reason we started, originally."

"What was?"

"Like I'm tellin' you, there were all kinds of things we wanted to talk about. We'd only just met."

It had happened after they had played a match and were sitting with the board between them. Matsubei had said to his opponent, "You really didn't seem to have your heart in it today."

Indeed, Yonesuke's father had been using nothing but oddball strategies.

"I said that, and then your old man got this clouded look on his face and blurted out, 'They're just so creepy, you know?'"

The two men had been talking about how the employment agency had been visited again and again by the same personages.

"Of course, even if we find jobs for them, that doesn't mean they'll keep at it for long. I'm not talking about them coming back to the agency often. I'm talking about the same person with the same face coming back every ten years or so, but with a completely different name and an entirely different work history."

Twenty years ago, he said, they had placed a young girl in a certain shop, and then ten years afterward, she had shown up again looking exactly the same as before, once again asking them to find her a place to work. However, the name was different and so was the birthplace. "I kept thinking that it was really strange, but I finally wrote it off as my mind playing tricks on me and found her a job. Then presently, I forgot all about her."

"Exactly ten years later, though, that same girl came again with a completely different name. 'I'm looking for a job,' she said. Even when we asked her, 'Didn't you come here ten years ago, and twenty years ago as well?' we were completely flummoxed. If it was the same person, she wasn't aging at all. That's why we thought it must just be an accidental resemblance to someone else. However . . ."

"However?" Yonesuke said leaning forward, his curiosity engaged.

"Your father apparently asked around quietly among other

people in the business to see if they had ever had a similar experience. It turned out that out of ten proprietors of placement agencies, just one man had had the same thing happen."

Regardless of age, regardless of form, Matsubei explained, these people, different only in name and work history, would return to that agency at certain fixed intervals to ask for help finding jobs.

"The master of that agency was older than your father, and when he was asked, he not only said he had had such experiences himself, but that his father—who had also worked in the family trade—had told him that he too had had the same thing happen. And that's when he admonished him."

There are people like this in the world, the proprietor had said. They don't age, they don't get sick, and they don't ever die. After they've been in the same place for a long time, though, that'll be noticed, and the people around them will start looking at them suspiciously. That's why every ten years at the most they had to change jobs. And why they would come to a placement agency. It takes a bit of effort to find a well-run placement agency, so they would come again and again to a place where they knew they could ask once and rest assured that they'd get a good place. They were the same way about workplaces. If one of them remembered being comfortable in the shop where he had worked for just eight years thirty years prior, he would go there to work again thirty years later, provided the place was still in business. If there was a branch shop, that would be fine too. After the passage of thirty years, not many people would remember the face of a maid or manservant who had quit, so there was really nothing to worry about. The circumstances were the same at the agencies too—because placement agents searched for workplaces for many young people, the ageless felt secure, thinking that nobody would remember their faces.

"However, people who become masters at placement agencies remember faces better than you'd expect," Matsubei continued slowly. "Even if their visits are ten years apart, if the same face shows up two or three times, it'll be noticed."

But even if you recognize them, you have to pretend that you don't. That was what Yonesuke's father had apparently been told.

"Folks like that, they aren't doing anything wrong. They just don't die, and they don't get old. That's all. So they live in hiding. They take care not to stand out. Because they could get mistreated and chased all over the place just for that."

Matsubei really knew the story well. He didn't stumble over his words at all.

"Your father was the one who told me about all this. He smiled just a little and told me, 'It's not that they're doing any harm; it's just a little creepy.' I was really shocked to hear this, because during the long years I'd spent working at first the Kawadzu'ya and later the Ogawa'ya, I had had something similar happen to me."

When Matsubei had been serving as an apprentice, there had been a young journeyman to whom the master was rather partial. He was a little fellow, but handsome, and the master's daughter had adored him. It was perhaps because of that that he was presently discharged and disappeared from the shop.

About twenty years afterward, when Matsubei was working as chief clerk for the branch store Ogawa'ya, the journeyman he had met during his apprenticeship at the Kawadzu'ya came there as a workman. He was the same age and had the same face as when he had been at the Kawadzu'ya. His name and his birthplace, however, were entirely different.

The only one who noticed was Matsubei, but because the resemblance was perhaps purely coincidental, he had said nothing about it. However, one day he had an opportunity to be alone with that man, so he said to him, "Back when I was a kid, I knew a journeyman who looked just like you." The other man had smiled and told him that he had no relatives in Edo. From that day forward, however, he had started to avoid Matsubei. And then after working for about five years, he quit. What the reason for that was, Matsubei didn't know. The master thought it was a real shame.

"But that same man, ten years later, showed up again, this time at the Kawadzu'ya once more. The name was different and his birthplace was different too. The master's daughter there, who long ago had taken a shine to the fellow, was now old enough that put together they looked like mother and son."

But the daughter of the Kawadzu'ya's master—she had long since married into another household and become a shop mistress herself—still remembered the face of her old sweetheart. It had been a terrible shock to her when a man who had the same face and form came back into her life.

"Because of that, well . . . she came very close to getting sent back from the home she had married into." Matsubei's lips twisted as though the words were hard to say.

"What happened to the man?"

"About the time when the daughter was approached with talk of divorce, he ran off. Nobody knows where he went."

"Matsubei . . ." Yonesuke aligned his knees, sat up straight, and looked deep into the old man's eyes. "I'm asking this just in case—you're not just pulling my leg about this, are you?"

"What reason would I have to lie to you?" Matsubei asked. His shoulders dropped, as though from exhaustion. "This isn't just some ghost story."

"In that case, I'm relieved. So, Matsubei, just now you were worrying over Rokutarō, correct? Would it be hasty of me, then, to assume you believe this Rokutarō—who just recently came to work at the Ogawa'ya—is also one of these strange ageless, deathless people?"

Matsubei slowly assumed a somber expression and nodded his head, as though he were being made to do so against his will.

"Long ago, I met him. Not just once. I met him twice."

"Twice as a shop worker?"

"No, one time he came as a groom from the Ito'ya, when it was getting along well with the Kawadzu'ya."

"He was adopted into the family? In that case, he shouldn't have been able to disappear so easily."

"But disappear he did. Just three years after he'd come to the house as a groom, he took money from the stationery box. At the time, I'd just been made a journeyman, so that makes it thirty-seven years ago."

"But this . . . He's just someone who looks a lot like that person back then."

"Everything about him looks exactly like him. Even his voice is the same. Even his way of speaking."

"Then maybe it's his son. There *has* been a thirty-seven-year gap, after all."

Matsubei shook his head. "I said I saw him twice, didn't I? Not once. The second time was fifteen, no, thirteen years ago; thirteen, because that was the year of the big fire in East Ryōgoku. That Rokutarō fellow worked at the Kawadzu'ya again for just two years, then cleared out."

Yonesuke's brow furrowed in thought. He had a feeling that his smooth face must be covered in sweat.

Matsubei was certainly not in good shape. His illness was a terminal one, and it must have been affecting his mind, making him say things like someone in a delirium.

"You don't seem to believe me." Realizing this, Matsubei was staring at him with tears in his eyes. "I can't say I blame you. Until I got together with your old man and traded stories with him, even I used to think something was wrong with my head."

"Matsubei, I'm not going to say anything like that."

Just as the conversation was about to become altogether perilous, the voice of the handmaid called out from the other side of the sliding paper door, as though to provide a much-needed respite. Matsubei answered her, and she came in with trays.

"It's time for lunch, so would you please join us? Sorry to serve what you brought for us, but I've made some mussel soup." Pleasantly, she offered a tray to Matsubei. "You must be tired of gruel all the time. See, we've got rolled fried eggs too. And this mussel soup, it's made with the Okura mussels your guest brought for you."

Matsubei didn't move his chopsticks, but the handmaid, determined to help him whether he wanted her to or not, looked at him with pleading eyes, and so making a visible effort, he began picking at the food on the tray. Yonesuke didn't feel much like eating either.

怪

After lunch was finished and the dishes cleared away, Yonesuke, feeling the time was right, said, "Well, I guess I'd better get going . . ." The strained atmosphere in the room had not changed in the slightest even when the trays had been taken out.

Sitting there miserably, Matsubei glanced at Yonesuke's expression, then said in a small voice, "Your old man knew about Rokutarō too. It's possible he may have left something behind in writing for you, for the day you took over the agency. Look for it."

"Matsubei . . ." Yonesuke unconsciously called out his name, but the words to follow it wouldn't come. *What a pitiful old man. He's completely possessed by these crazy ideas.*

"The important thing is to act like you don't know," Matsubei said. "As long as they don't realize they've been found out, they won't do a thing. I feel kind of sorry for them because of that. Never dying also means hardship without end. If they should slip up and be found out, they'd be chased around all over the place by people blinded by greed, demanding the secret of immortality."

He went on, hardly parting his lips as he mumbled, "Anyone with a heart pretends they don't know and never lets the pretense slip."

For Yonesuke, the story finally became unbearable. He quickly made his excuses and departed.

怪

The day after Yonesuke came to visit him, Matsubei died at the villa in Mukōjima.

No matter how long he had served there, he was still just a workman, so the Ogawa'ya was not about to put on some showy funeral for him. Even so, they did invite a small number of people with whom Matsubei had been friendly during life and were holding a modest wake in the room at the dormitory where he had lain ill. Yonesuke decided as well to hurry over to attend.

A strong wind was blowing that night. Luckily though, there was a full moon and the road was brightly lit. There was no need for a lantern, and Yonesuke cast a clear, sharp shadow on the ground.

Yonesuke didn't leave until the office closed, so he arrived quite late. This time yesterday, he wouldn't have believed that the old man would be dead now. Had it been a peaceful death? He hoped that he hadn't suffered. And he wondered: had he been the last one to hear the old man's strange ravings?

Tonight, that Rokutarō fellow was standing at the servants' entrance through which the handmaid had come out to greet him the day before, welcoming guests as the strong night wind set the sleeves of his kimono flapping about. He spotted Yonesuke's face from afar and bowed toward him with great politesse. Yonesuke returned the bow and started toward him at a light jog.

Just then, a gust of wind struck him from the side like a strong right hook, and Yonesuke threw up his hands as he tottered forward. Flapping in the wind, the hem of his kimono got tangled with his ankles, and his foot came halfway out of his sandal.

Realizing that Yonesuke was about to trip and fall, Rokutarō, thinking quickly, moved forward and held out his hands. "Ah, this wind's really something!" he said.

"No kidding," Yonesuke said, as Rokutarō caught and steadied him.

It was at that moment that Yonesuke, face downturned to shield it from the wind, happened to look down at the ground.

The moon was shining directly overhead. Everything around was suffused with its blue light.

The shadow that Yonesuke cast on the ground was in an odd position, being held on to by someone. No, that wasn't right. The reason its position seemed odd was that the shadow of Rokutarō, which should have been beside his, wasn't there.

Rokutarō had no shadow.

All this happened in one brief instant. Yonesuke looked up right away, meeting Rokutarō's eyes when he did so.

The important thing is to act like you don't know.

"This way, please." Rokutarō was smiling, albeit with solemnity proper to the occasion, as he began to lead Yonesuke inside. Yonesuke felt as if he were growing damp with a sweat that had started to break out from the places where Rokutarō's arms had just now been supporting him.

Matsubei, chief clerk of the Ogawa'ya, had died with his face twisted in torment, it was said. "Dropsy's a frightening thing," the people whispered to one another all around.

怪

Yonesuke, proprietor of the employment agency in Yanagibashi, was an unusual fellow. After running away from home at a young age and living the life of a wanderer for many years, he had just five years ago turned around and come home, then taken over the business of his father who had died almost immediately after. A youth spent drifting aimlessly from place to place was not a respectable past to have, but the man himself was of an unexpectedly mild and serious character, so his reputation in the neighborhood was not at all bad.

However, one thing did seem very odd about Yonesuke around this time: he turned his house upside down looking, he said, for writings that his father might have left behind. The caretaker who had been his late father's good friend he also called over to his house and sat knee-to-knee with him, questioning him like a suspect: "Do you remember anything from long ago?"

"What do you mean, from long ago? What kind of things?"

"Ah, sorry. Did he ever tell you any weird stories?"

"What kind of stories are weird stories?"

"I can't say. I'm afraid to talk about it."

The neighbors wondered if Yonesuke might be touched in the head.

"Now, when was it he started to get like that?"

"Hey, now that you mention it, didn't this all start when the Ogawa'ya's chief clerk died, and he came back from the wake looking all . . . haunted?"

While such rumors were being whispered, Yonesuke was hardly able to keep still as he continued to dig around in his house. Then, on the sixteenth day after the death of Matsubei of the Ogawa'ya, he disappeared.

It was another three days afterward that Yonesuke's mutilated corpse was found floating in berth number four of Asakusa-Okura.

The damage to the body was so severe that they couldn't even determine the cause of death. He was covered in countless wounds both large and small, which all appeared to be the result of fishes eating at him. Both his eyes were completely gone. And the insides of both sleeves of his kimono were for some reason tightly packed with mussels.

Because of this, for some time afterward the Okura mussels, which would normally sell for four or five times the price of regular mussels, dropped to less than half of their regular price.

And that wasn't all. There was also the unpleasant fact that Yonesuke had been a frequent purchaser of Okura mussels. In the end, stories were even going around claiming that "that man was killed by the grudges of all those mussels he'd been eating."

Again and again, graffiti appeared slapped across walls around Okura, with messages such as this one, which played off Yonesuke's nickname and the tendency of the mussels to eat actual rice grains:

> The terror of the
> Mussels of Okura, who
> Eat Rice, and avenge!

This was a troublesome state of affairs indeed for fishmongers in the area who had profited so handsomely thanks to the Okura mussels. They put their heads together and worked out a plan.

And then, at the fourth of the eight berths at Okura—by the side of the very berth in which Yonesuke's body had been sunk—they laid a foundation of stones bearing strong resemblances to mussel shells and built a little shrine, deciding that they would worship it as a burial mound for the mussels.

This occasioned at last a return to proper pricing for Okura mussels. According to the locals, that little mussel mound continued to be worshipped by townspeople after the Meiji Restoration and all the way up to the close of the Meiji Period. Although the rice storage facility from which Okura drew its name disappeared, the spilled grains of rice disappeared, and even the difference between Okura mussels and regular mussels disappeared as well, the oral tradition remained.

They say there's even an elderly man living in Asakusa-Torigoe-chō who turned eighty-eight this year and can still remember his father, a former bar worker, telling him about this when he was a child.

"What? No, somebody made that up. I mean, if that's not the case, then what that Yonesuke fellow believed would've never come up in the flow of the story. 'Cause at the time, they weren't thought of as scary or anything."

At that time, there had been a woman whom the old man's

father had known very well. Although she had been a barmaid, she had also possessed quite a refined beauty, with a mole that stood out on her left cheek just below the eye. The old man's father had been intimate with her for a number of years, and it was said that the woman had doted on his son as well. However, their secret relations ultimately became known to the child's mother, and his father had broken things off with the woman.

"When my father died at age seventy," the old man said, "that woman came to the wake. She was a rare beauty that I can't forget. The mole under her eye was right where it was supposed to be. She hadn't changed a bit since she was young, and she smiled when she saw me. I had never been so shocked in my life. Because of that, the story I'd heard when I was a kid came back to me."

The night of that wake, they say it rained heavily, and in the absence of moonlight, he was unable to check and see whether the woman cast a shadow.

"I reckon it's best if you pretend not to know, after all," the old man said.

About the Author

Miyuki Miyabe's first novel was published in 1987, and since that time she has become one of Japan's most popular and best-selling authors. Miyabe's 2007 novel *Brave Story* won The Batchelder Award for best children's book in translation from the American Library Association. Seven of her novels have been translated into English, and *Apparitions* is her first short fiction collection to be so translated.

About Masao Higashi

Masao Higashi is an anthologist, literary critic, and editor of the magazine *Yū* (Ghosts), which specializes in Kwaidan, the traditional ghost stories of Japan. He is the editor of *Sekai Gensō Bungaku Taizen* (Global Encyclopedia of Fantasy Literature), *Kaiki: Uncanny Tales from Japan* (Kurodahan Press, English language), and several collections of ghost stories and critical works. In 2011 he won the 64th Mystery Writers of Japan Prize for his work *Tōno Monogatari* (Tales of Distant Fields).

A Note on the Cover Art and Artist

The cover image, *The Plate Mansion* by Katsushika Hokusai (1760–1849), depicts the legend of Okiku and the Nine Plates, a story that exists in several versions. The maid Okiku was bound and then flung down a well by her master after one of a set of ten finely made plates had either been destroyed or gone missing. The spirit of Okiku is rising from the well into which she was thrown, counting "One, two, three . . ." all the way to nine.

Hokusai was an Edo era printmaker and artist. He was known for his *ukiyo-e* (pictures of the floating world) woodblock prints and paintings. "Floating world" images depicted landscapes, city life, Kabuki actors, supernatural events, and sexual images for consumption by the wealthy merchant class created by the urbanization of the period. Hokusai was influenced not only by traditional Japanese art schools, but also by French and Dutch art, which he gained access to thanks to trade with the West.

HAIKASORU
THE FUTURE IS JAPANESE

THE MELANCHOLY OF MECHAGIRL BY CATHERYNNE M. VALENTE

A woman who dreams of machines. A paper lantern that falls in love. The most compelling video game you've never played and that nobody can ever play twice. This collection of Catherynne M. Valente's stories and poems with Japanese themes includes the lauded novella "Silently and Very Fast," the award-nominated "Thirteen Ways of Looking at Space/Time," and "Ghosts of Gunkanjima"—which originally appeared in a book smaller than your palm, published in a limited edition of twenty-four.

Also included are two new stories: the semiautobiographical, metafictional, and utterly magical "Ink, Water, Milk" and the cinematic, demon-haunted "Story No. 6."

ALSO BY MIYUKI MIYABE
ICO: CASTLE IN THE MIST

When a boy named Ico grows long curved horns overnight, his fate has been sealed—he is to be sacrificed in the Castle in the Mist. But in the castle, Ico meets a young girl named Yorda imprisoned in its halls. Alone they will die, but together Ico and Yorda might just be able to defy their destinies and escape the magic of the castle.

Based on the video game filmmaker Guillermo del Toro (*Hellboy*, *Pan's Labyrinth*) called a "masterpiece," Japan's leading fantasist Miyuki Miyabe has crafted a tale of magic, loss, and love that will never be forgotten.

THE BOOK OF HEROES

When her brother Hiroki disappears after a violent altercation with school bullies, Yuriko finds a magical book in his room. The book leads her to another world where she learns that Hiroki has been possessed by a spirit from The Book of Heroes, and that every story ever told has some truth to it and some horrible lie. With the help of the monk Sky, the dictionary-turned-mouse Aju, and the mysterious Man of Ash, Yuriko has to piece together the mystery of her vanished brother and save the world from the evil King in Yellow.

BRAVE STORY

Alone after his father is hospitalized and his mother attempts suicide, Wataru Mitani ventures from the real world to the land of Vision, where he seeks five magical gemstones representing the qualities of charity, bravery, faith, grace, and the power of light and darkness. With these, perhaps Watari can change his fate and bring his family together again.